Critical Praise for Kaylie Jones

DISCARD

"Although we've got used to second-generation actors equaling or surpassing the accomplishments of their parents, the same hasn't happened with second-generation novelists. Nonetheless there are a few . . . and added to their small number ought to be Kaylie Jones."
—New York Times

For *Lies My Mother Never Told Me*

"A bright, fast-paced memoir with an inviting spirit. There is real immediacy to the family portraits here . . . There's also great daughterly love for James Jones . . . and palpable pride in his achievements."
—Janet Maslin, *New York Times*

"Unadorned, poignant, and honest to the core, Kaylie Jones's memoir is a light emerging from the shadows of a writing life."
—Colum McCann, author of *Let the Great World Spin*

"Searing, brutally honest . . . What makes *Lies My Mother Never Told Me* such an uplifting book despite all the pain and turmoil it recounts is its revelation of how Kaylie Jones has matured as a person in dealing with her twin legacies, literary and alcoholic, and also as a writer . . . Like D.H. Lawrence, she is entitled to say 'Look, We Have Come Through' —and triumphantly."
—Washington Times

"[*Lies My Mother Never Told Me*] contains juicy celebrity anecdotes (oh, Frank Sinatra!), but its poignancy comes from the journey of a talented woman wrestling not just with her own demons, but with those of her parents, and discovering a strength she once thought unattainable."
—*New York Observer*, Very Short List

"Shattering, totally scary, yet beautiful . . . A splendid, splendid book . . . completely gripping from start to finish, and written with grace and zest . . . What a fine book."
—Tim O'Brien, author of *The Things They Carried*

"Brilliant, touching . . . Absolutely addictive, this story of struggle and triumph is a joy to read, thanks to Jones's gift for handling dark material with humor and grace. A rare child of privilege capable of looking on herself and her family objectively, Jones has produced a memoir [that] will be a treasure for fans of literature and literary memoirs, as well as anyone who's coped with alcoholics in the family."

—*Publishers Weekly* (starred review)

For *A Soldier's Daughter Never Cries*:

"The daughter of James Jones here offers a discerning, brightly written, apparently semiautobiographical bildungsroman." —*Publishers Weekly*

"Jones's third book, a delightful account of Americans living in Paris, captures the essence of childhood . . . Jones, the daughter of James Jones, writes with sensitivity and compassion. Highly recommended."

—*Library Journal*

"Every page is a joy." —*Self Magazine*

THE ANGER MERIDIAN

THE ANGER MERIDIAN

by Kaylie Jones

Published by Akashic Books
©2015 Kaylie Jones

Hardcover ISBN: 978-1-61775-350-3
Paperback ISBN: 978-1-61775-351-0
Library of Congress Control Number: 2014955091

Akashic Books
Twitter: @AkashicBooks
Facebook: AkashicBooks
info@akashicbooks.com
www.akashicbooks.com

For my cousins Joanie Mosolino Wall and Kate Mosolino Sotirdy
and for Dayle Patrick

"A real friend is one who walks in
when the rest of the world walks out."
—Walter Winchell

PART ONE

"It's a sad day when you find out that it's not accident or time or fortune, but just yourself that kept things from you."
—Lillian Hellman, *Pentimento*

CHAPTER ONE

A PERSISTENT FOUR-TONED GONG rings in my ears and I am suddenly back in the dusty courtyard of the École de Sainte Thérèse de Lisieux in Cameroon and the church bell is announcing the end of the school day. The children are shouting, their deafening din rising in the hot air as they break ranks and run wildly about—but not me, I remain firmly in line. The nuns have rulers and they'll smack you hard but most of the kids don't care. The tolling doesn't stop and I know this doesn't make sense because the bells only toll on the hour at Sainte Thérèse and school ends at four. My eyes flutter open and above me the incandescent solar system and stars of Tenney's ceiling glow dimly. I must have fallen asleep while scratching her back.

It's the doorbell, the sound growing more impatient. Beau must be a little drunk. Sometimes he can't manage the lock. I glance at the Winnie the Pooh clock. It's 3:35 a.m. I lift my hand to my forehead. I have written on my palm: *Ne lui dis pas qu'il boit trop*. I don't need this reminder, I never tell him he drinks too much.

I rush down the hallway, pulling tight the unraveling knot on my robe's belt. As I'm about to open the front door, I notice a line of white masking tape stuck to the door just at my eye level and on it are the words: *Ne lui demande pas où il était*. Of course I won't ask him where he was, though the impulse to blurt it out is always present and that's why I have to warn myself. I rip the tape off and ball it up, putting it in my pocket, rolling it around to get it off my fingertips. I take a moment to gather myself, prepare my unconcerned, relaxed face for him, and open the door. But it's not Beau.

Two large, uniformed policemen stand there, one pale and blue-eyed, the other dark.

"Mrs. Huntley?"

"Yes?"

They wear short-sleeved uniforms that expose their bulging forearms. The policemen's eyes seem already old in their smooth, unlined faces, and they are scowling at me with such grave expressions I'm once again reminded of Sainte Thérèse de Lisieux and the stern faces of the nuns.

The pale one, whose name is Johnston, says, "Mrs. Huntley, may we come in?"

"Yes, of course, come in." I step aside. If Beau got pulled over for drunk driving again, this time they probably arrested him and I'm going to have to go pick him up. He'll be absolutely furious. Anticipating his rage, my face grows hot, my heart starts to pound, my mouth goes dry.

"Please, Mrs. Huntley, sit down," the young policeman says, guiding me into the living room where I perch myself expectantly on the armrest of the couch. "I'm sorry to have to tell you this, Mrs. Huntley, but your husband was in a car accident and he didn't make it."

For a moment I am so stunned I can't even speak. My first thought is: *It's over.* I work hard to force my face muscles into an appropriate expression of horror.

"Hit a tree head-on," says the other policeman, Officer Gutierrez. "He probably didn't feel a thing."

I stand, and I stumble, as if my knees can't hold me at

this news, and Officer Gutierrez takes my elbow to steady me. "Please sit down, Mrs. Huntley," insists the young man, so I sit back down on the armrest.

Officer Johnston clears his throat. "Look. You may as well know this now because you're going to find it out soon enough. There was a girl in the car."

My mum used to say, *Lying is necessary. Not only necessary, but good. When you tell a lie, make sure you keep it as close to the truth as possible, because it will be easier to remember.* The problem is, right now I'm having a little trouble remembering what's a lie, and what's the truth.

Officer Gutierrez reaches into his pocket and pulls out a little notebook and reads: "*LouKeesha Smalls.* L-o-u-K-e-e-s-h-a. Do you know this person?"

Just last weekend we were at that place the Blue Bayou with Bucky and Bucky's wife, Jocelyn. LouKeesha was Beau and Bucky's favorite waitress and they loved to banter back and forth with her. I do my best to look positively stunned.

"She's . . . LouKeesha's a waitress at the Blue Bayou," I tell the officer helpfully.

The young men glance at each other. They must think I'm a fool. I'm sure they feel sorry for me, the Yankee in the Court of King Beau. My mum always said, *Acting like a damsel in distress is often extremely useful, just as long as you realize it's just an act.*

"What is it?" I ask, my voice tight in my throat.

"Well," Officer Johnston sighs deeply, "she was killed too."

"Oh God, no! That poor girl, she was so young!"

They just stare at me and it's clear what they are thinking.

"He was probably giving her a ride home," I explain. "That's the way Beau was—always going out of his way for people."

Officer Gutierrez snorts. I would like to snort myself right now. He shakes his head, making a wincing face. "Uh . . . it's gonna be a little hard to explain . . ."

In my mind I have a vision of that scene in *The World According to Garp*. They seem a little perplexed, almost frowning, and I realize I'm giggling. I'm having an attack of nerves. I shake my head and cover my face with my hands.

In a kind of stunned stupor I sit while they explain that I will need to identify the body later on and they warn me Beau's in pretty bad shape. They want me to call someone to come sit with me but I don't want to call anyone. I just need a little time to think by myself, before the sun comes up. The real cataclysm is that Tenney's life will never be the same. And I have tried so hard to keep this ship afloat. All along I was dancing to the band and the deck was tilting beneath my feet.

Eventually I get them out the door and I tiptoe back to Tenney's room. She's lying on her stomach, her left hand hanging off the bed in a fist, her silver medical-alert bracelet glinting in the yellow glow of her night-light. Poor Tenney. What am I going to tell her? I slip under her quilt and snuggle up to her warm body. I can feel her rib cage through her nightgown. She's so thin. I nestle my face into the back of her head and breathe in her little-girl scent. She is too young to understand that we are free.

The phone is ringing. I sit up, suddenly remembering. It's 8:28 a.m. by her Winnie the Pooh clock.

The phone rings and rings, and after a while voice mail picks up. I can hear murmurs but not words.

Two more calls. I get up, tiptoe out, shut the door. The cordless phone and its built-in answering machine stand in the hall on a delicate cherry wood console table. The phone trills again. "*Hi, honey, it's Jeanne-Wallace, are you there?*" Beau's executive assistant, that slut. *"Pick up, honey. Please."* Her high, sweet voice is shaky and uncertain. *"Merryn, ah am so, so sorry, ah don't even know what to say. A reporter called . . ."* Jeanne-Wallace starts to cry, and through her hiccuping says that Bucky is away on business in Houston and she's got to call him immediately but she wanted to check in with me first. She'll call me back in a few minutes to see if there's anything she can do, anything I need . . .

Ringing again. This time it's Bucky's wife. Jeanne-Wallace must have already called her. Of course she'd call Jocelyn, the Dallas cowgirl, before she'd call me, the Yankee. I pick up the phone.

"Oh, honey," says Jocelyn Buckingham, "Ah am *so* sorry."

"Thank you." Suddenly I feel choked up.

"Ah told Bucky, like, *months* ago, ah said, *Bucky, you tell him to* just *quit it. Runnin around with a waitress!* Honestly. Now how can that be good for business?"

So they knew. I thought *I* was the only one who knew—not specifically, but generally. They never would have told me. I'm the outsider who doesn't play well with others.

"Don't worry, honey, no one knows except Bucky and me. Ah mean, we never expect them to keep their pants on *all* the time—but Beau . . . all the way back to college he had a real appetite for the help. A real virgin-and-whore thing. Ah told Bucky *someone* was going to get into trouble."

This does not require a response from me, so I remain silent. I have a feeling Jocelyn is enjoying herself. I'm too judgmental of people. It's really a terrible character defect. I never give people the benefit of doubt.

"Honey, do you know what hotel Bucky is stayin' at in Houston by any chance?" she asks. "He went off in such a hurry I plumb forgot to ask and he isn't answering his cell."

I manage to say I have no idea and she promises to stop by later with a casserole.

I flee to the kitchen, open the freezer, and stick my head in. There's a little strip of white masking tape on the back wall: *N'oublie pas de mettre sa vodka au congélo.* Not only did I not complain about his drinking, I even reminded myself to put his damn vodka in the freezer for him. Four years of Spanish in college and Beau couldn't speak a word, so I never worried for a second that he'd be able to read my French Notes to Self. He was not a detail person, especially not when the details pertained to me.

The icy air feels good on my face. I feel like I can't breathe. The walls are closing in. What am I going to do?

I should call my mum down in Mexico before someone else does. She'll know what to do.

A doctor once told me to breathe into a small paper bag when a panic attack comes on, so I keep a stash of brown lunch bags under the silverware drawer. I grab one, place it over my nose and mouth. Okay. Breathe. Breathe.

The phone trills. I let the machine answer. Jeanne-Wallace, sobbing hysterically, says, *"Pick up, honey, it's important."* I pick up, the bag still over my face.

"Oh, Mer-r-y-yn, ah can't tell you how bad I feel about this but I need to tell you before someone e-else does . . . Beau and I . . . well, me and Beau, we . . . ah mean, it only happened once and we were both real drunk and it was absolutely clear that this had nothing to do with your marriage. It's important to me that you believe that, Merryn," she sobs, waiting for my response.

"You know what, Jeanne-Wallace?" I say, crumpling the paper bag in my fist. "There is something you can do for me, actually."

"Anything, M-m-m-erryn . . . anything."

"You can go to hell."

I hang up. I feel a little better, but then I feel much worse—guilty for being rude. I'm reaching for the phone to call her back and apologize when it trills again.

"Mrs. Huntley, this is George Strong at Wells Fargo. Sorry to trouble you at home, but I've been attempting to contact Mr. Huntley at the office and I'm unable to reach him. This is in regards to the mortgage payments that are past due. My apologies, but I am going to have to start—"

Tenney appears at the end of the hall; I press the disconnect button. She walks toward me carrying Blueberry, her talking bear with black velvet paw prints on the soles of his large feet. She stops and rubs her eyes. Her yellow nightie is frayed at the bottom. It seems she hasn't grown at all in three years. This nightie is a size six.

I try to compose my face.

"What's wrong, Mommy? Are we in trouble?" Her eyes search mine for a clue. They are so perceptive at this age. I try to unclench my jaw and soften my eyes.

"No, no. We're not in trouble. Daddy had an accident. He . . ." I can't go on. My eyes fill with tears.

Tenney approaches, gripping her bear to her chest. "What happened to Daddy?"

I throw the paper bag into the wastepaper basket under the phone table, drop to the floor, pull her onto my lap, and wrap my arms around her. She is so bright. People always underestimate children. I never make that mistake.

"Daddy was in a car accident. He . . . Daddy died. But it was very quick and he didn't feel a thing."

Tenney heaves big sighs and her lips begin to tremble. My heart feels torn to shreds. I lay my hand on her back and rub in silence as she cries. After a while, she sits quietly in my arms with her head pressed into the crook of my neck and I rock her.

Why should Tenney have to feel shame? Why should she have to walk around with everyone whispering behind her back?

I hate Dallas, Texas.

No. No, that's not fair. It's not Dallas. It's my fault. I never fit in. I never tried. I'm a bad person.

But we need to leave. I don't want this for Tenney. I don't want her poisoned by this scandal. We'll go stay with my mum in Mexico.

"Can I see Blueberry for a minute?" I ask. Curious, sniffling, Tenney relinquishes the bear. I turn him over and lift a flap of blue fur on his back, open the battery compartment, and remove the batteries.

I take off my frozen pond of an engagement ring and my Rolex Oyster and put them in the battery compartment.

I remember quite clearly how, when we were living in Cameroon, my father, the Deputy Head of Mission for the US, made a public statement about civil rights that enraged President Paul Biya, and Biya gave us twenty-four hours to leave the country. *Sometimes you just have to cut your losses and run*, Mum said to Dad. *No point acting the hero.* We took only what was necessary, one little suitcase each. We had to leave our dog with the neighbors. Mum hid her jewelry and all our cash inside my Raggedy Ann doll, which I carried quite proudly through the gauntlet of soldiers onto the plane.

"You know where Daddy keeps the emergency cash?"

Tenney nods. "In his cigar box."

"Want to get it for me?"

She jumps off my lap and takes off running. In a moment she's back clutching a stack of hundred-dollar bills that smell of expensive tobacco and his Clive Christian cologne.

"How much is there?"

She crouches and quickly counts the bills. "Two thousand five hundred," she says.

I stuff the money into the battery compartment and close it, then hand the bear back to Tenney. "Let's go pack your suitcase. We're going to start our summer vacation early and go visit Bibi in San Miguel."

. "What about school? And chess camp?" Tenney asks.

"Don't worry about school. And I'll call Mr. Khlebnikov about chess camp. We'll find a place for you to play down there."

In her room, I open her closet and reach for her rolling Harry Potter suitcase, stored on the top shelf. There is a piece of tape on the edge of the shelf: *Ne lui parle pas de ses habits, ça l'ennui.* Yes, talking to him about her clothes for some reason made him antsy and aggressive. I suppose we bored him.

"What's going to happen to us?" Tenney asks, worry crossing her brow.

"We're going to be fine."

"Are we going to be poor?"

"There's nothing wrong with not having a lot of money, Tenney. You'll always have everything you need. I promise."

"So we're going to be all right?"

"We are absolutely going to be all right. But we should get ready, honey. You decide what you want to bring, and I'm going to get our plane tickets."

Tenney walks slowly once around her room. The first thing she reaches for is her portable chess set, a small leather case with embossed red roses and delicate white and pink alabaster pieces, which Beau gave her last Christmas. Sometimes Beau would play with her on Sunday mornings. He'd sit across from her with a look of bemusement, a slightly baffled smile breaking over his face. *When you play a seriously good player, you have to consider every contingency. The game becomes about how many moves ahead you can calculate. Think ten steps ahead.*

Well, he certainly didn't plan on this contingency. My lungs start to seize up again.

I rush to my laptop, which is lying on my bed across the hall. On the left corner of the base, another piece of tape: *N'essaye pas de savoir ce qu'il fait.* I did try to find out about his work through Google searches. This made him so angry he threw my previous laptop across the room and smashed it against the dresser mirror. I never made that mistake again.

I check flights to San Miguel de Allende, Mexico, from Dallas/Fort Worth. There are flights to San Miguel all day long and spring is the least popular time to visit due to the heat and drought. We can make the flight that leaves in two hours. I book two seats and type in my Visa number.

Credit card rejected.

I type in my AmEx Platinum number. Rejected. I type in my debit card number. Rejected.

Time for another brown paper bag.

In a few minutes I return to Tenney's room and find her pulling her colorful swimsuits out of the bottom drawer and throwing the little bikinis she no longer wants behind her into the air. They fall around the room like confetti on New Year's Eve.

"We're going to drive to San Miguel, Tenney. That way we won't have to rely on Bibi's car if we want to do a little traveling . . ."

She looks up at me, assessing. She knows that I know that she knows that I'm lying, but she doesn't know why. "Can we go to the hot springs amusement park, like, *a lot*?" she asks defiantly.

"Of course!" I say, trying to muster a light tone.

I step into her bathroom and gather her toothpaste and toothbrush. On the mirror above the sink: *N'oublie jamais ses medicaments.* I never forget her meds. Well, yes, I have in the past and that is why I need the reminder.

There's a box of EpiPens on the top shelf inside the cabinet. There's a box in the kitchen, and one in our bathroom too. In case she inadvertently eats something containing cow's milk, or casein, or caseinate, or ammonium caseinate, or calcium caseinate, or hydrolyzed casein, or iron caseinate, or magnesium caseinate, or anything of the kind.

I need to pack some safe food. She'll have to eat in the car. I throw a couple of ice bricks into a cooler and fill it with Tenney's favorite snacks.

I can pack in seven minutes and thirty-eight seconds. I know how to do this. I am always prepared to go at a moment's notice. I am Superpacker. In my rolling suitcase I even have taped a list of items I must never forget. This is an extremely useful list to have.

My silver Honda CR-V is parked in the building's basement. Beau never liked my car—he wanted me in something more substantial. Here in Texas they think oil is their personal property and the rest of the world can go to hell. My small act of rebellion, taking a stand for the environment, made him wince and call me a hypocrite. Okay. I am a hypocrite, I readily admit it.

The elevator heads right down to the garage so we don't have to talk to the doormen. Our two rolling suitcases go into the hatchback. Tenney pushes the garage opener and the gate slides open and sunlight floods the rectangular opening.

Perhaps we really will be free.

CHAPTER
TWO

Friday

L ATE AFTERNOON, Tenney and I have reached the outskirts of San Miguel de Allende, Mexico, elevation 7,000
feet. It feels like a detonation went off inside my head
just below my ear. I've been driving for 16.46 hours, not including stops. In the rearview mirror I see Tenney's face pressed up
against the backseat window, watching the world go by. Blueberry sits strangled in the crook of her arm, his legs splayed out
with his black paw prints facing the ceiling.

"I can't wait to see Bibi!" says Tenney.

The pain in my head expands like a mushroom cloud. I
breathe slowly, in my nose, out my mouth. The cars behind us
start honking. I must have hit the brakes.

"Remember what we talked about, Tenney?"

"Yes," she says glumly. "If Bibi asks me what happened,
don't say anything."

"I didn't say *don't say anything*, Tenney, because Bibi's very
push—"

"Right," she cuts me off. "I'll tell her I don't know anything."

"Exactly."

"And do you remember what we discussed about our cash
situation?"

She sighs, as if she is being asked to recite her multiplica-
tion tables. "All our cash is inside Blueberry's battery compartment. It's the safest place because no one would ever think that

a little girl would be responsible for that much money. But it has to last us for a while so I have to be really careful and keep Blueberry with me at all times."

"Very good!" I say. "I'm proud of you."

"Isn't that lying, though, Mom?"

"Lying is sometimes necessary, sweetie. But anyway, not telling anyone about Blueberry is not lying, per se. It's withholding information. Withholding information gives you an excellent advantage. When you have information that others don't have, that puts you in a position of power. Do you understand?"

"It's kind of like chess."

"It's exactly like chess."

The outskirts of San Miguel look like any other medium-sized Mexican city, with a huge, ugly mall and a prison with high walls and barbed wire at the top and gas stations and steaming parking lots. After several dusty turnabouts, we begin our descent into the valley on a steep two-lane road. Houses and tiny bodegas line the left side but all at once, there are no more houses and the city sprawls out before us across the bowl of the valley. The brightly painted houses with their red tile roofs and the church domes shine brightly in the afternoon sun. Above all the others, the Gothic steeple of the *parroquia* reigns—a rosy and unapologetic queen. I love the story of the illiterate stone mason who only had a little postcard of a French Gothic cathedral on which to base his vision. I have always admired his exuberance.

We finally reach the Balcones neighborhood on the opposite edge of town and drive up the steep, winding street paved with rounded cobblestones where Bibi's red house stands perched at the cliff's edge. High walls block the view of the house and its green terraced gardens from the street.

I get out and stretch my cramped back and legs and turn my head from side to side, trying to loosen my neck. The air is filled with dust, chalky in the mouth, and the heat radiates up from the uneven cobblestones in waves, right through the soles of my sandals. April and May are the driest and hottest months in San Miguel—little rain and temperatures remaining steadily in the mid-90s. The road is deserted.

A few weeks ago Bibi—that's what she wants to be called now, since she became a grandmother—left a message on our answering machine. We hadn't heard from her in weeks. *"I just wanted to let you know that I have a sinus infection, but I called the doctor and he's put me on steroids, so I should be feeling better in a few days. I just didn't want you to worry."* I called her back immediately, and she said that this year she decided not to go to France and will be staying in San Miguel. With no money and no credit cards I wouldn't have been able to escape to France, so it's a good thing she stayed in San Miguel.

I press the buzzer by the heavy, dark wood door. Marta the cook opens the outside door and peers at us without expression, which is not a good sign. The more drama is raging in the house, the more Marta's face flattens out, a boulder in a hurricane. Tenney runs ahead of me, down the stone steps and through the elegant stone archway of the outdoor entryway, into the large patio garden, calling out, "Bibi! Bibi! We came to visit unannounced!"

Marta tells me *no se preocupa*, she will get Pedro to move the car into the garage and take care of the bags. Marta has been a widow for thirty years and thinks not so highly of Pedro, who is a bit of a lout. Every time she says "Pedro" she rolls her eyes. I thank her, and step through the archway into the patio that is steeped in shadow and ten degrees cooler than the street. No matter how hot it is a breeze always blows through this lush, green space. Flagstone paths separate the garden into sections. The banana, lime, and ficus trees are a little dusty and wilted, despite Pedro's constant ministrations. The fig tree leaves are five-fingered, flat and wide, like the hands of green giants, and they caress my arm as I pass. The ground is covered with a variety of pointy agaves and aloes and juicy jades that look like rubber; and all year wild white roses bloom in the center, around a fountain that burbles with a calming sound. Crimson bougainvillea and white jasmine vines climb the thin pillars hewn from a light, porous stone called *cantera*, gray and speckled like birds' eggs, which surround the patio in the style of a Roman villa, creating a covered walkway on three sides.

It's cocktail hour and I see Bibi reclining on the west-facing balcony in the shade of the wide archway, in a comfortable armchair upholstered in white canvas, with her tanned bare feet up on a matching ottoman. The balcony has a view of downtown San Miguel, the parroquia's steeple, and the sunset—the whole point, Bibi always said, of buying this house so far up the mountain. With her is Faye Peabody, the Houston oilman's widow who introduced me to Beau.

Eleven years ago, I came down to San Miguel from New York City for Christmas vacation, and Faye Peabody brought him over for "a little cocktail party." PGT Beauregard Huntley V, known to all as Beau, was a sight to behold. Tall, wide-shouldered, fair and solid, he was a Dallas real estate tycoon who came from a long line of Southern aristocrats from Charleston, South Carolina. Their ancestor had been at Fort Sumter with PGT Beauregard in 1861 when the first shot of the Civil War was fired. Once divorced, no children, at thirty-five Beau was, in Mum's opinion, an excellent catch. "And you, my dear," she had pointed out, "are getting a little long in the tooth to be so picky."

He was not terribly impressed with my lowly ESL teaching position at Hunter College; however, he seemed quite taken with Mum and her sprawling house and the photos she had everywhere of herself with the most important dignitaries of the twentieth century. She urged me to go out with him if he called me the next time he was in New York. "The only problem I can foresee," she'd said with her usual prescience, "is that if you marry him and have a son, we will be forced to name the poor child PGT Beauregard Huntley VI."

The way she is backlit by the sun, she seems like a painting, and I have a strange vision of myself kneeling at her feet with my head in her lap. Perhaps she might even stroke my hair. What nonsense! She is an Amazon. She doesn't have an ounce of natural compassion in her, which is why her life is such a success.

Tenney collides with Bibi and throws her arms around her grandmother's neck. Bibi seems only slightly startled and raises her torso just a fraction. "Ah!" she exclaims, patting Tenney's head with her long, elegant fingers. "My baby is here!"

She turns and glances over her shoulder, her sharp blue eyes searching for me. My pupils are adjusting to the shifting light from the shaded patio to the balcony, where the glare of the sun slowly sinking in the white sky is like a camera flash on the retina. Faye's eyes drill into me as well, assessing. I step forward and greet them with a shaky smile. My jaw aches from the effort.

"I thought you might come," murmurs Bibi, "but really, you should have called."

Off slightly to the left, in a shadowy corner, sits a hunched figure in another matching armchair, a young man with long, straight black hair, a dark complexion, and a morose expression on his face. I smile at him in a friendly greeting; there's no response but a brooding frown. I can almost see the storm cloud of general disapproval hanging above his head.

"Calisto, this is my daughter, Merryn. Merryn, this is my protégé, Calisto. He's a brilliant philosophy student at the university." She beams at him, her face animated and lovely.

"Ah . . . the university," I reply, as if this makes perfect sense to me. What university? Is there a university in San Miguel?

Has she told me about Calisto? I don't think so. Regardless, she will say she has and I will agree that she has, because I am the silly little fool who has the memory of a flea and has caused her nothing but trouble. That's okay, her perception of the world has always been egocentric; I'm used to this. But maybe she really did tell me about Calisto and I'm just so self-centered myself that I can't remember.

"Ha-ha!" she laughs lightly. "You have the memory of a flea! But I told you all about Calisto just . . . why . . . just last month on the phone!" She looks at me, eyes widening with the expectation of a response, so I nod, smiling, of course she did. "Anyway, I am his new patron, and he is living here with me while he's working on his dissertation." She turns her bright smile in Calisto's direction.

Calisto nods, barely glancing up, and doesn't say a word. He takes a deep drag off a cigarette, his head suddenly enveloped in smoke.

"Why haven't you returned my calls?" asks Bibi, her expression sour as she turns back to me. "Good God in heaven, Merryn. What in the world! Daddy would have been appalled!"

She means her daddy, not mine. When I was little Bibi let me know in no uncertain terms that her daddy was smarter, nicer, better, richer, and certainly more intelligent than mine. Her daddy was the US ambassador to the Soviet Union during World War II, and my dad was only a lowly attaché in Cameroon, a job he couldn't even keep.

"The papers are always so cruel," Faye murmurs. I am jolted back to the present, realizing that Faye is talking about Beau. Bibi shakes her head slightly, indicating Tenney with her eyes, and the conversation dies out. Bibi calls over her shoulder to Marta to bring another margarita. Bibi reaches for her own stemmed glass, which stands on a low wrought-iron table along with a bowl of guacamole, another with spicy pico de gallo, and a basket of chips. Tenney dips a chip into the salsa.

"Always ask first, Tenney. Ask what's in it," I remind her, though I know there's no casein in the chips or salsa.

"You are just *so* dramatic, Merryn," Bibi says. "You're going to turn the child into a neurotic. Anyway, milk never hurt *any*one. Isn't that so, Tenney?"

Tenney seems to be giving this statement some thought. I don't bother to respond. It's an exchange we've been having for seven years, since Tenney was two and had her first anaphylactic reaction to a simple glass of milk. Bibi is convinced allergies don't exist and are psychosomatic. I am on my guard around Bibi, because she is perfectly capable of accidentally giving Tenney something that contains cow's milk, or casein and all the other derivatives out there. No worries, though, I am always armed with EpiPens.

Marta approaches me with a handblown, frosty blue, long-stemmed martini-style glass with rock salt around the rim. Normally I don't drink alcohol because I cannot abide a loss of control, but for propriety's sake, I thank her and pretend to take a sip. Bibi likes her margaritas shaken over ice like martinis, a couple of ounces of good, dark tequila with a finger of fresh squeezed lime, a spritz of triple sec, and just a *soupçon* of Angostura bitters, then a good shake in the martini shaker—the winning combination. *Why is my mind floating off like this?* It must be this headache. I can't stay on track. I set the drink down on the balcony's balustrade.

"Tenney," Bibi says, "how about a nice swim in the pool? Allegra can watch you."

Tenney glares at her grandmother suspiciously, understanding perfectly well that she's being dismissed so the grown-ups can talk. Bibi doesn't realize how smart Tenney is.

"Go ahead, Tenney," I say, and secretly wink at her.

"Can I swim naked?" she asks.

"Of course!" says Bibi. "It's the only way to swim! Allegra!" she shouts over her shoulder.

I stand before the two lounging ladies and the silent young man like the accused in front of a Roman tribunal. I lean my hip against the balcony's red-tinted, polished-concrete balustrade so that I can gaze down at the pool where Tenney shouts like an Apache and launches herself naked into the deep end. Quiet Allegra stands nearby and watches, stepping back to avoid the splash.

I turn to face them and now the sun is at my back and in their eyes. But my head is suddenly pounding again. Bibi lifts her hand at eyebrow level. She wears several silver rings with large, chunky turquoise stones. Her hair is ebony-dark with soft reddish highlights, tied back in a ponytail by a bright red scarf in a complicated bow that looks like a flower. The skin around her chin is taut, not a sag or line. Apparently they get a group rate; the more ladies who go together to the "spa" in San Luis Potosí, the bigger the discount.

"There was a girl with him in the car, the papers said," Faye intones, patting her platinum hair into place. "Black, if the name is any indication."

"Well then," Bibi shrugs. "It's obvious. He was giving her a ride home." She picks up her stemmed glass with two slim fingers and takes a long sip. "I hope you have a copy of his last will and testament."

I realize I've been gripping the balustrade; I let go and my palms leave sweat marks on the polished concrete.

"I never thought to ask him about—"

"As far as men go, Beauregard was a perfect Southern gentleman," Bibi interrupts.

"He was a gentleman through and through," I agree.

"Well, at least you have your solitaire," Bibi adds after a pause.

I glance down at my ring finger, naked now with only the platinum band. Mr. Liebenthal at the International Diamond Exchange on Belt Line Road told me yesterday morning, after inspecting my diamond through a magnifying lens and consulting with his son the Harvard graduate, that while it was a *big* diamond, it was also quite flawed—*murky*, he said—and only worth $20,000 on the market. Mum told everyone that Beau told her the ring cost "a hundred thou." I weighed this information as I sat before Mr. Liebenthal, at ten thirty a.m. on the morning of my husband's death by blowjob, and decided that, under the circumstances, there was no reason not to believe the jeweler. He offered me $17,000 in cash. But how much for my 18-karat gold Rolex Oyster Perpetual Datejust Masterpiece? I wanted to know, a belated anniversary gift from my loving husband. I was hoping for another $20,000. The Rolex was a fake, said Mr. Liebenthal sadly. A good fake, but a fake nonetheless. I never even wanted a fancy watch in the first place.

I took the $17,000 and left the watch on the counter. It didn't work right anyway. The cash, all the cash I have in the world, is now rolled up inside Blueberry's battery compartment.

"Truth be told," Bibi says, "you've never been able to handle anything in your entire life without my help. What would happen to you, Merryn, if I weren't here to take care of you?"

No one says a word. The ubiquitous San Miguel drought dust that already coats my skin feels chalky in the back of my throat, like pulverized bone. I turn away and stare down at the pool where Tenney is splashing up a tsunami. A hot zephyr blows up from the valley and the dust seems to suck all the moisture from my eyes. I turn back to my Roman tribunal, contrite, shoulders hunched, beaten down by my own inability to stand up for myself.

"Ah, see now, my margarita has gone warm," murmurs Bibi. She yells to Marta to bring fresh drinks. I can hear the ice crashing around in the cocktail shaker all the way from balcony; Marta has anticipated her request.

"You're the best mum in the whole world," I say, my voice trembling.

"Yes, I am. Well, I'll just have to call Harvey Berger in New York. He's a horrible man but he's a great lawyer. I'm sure he'll figure out a way to put a lid on this slanderous gossip." Bibi picks up the cordless phone and stares at it for a moment. "Harvey's on speed dial, but it's not like I call him every day. Just getting through the pleasantries costs me two hundred dollars. I swear the man couldn't speak more slowly if he were in Congress."

She finally chooses a button and presses it with dramatic flair. After a moment of listening, her entire demeanor changes and she smiles brightly, as if she's on camera. "Yes, dear, this is Vivienne Alderman. I must speak to Mr. Berger immediately. Well, I don't care if he's in a meeting. Of course I'll hold."

The ground tilts at a dangerous angle beneath my feet. The pain in my head makes me feel sick to my stomach. I drag myself across the patio and into the kitchen and open the freezer side of the American refrigerator and stick my head in. I take slow, deep breaths. I hear Marta shuffling around behind me; she asks me if I need anything. I can't pull my head out just yet to respond.

"What in the world is wrong with you, Merryn?" Bibi pokes me in the ribs. "If you need something, just ask Marta. That's what she's here for."

I pull my head out of the freezer and stand up straight.

"Harvey is going to call you back. Honestly, do I have to take care of everybody and everything? You don't look well, Merryn. You'd better go lie down."

I lie on the king-size bed in the darkened bedroom just off the patio that has always been my room when I've come to visit. The fountain burbles peacefully beyond the open windows as the fan turns languidly overhead. Tenney has fallen asleep beside me, reeking of chlorine, her hair still wet, and I mentally backtrack to the beginning, following the little white pebbles out of the deep, deep woods . . .

Last year, at the Bootstraps for Dallas fundraising gala, I wore a luminous silver vintage Givenchy gown that Beau didn't like because I'd bought it at a consignment shop. Bootstraps for Dallas was a good organization. When Beau bought a commercial building he left spaces vacant for startup boutique companies that had great ideas but were unable to get low mortgages from banks. Some of them did really well. I loved hearing about the success stories. Bootstraps also did nonprofit work in Afghanistan, building housing and schools, helping refugees get back on their feet. While we sat listening to the mayor give a speech about how important Beau's brick-and-mortar, grassroots organization was for the Dallas economy, and how I'd been volunteering for the community as his abiding wife, Beau, in his exquisite Brooks Brothers tux, leaned toward me and murmured, "We sure look good on paper."

I smiled back at him with all the brightness I could muster while my heart started to pound and I had trouble catching my breath. I'd have to excuse myself and make do with cupping some paper towels around my mouth in the ladies' room.

Later, after the toasts, Beau's Saudi business associate, Ibrahim Ansari, who was sitting to my right, placed an unassuming black velvet drawstring purse on the white tablecloth before me. His eyes were glittering. For a moment, I thought he was giving me a bag of marbles. He looked like a South American billionaire playboy in his black Armani suit and Hermes cuff links, drinking champagne.

"Open! Open!" Ibrahim pointed to the black velvet bag, smiling, showing his white teeth. I untied the knot and out poured a choker of the largest, most lustrous pearls I'd ever seen in my life. A tiny platinum *M* hung near the elegant clasp.

"Mikimoto!" Ibrahim beamed.

"Oh no, Ibrahim, I couldn't possibly."

He drew his lips back and made a wolf face. "You could! It is done, they are yours."

I slid the velvet bag into my clutch.

While I had no problem selling my engagement ring to Mr. Liebenthal, I did not feel the urge to part with the Mikimoto pearls. I had a vision of placing that perfect strand around Tenney's neck on her wedding day . . . *something old*. They would be hers. For now, they are nestled in with the cash in Blueberry's battery compartment.

After all, I worked hard for them. Keeping my mouth shut, keeping his world perfect and uncomplicated, was a fulltime job.

I am wrested from unconsciousness by loud banging on our bedroom door.

"Merryn! Come out here right now!" It's Bibi.

I rush out in my wrinkled cargo pants and T-shirt that I've been wearing for two days. Night is falling, the garden greens fading to blue.

"Harvey," she rolls her eyes toward the sky, "I'm sure that's all fascinating but you're only going to have to repeat it all for Merryn anyway so please, *please* stop talking. She's right here."

Bibi thrusts the phone into my hands and throws her arms up in frustration. "The man simply can't stop talking!"

I put the receiver to my ear. "Merryn," says Harvey, his voice low and commanding, "I haven't seen you since . . . aahh . . . you were a teenager. Are you well?"

I've only met him twice, once when I was a girl and we were visiting from Cameroon and stayed with him in his huge Central Park West apartment; and the second time, at my dad's funeral. They were roommates at Columbia through their college years.

"Let me start off by saying . . . aahh . . . my condolences on your loss . . . but . . . however . . . Merryn . . . there seems to be some very serious trouble brewing. Do you know anything about this?"

"Trouble?" I say, my voice unsteady. "What kind of trouble?"

"Your husband and his company are being investigated by the FBI."

"The FBI?"

"Well, needless to say, I immediately put a call in to the US attorney in Dallas and he's going to call me back. He's an old friend of mine, which is an incredible stroke of luck, Merryn."

"Mr. Berger, did the FBI block all our accounts?"

"Well, if the accounts are linked to the company and the company is being investigated, Merryn, then yes, presumably they might block the accounts. Yes. I'll check on that. Meanwhile, is there anything else I need to know right now, before I talk to the US attorney? Anything you need to tell me?"

"I . . . I have no idea, Mr. Berger. This is a complete shock to me." And I start to cry.

CHAPTER THREE

EIGHT THIRTY A.M. Tenney and I are sitting at the mahogany Spanish Colonial refectory table with eight beautifully carved chairs in the long, vaulted great room, where breakfast has been laid out by Marta—different types of fresh-baked breads, including the sourdough and the margarine I brought from the States, and Marta's fresh jams, and slices of papaya and melon; coffee, and a large glass pitcher of tomato juice spiced with Tabasco and lime—and I'm watching Tenney pretend to eat. I didn't sleep well. I had to take an Ambien but it knocked me out for only two hours. And this damn headache just won't go away.

"Stop picking at your food, Tenney, and eat it right now," I say in a clipped tone.

Bibi glides in, dressed for her Zumba class at the Bellas Artes in the Centro, black leotards and a tank top, her hair tied back in a shiny gold and red scarf. Her Capezio cross trainers are in a mesh bag hanging from her shoulder. Over her workout clothes she has thrown on a tailored red linen jacket with big buttons and on her feet she wears a pair of San Miguel sandals, black rubber-soled shoes with two thick elasticized bands to hold the foot, this pair adorned with red and gold stripes. She must have three hundred of these in every color imaginable. I can't wear them; my arches are too high. Every year Bibi buys me at least two pair and I thank her so much then give them away as soon as I get back to Dallas.

I'm already on my third cup of Marta's dark, rich coffee, black and piping hot. Bibi goes to the bar and pours a long stream of vodka into a glass and returns to the table to add tomato juice, stirring the Bloody Mary with a celery stick. She takes a sip and wipes her mouth on a peach-colored cloth napkin, leaving a sharp red lipstick imprint. She lights a Virginia Slim and blows the smoke out her nose in a roiling plume, giving the impression that something inside her is on fire.

"You really shouldn't drink so much coffee," she says to me over her shoulder. "It'll kill you, you know."

I'm admiring the brick masons' handiwork in the vaulted ceiling. They apparently don't begin with a plan, they just start laying the bricks in a herringbone pattern, letting the domed shape develop naturally, allowing it to dry each night, before taking up the work again the next day. When the dome is complete, they fill in the spaces for the floor above with light lava stone, then pour concrete on top, in order to build a second story. Magnificent work.

"What's the matter with you, Merryn? Are you listening to me?"

My eyes drift to the wall of rectangular glass panes separated by a metal framework that leads to the north-facing flagstone terrace. The terrace lies atop a thick stone and concrete retaining wall that seems carved right out of the mountainside. The eighty-degree slope must drop two hundred feet or so to the first natural ledge, then two hundred feet more, at a slightly less slanted angle, to the bottom of the ravine. Rocks and shrubs of various types pepper the slope, but due to the drought they are almost the same sandy color as the rock. In summer and fall, the mountainside is a muted, brownish green. To the right, round-topped mountains rise high into the blue sky, shining golden-orange in the morning light while casting a blue shadow

on the riverbed and reservoir far below. This is the only time of
the day that won't be stupefyingly hot.

"Please don't tell me you're having one of your *episodes*,
Merryn."

"I'm listening to you, Bibi." I put my cup down and push it
away.

"I swear, sometimes I almost believe that idiotic French
child psychiatrist we took you to in Cameroon who said you were
slow."

Tenney glances at me, suddenly ramrod straight, as if she's
received an electric shock.

"She's just in a bad mood," I whisper, feeling slightly ill.

Bibi glances at her watch, "I'm going to be late for Zumba.
Calisto!" She steps through the opposite glass doors that lead to
the patio and calls up the outside stairs, the only way to reach the
second-floor master suite and guest rooms. If it's raining, you
get wet coming down. Across the patio, beyond the thick green
plants and burbling fountain, beyond the pillars and archways,
is our room.

"Calisto!" she shouts, "we have to go!" Her cordless phone
rings. "Hello? Hello? I can't hear you . . . What?"

My heart starts to pound, sending shock waves of pain into
my head.

Pedro knocks on one of the patio doors, looking sheepish.

"Just a moment, please!" Bibi shouts into the phone, and
turns to her gardener. *"Qué pasa,* Pedro?" she asks with an annoyed expression. He mumbles something about *el jazmín* not
doing well because of the heat—the jasmine that fills the night
air with its intricate perfume. *"Yo no soy jardinera,"* I am not a
gardener, she says, adding, "it's your job, not mine!" And turns
back to the phone. "Ah, Faye . . . why can't I hear you?"

My eyes travel down the long room, gazing at the familiar

photographs in silver and gilt frames that adorn every surface, a younger Bibi posed with important political figures, everyone in cocktail or evening attire. The frames crowd the slim strips of wall between the glass panes and French doors; they're on the side tables, the cabinets, the upright piano. American Presidents (JFK, Johnson, Carter, Clinton); Senate Democrats; foreign dignitaries (Sadat, Boutros-Boutros Ghali, Gromyko, Mitterand); the only Republican is Henry Kissinger, with his hand around Bibi's back (probably on her behind). At the other end of the great room is a fireplace with more photographs on the mantelpiece. The sitting area has a lovely deep, coral-hued sofa, armchairs and ottomans, and a smoked-glass coffee table.

"Ha-ha-ha! Lizzie is having an affair, that slut! NO! With *our* Doctor Handsome! . . . Well . . . everyone knows that our Doctor Handsome can't keep his pants on. You'd better watch out, Faye, or he might try to seduce *you* and get you to leave him all your money . . . Faye, I'm already running late for Massimo's class. Marta!"

Marta comes shuffling out of the kitchen. "*Sí, señora?*"

Bibi explains that she won't be home for *comida* but to prepare something for *cena* tonight and to leave it on the stove. No need to stay late today. It's Saturday, after all.

The phone rings again, and again my blood pressure seems to rise.

"Oh hello, Lizzie. We were just talking about you and wondering how you are, and why you've practically disappeared. I'm on my way out, I can't speak right now . . . No, I'm going to Massimo's Zumba class . . . Zumba. Oh, for goodness sake." Bibi clicks off and tosses the receiver down on the table, such a beautiful, rich chocolate brown, the seams in the wood grain as pronounced as the lines on a topographical map. I wish she wouldn't throw the phone down like that; she might scar the wood.

"Calisto!" she shouts again. He saunters down the outside stairs, his eyelids at half-mast and his long hair uncombed. He's wearing a dark blue button-down shirt with the sleeves rolled up. He seems to be going for the relaxed look, with the hems of the shirt untucked and his hands in his jeans pockets, but the jeans are so tight he can only squeeze in the tips of his fingers. He doesn't look any happier today than he did yesterday.

Bibi upends her Bloody Mary, drinking it down in three gulps. "We are meeting Faye in the Centro," she tells me. "Marta!"

"Sí señora?" Marta returns once again from the kitchen.

"Huevos rancheros for the *niñas* Marta!" She turns back to Tenney and me. "Daddy always said, *Start the day with protein,* and I have always taken that to heart."

I am feeling suddenly exhausted despite the coffee, and here comes Marta with a second steaming pot. I explain to her as best I can, in my limited Spanish, "*Por favor Marta es muy importante: no leche en los huevos, no queso. No leche de vaca para la niña. Nunca.*" No milk in the eggs, no cheese. No cow's milk for the little girl. Never.

"No se preocupa Señora Merryn," she murmurs. Don't worry. Marta has never let us down.

Once again, the phone trills, and Bibi, who has finally made it out to the patio, rushes back in. She is not one to rely on voice messaging, too afraid she may miss something. She plucks the receiver from the table. "*Hello?*" she says in a deeply frustrated tone. "Ah, Harvey! Don't waste another moment talking to *me,* Merryn is right here." She thrusts the phone at me and walks away without a backward glance.

Tenney stares at me solemnly as I press the receiver to my ear.

"How are you, Merryn?" asks Harvey Berger. Then he says, in the tone of an undertaker, "I spoke to the US attorney in Dallas . . ."

I can hear Bibi's voice as she and Calisto hurry toward the arched stone entryway, her words carrying so clearly as they echo off the patio's walls, it's as if she were still in the room. Once the outside door thuds closed, a profound silence descends upon the house.

"Well, we have a major problem," Harvey says with ponderous calm. "You signed papers that make you a VP of Bootstraps for Dallas. That . . . aahh . . . charity, they say, was really a money-laundering scheme for some wealthy Arabs who *allegedly* are opium dealers in Afghanistan. They also . . . hmm . . . *allegedly* fund extremist organizations."

This is not possible. I feel as if I'm being held underwater by powerful hands pressing down on my chest.

Marta places two plates of huevos rancheros before us. Tenney stares down at the eggs, then across the table at me.

"Just a moment, Mr. Berger."

I rush into the kitchen and open the freezer, phone in hand. I breathe in the icy air, blowing out steam. I close my eyes, trying to slow my breathing. "This is not possible," I manage to say. "Extremists? B-Beau was a Republican."

I feel Tenney's presence behind me. I shoo her away. She doesn't move. I shoo harder. Reluctantly, she turns and walks out the side door and listlessly crosses the patio toward our room.

"They think Beau set up an offshore account . . ." says Harvey Berger.

"An offshore account? I can't believe it!"

Funding terrorists? Beau was capable of many things, but funding terrorists? He couldn't have known about this. But then . . . his family used to own slaves. They turned a blind eye while their overseers whipped people to death. What high horse am I sitting on though? I turned a blind eye to quite a few things myself.

"Do you know this fellow Ibrahim Ansari?" asks Harvey Berger.

But none of this has anything to do with me.

"Ibrahim is a Saudi prince or something. A rich playboy. He drinks, he plays polo. He has all kinds of girlfriends. I don't know anything, Mr. Berger. Beau took care of all the money. I wasn't really a VP. Beau told me he wanted me to be a VP in name only. I wrote checks for incidentals on the Bootstraps account. That's all. He thought it looked good to have his wife involved with the fundraising. The only thing I ever did was help organize the galas."

"So you never asked him about his work?" Harvey's tone is sharp-edged now.

N'essaye pas de savoir ce qu'il fait.

I close the freezer and return to the great room. Tenney is setting up her chessboard at the square game table that has two lovely armchairs upholstered in faux-leopard velour. She hums to herself quietly, hunched over her pieces. I return to the kitchen.

"Early on, when I would ask questions," I mumble into the phone, my voice barely above a whisper, "Beau would get short-tempered and tell me to just stay out of stuff I didn't understand." I don't mention the demise of my former laptop.

"I am . . . *deeply* reassured to hear you were not involved—I couldn't believe that you were, but still . . . Time is of the essence, Merryn. The FBI is keeping a lid on this because they don't want to scare away the partner, Edward Buckingham, or Ibrahim Ansari. You won't see a word about this in the papers. That's already a good thing. I will see what I can do and call you back as soon as I have something to report."

I return to the table on jellied knees and sit, surrounded by profound silence. I feel as if I'm plugged into a wall socket or

something, my whole body is buzzing. What I need to do is practice my yoga to ease this tension.

I change into yoga clothes as Tenney throws herself onto the
king-size bed with her Harry Potter book and one arm around
Blueberry, our secret bank. I carry my Jade yoga mat that I found
in the back of the car out to the terrace, and work my way through
my six Surya Namaskaras.

I am on the last set, sweating heavily, when Calisto and Faye
stagger into the great room practically carrying Bibi and shouting hysterically that she fainted during Zumba.

"I've been telling her for weeks," says Faye, out of breath
herself, "she needs to start taking her medication."

"Do you mean the steroids?" I ask, perplexed because my
mum seemed perfectly fine.

"This is *not* open for discussion," Bibi counters irritably,
her long fingers fluttering as if she were shooing away a fly. I
am drenched in sweat, my yoga pants and tank top clinging to
me. Bibi stares at my clothes as if I've just walked in from mud
wrestling. "What's wrong with you?"

"I was practicing my yoga."

"Yoga, yoga. If you spent half the time you spend on that
foolishness doing something productive—" she starts, but Faye
interrupts.

"No. This time, Vivienne, you're not changing the subject."
Faye turns to me, her eyes filled with concern though not a wrinkle mars her forehead, smooth as vanilla icing on a cake. "Your
mother's asthma has been acting up and I think she still has that
sinus infection. She's been taking taxis back from the Centro."

"Nonsense! I have never taken a taxi back from the Centro
in my life, except late at night. I had a little attack, that's all."

"She's been having these attacks almost every day. *Every*

day!" Faye repeats, then gets up and reaches for the cordless phone charging in its cradle. "I'm calling Doctor Handsome."

"You are not calling anyone!" Bibi cries out. "Daddy had bronchial asthma but it never stopped him from leading a full, productive life." But suddenly her breath catches and she collapses dramatically onto the sofa. Calisto lets fly the longest stream of words in Spanish I've ever heard him utter, and Bibi stares at him, eyes wide and mouth agape. He's saying something I can't quite make out about Doctor Handsome—Calisto is apparently not happy about Faye calling him.

I remember from phone conversations with Bibi over the past few months that Faye Peabody was never ill a day in her life until her boyfriend, a young man named Pablo whom she'd met while dancing at Mama Mia's, attacked one of her aging gay friends who'd stopped by for a drink. Apparently Pablo was in a jealous rage. After the police carted him off to jail for striking the elderly Maurice with his own cane, Faye came down with a pain in her chest that Doctor Handsome diagnosed as anxiety. He recommended antidepressants, which she took for two days, then threw away because Bibi told her they were crazy-people pills. This happened a few months ago and ever since, according to Bibi, Faye has been "ill" at least once a week. Doctor Handsome apparently makes house calls, and Faye has him running at her beck and call.

"First of all," says Bibi, holding up an elegant index finger, "I've decided to change doctors. I don't like that Doctor Handsome one bit. Why, he stopped by unannounced just the other day, presumably to check in on me, but what he really wanted was a donation for his children's clinic. He may very well have wanted to seduce me, for all I know! Everyone is aware that he got the money to start that clinic from that filthy-rich Anna James, and Anna James told me herself that they were lovers!"

Calisto throws himself into a deep armchair and crosses his arms in a pout.

What I want to know is why this Doctor Handsome is practicing medicine in San Miguel de Allende. Where did he go to medical school? It sounds like he really is taking these old ladies' money in exchange for God knows what. And why is Bibi not better? But it is not my place to ask questions, and anyway, Faye has made the call and Doctor Handsome is on his way.

I shower quickly and change into a simple yellow sundress, careful not to wake Tenney who has fallen asleep with her book on her chest. As I'm coming out of our room, I hear three short, insistent bursts of the buzzer and Marta shuffles out of the kitchen toward the door. I tell her I'll get it; I want to have a look at this Doctor Handsome.

Our inner patio is still in shadow at midday, despite the staggering force of the sun, and when I open the outer door I'm blinded by the glare from the street. All I can see in the flood of white light is the silhouette of a fairly tall, thin man. I bring my hand up to shade my eyes. He is dark-haired, unshaven, carrying a backpack and a motorcycle helmet. I glance over his shoulder and indeed there is a motorcycle of some kind parked on the sidewalk. Once the outer door is closed and he moves into the shade of the open-air entryway, my eyes begin to adjust and I see that he's wearing a white guayabera shirt with two columns of little red flowers embroidered down the chest and over the pockets—not what one would expect from a doctor. He doesn't even have a doctor's case. He wears faded jeans and tan-colored, ostrich cowboy boots that are all scraped up. No older than thirty-five is my guess, with a dark tan that suggests he is not toiling away in an office. I must be looking at him suspiciously, because he introduces himself quickly, stepping forward with his hand extended, "I'm Dr. Fuller."

He smiles reassuringly in that friendly way one expects from doctors, but I am far from convinced. I step back and allow him to follow me, turning to him slightly as I murmur over my shoulder, "My mother had an attack of dizziness this morning during her Zumba class."

"I've been trying to get her to let me run some blood tests, but she's very stubborn."

I lead him across the patio, past the gurgling fountain, and into the great room where Bibi is now sitting up with a vodka tonic in her hand. All three of them are holding lit cigarettes and the air is filled with smoke.

"Here she is," I say, and move toward the terrace's French doors. This way the light is at my back, and for them I am now in shadow.

Bibi, Faye, and Calisto look up at Doctor Handsome at once. Faye and Bibi put out their cigarettes; Calisto continues to smoke, deep in his armchair. If he were a cartoon character he'd have a black cloud over his head.

I gaze out across the flagstone terrace and down the mountainside. In the midday sun, the northeastern edge of town deep in the valley appears bleached of color; even the shrubs have lost their luster and the reservoir glitters like mercury. The sun is so bright it hurts my eyes. Not until late afternoon will this brightness subside, when the sun sinks toward the distant mountains to the west and lights up the whole of San Miguel below us in lilac and coral hues. My mind is floating off again. I turn back toward the great room with difficulty.

Doctor Handsome, his jaw set, removes his instruments from the weather-beaten backpack and goes about taking Bibi's blood pressure, temperature, and listening to her lungs. Faye, Calisto, and Bibi sip their vodka tonics as if this were ordinary pre-comida cocktail hour. The doctor looks down Bibi's throat, up her nose, and into her eyes with a little flashlight with a cone-shaped attachment; he then palpates her stomach below the rib cage.

"Stop, that tickles!"

The doctor says, in a completely calm tone, "Have you cut back on your drinking like we talked about, Vivienne?"

I can't believe what I'm hearing and feel the urge to run. No one ever says anything to Bibi about her drinking. And anyway, she really doesn't drink that much. She's just a heavy social drinker. I stand in my corner, half of me outside on the terrace and half in. I feel like a soldier in a foxhole into which a live grenade has just been dropped. But I really need to hear what he says, in case it is something like, *You may have lung cancer and must fly back to the States immediately*, or something equally horrifying that she will resist.

"Of course I haven't cut back!" Bibi replies with a snort. "You're a zealot. From now on I'm going to call you Carrie Nation, after that pillar of the temperance movement."

"Ha-ha-ha-ha!" Faye laughs uncomfortably. "Carrie Nation! Vivienne, you're too much!"

"How many drinks have you had today?" he asks.

"This," she says, holding up her glass, "is the first."

I am constantly inspired by her ability to lie with a perfectly sincere expression. It is a true talent. I must practice that steady, unflinching look myself.

"Well then, how many cocktails would you say you've been having per day, on average?" he persists.

"Four," Bibi says.

She had four margaritas yesterday during cocktail hour alone, and then four glasses of white wine with dinner, followed by a cognac. A Bloody Mary or two this morning for breakfast. Now, a pre-comida vodka tonic. Is this more than usual? This must be more than usual. But she's under stress. And what about Faye? They always have cocktails together, matching each other one for one. This has been going on for years. Beau always had several drinks when he got home and drinks when he went out with clients and drinks at lunch and dinner on the weekends. *Ne lui dis pas qu'il boit trop*.

Everyone drinks this way. Everyone except me, since I don't like that feeling of losing control.

"Vivienne, I've already told you, your liver is enlarged. It's huge." Doctor Handsome continues to palpate her stomach and I can tell by the tiny pulse of her jaw muscle that she's in pain.

"Nonsense," she says. "The only thing wrong with me is that I have trouble with my sinuses."

"You've developed an allergy to the fermentation in alcohol. I'd like to run some blood tests—"

"There is no such thing as an allergy," she tells him, laughing harshly.

"You don't have an infection but your sinuses are inflamed. Have you been using the nasal spray?"

"It makes me jittery," Bibi complains. "You never give me anything that works. And your pills upset my stomach. You're a Doctor Feelgood is what you are. You're not a serious doctor at all."

"Your symptoms may be exacerbated by stress," he says, ignoring her barbs. "Anything unusual going on?"

"Well!" she cries, throwing up her hands. "Besides the fact that my son-in-law was killed in a car accident three days ago and his reputation is being slandered all over Texas and the whole of San Miguel is talking behind my back—no, nothing!" She turns and glares at me, making sure all know whose fault it is, then looks back at Doctor Handsome.

Maybe doing my Surya Namaskara in the noonday heat was

not such a good idea. Suddenly I'm feeling sick to my stomach again. Gritty dust coats my teeth and throat, making me feel like I'm going to gag. I edge toward the kitchen on tiptoe to get myself a drink from the water cooler. I take the opportunity to open the freezer and stick my head in.

"And why aren't you in the States, anyway?" I hear Bibi ask Doctor Handsome. "What are you doing here in the mountains of Mexico, criticizing decent widows? You're much too uptight. You need to have one of Marta's margaritas. *Marta!*"

"No, thank you," I hear him say.

I pull my head out of the freezer. Marta, her face impassive, doesn't even blink at the sight of me with my head ensconced in her ice. She dutifully shuffles off to see what Bibi requires.

"I'm feeling much better now anyway," Bibi is telling Doctor Handsome when I return. Then she dismisses him, opening her purse and asking how much she owes him, as if he's a waiter. He says she owes him six hundred pesos for the house call, but if she'd like to make a donation to his free children's clinic, she can do that as well. While she's digging through her purse she turns to Faye and asks her what she thinks of a certain young Mexican potter who is showing in one of the high-end Centro galleries. Bibi hands Doctor Handsome two five hundred–peso notes and tells him to keep the change. He folds the bills and sticks them in his guayabera shirt pocket, then calmly packs up his instruments and heads toward the patio doors. I tiptoe along the wall and follow him out.

"I can find my way, thanks," he says.

"No, that's okay," I respond, trying for a smile. His lips stretch into a thin line. Is he smiling too, or just annoyed?

"Mom! Mom!" Tenney comes running. "What's wrong with Bibi?"

"Bibi's fine, honey pie. She just felt a little dizzy." I look up at Doctor Handsome, who is gazing down at Tenney impassively. Is he surprised I have a child? Why would he be? "This is my daughter, Tenney."

"Hello." He puts out his hand, as if he is being introduced to an adult. She dutifully shakes it. Tenney is not afraid of grown-ups.

"You're Doctor Handsome!" she says, and he blushes. "Well, see you." She waves and tears off back toward the great room.

"Bibi really doesn't drink that much." Who is he, anyway, to say what is too much?

"If she says four, it's probably more like twelve."

"She's always been a heavy social drinker," I explain. He snorts. The nerve. He probably got his medical degree at the University of the Central African Republic. And people have been snorting way too much around me lately.

He reaches for the latch on the outside door, but pauses for a moment. "Why aren't there any photos of you or your daughter in the house?"

"Excuse me?" I'm trying to picture the photos that adorn Bibi's great room, her quarters upstairs, and her parlor. "Of course there are," I say dismissively, finding it hard to focus on his face; the sun is really bothering my eyes and they are stinging from the dust.

"Here, take my card. Just in case." His card reads:

Estéban Fuller MD
San Miguel Free Children's Clinic
Clínica gratuita para niños San Miguel

Below that are two phone numbers.

"You're a pediatrician?"

"Not specifically. But the poor desperately need doctors . . ."

His voice trails off, as if he's just plain tired of explaining this to American tourists.

He turns the latch and steps out into the blinding white sunlight and I close my eyes against the glare. All that's left behind my eyelids is the bright white image of his outline.

CHAPTER
FOUR

Sunday

THE FIRECRACKERS AND FIREWORKS start just before dawn. Sunday is often the only day people have off so Sunday mornings are not peaceful in San Miguel. When a child is born or a person dies, a relative will climb to a high spot on a mountainside and light fireworks to let God know they're coming. The earlier the relatives awaken and perform this task, the more dutiful and loving they believe they will appear in the eyes of God. Then the church bells start ringing, welcoming the people to mass.

Finally I sink into a restless sleep, but I'm pulled back up to consciousness by a loud banging on the bedroom door. I rush to open it, still in my pajamas. The light seems diffused, the colors muted, the patio is still deep in shadow behind Bibi, who stands there in her crimson silk negligee with mauve piping and the phone pressed to her ear.

"What sane person calls at the crack of dawn on a Sunday?" she says into the phone. "You're mad as a March hare, Harvey." She thrusts the phone into my hands. "I am going back to sleep. Please do not disturb me until noon at the earliest. This is just simply untenable." She turns and clicks across the patio and pulls herself up the outside stairs, gripping the banister as if she were on the last few steps of the Eiffel Tower.

I close the bedroom door and stand by the bubbling fountain, which sends a cool mist into the air and a little chill down my back.

"Hello, Mr. Berger."

"Please, dear, call me Harvey. How are you, Merryn?" After a moment, his voice somber and sonorous, he says, "They're sending two FBI agents down to San Miguel to talk to you—"

"*What?*"

"—today. Time is of the essence, Merryn, do you understand? They need to move fast in order to catch Ibrahim Ansari before he gets wind of this investigation and tries to flee the country. Have you heard from Ansari?"

"Me? From Ibrahim? No!"

"Apparently he's in New York. And he's been calling your mobile."

"What? What does he want with me?"

"That is exactly what the FBI would like to know."

"I haven't checked my voice mail since I left Dallas." For some reason I'm having trouble controlling my voice.

"You haven't checked your messages?" Harvey Berger sighs deeply. "Please check your voice mail immediately after we hang up. Do you hear me, Merryn? And don't erase any of Ansari's messages."

"Okay." I can't remember from all the television crime shows I've watched whether or not a deleted phone message can be recovered. Surely if they can land a robot on Mars and send back computerized images and information, they can recover a deleted message.

"Now, listen carefully," says Harvey Berger. "The US government has something called ICE, Immigration and Customs Enforcement, and they are in a task force with Mexican law enforcement, which gives them the authority to investigate US drug- and money-laundering operations in Mexico. Technically speaking, this crime falls under their jurisdiction because the issue is money laundering. The jurisdiction is not intended for . . . aahh

. . . a Saudi investigation, but this is a classic law-enforcement ma-
neuver. They call this *bootstrapping*—ironic, I know."

"But . . . but . . . Harvey, they're coming here *today*?"

"They should arrive by late this afternoon," he says. "And I
can't get there myself for at least two more days. I have a major
court case coming to a head here in New York. But I'll be con-
ferenced in on the meeting. Don't worry. I'll go over the questions with them beforehand. Now, you'll have to sign a proffer
agreement . . ."

I have no idea what he's talking about but it sounds awful.

"Merryn . . . I must ask you again, did you have any idea what
Beau was doing? Did you ever ask him about his work?"

"No. He didn't like to talk about his work. He never even
wanted to tell me about why he had to travel so much. He was
always coming back jet-lagged. Beau would get annoyed and say,
*I always take care of you and Tenney, don't I? Why are you question-
ing me?*" There is a long silence. "Harvey . . . are you there?"

"Seems to me Beau isolated you, just like your mother did."

"Isolated me? What do you mean?"

"Your father used to worry so much about you, Merryn."

"I have no idea what you're talking about, Mr. Berger."

"Your mother never let you have friends, and she never
really had friends herself. It was always just the two of you
together."

"Well, you must have misunderstood him. We had a perfect
life. And I had a wonderful childhood."

Harvey Berger coughs. "Well, hmmm, let's focus on the issues at hand, shall we? Ahhhh . . . you're sure there's nothing
else, Merryn? This is the moment to discuss it if there is anything . . . in the back of your mind that you want to talk through."

"I'm still just so stunned."

Harvey Berger was my dad's closest friend. His job will be to defend me, and he will defend me no matter what. Mum always said, *Men love to be knights in shining armor; all you have to do is give them the chance.*

"Merryn . . . they think you're guilty of something because you fled Dallas the day of your husband's death."

"I didn't flee," I say. "I was trying to protect Tenney from exposure to cruel gossip. I had no idea the FBI was interested in Beau's affairs."

Except that all our credit and bank cards were frozen. Except I knew he was a liar and a cheat.

"Well," Harvey says with a sigh, "it would be best if we . . . aahh . . . keep using your mother's landline. If they're tapping your cell phone, they're supposed to turn it off when you're talking to me—but still. I'll call you as soon as . . ."

Tenney opens the bedroom door and steps out in her frayed yellow Tinkerbell nightie and bare feet. "What's going on, Mommy?"

"Nothing at all is going on," I tell her, pressing the disconnect button and clutching the phone to my chest. "Everything is fine." I smile brightly but can feel my face muscles pulling against it.

Can she tell? She's watching me closely. It took me years to be able to tell when Bibi was lying and sometimes I'm still not sure. But Tenney is much smarter than I ever was.

"How about breakfast in the kitchen, since it's just us?" I suggest.

Tenney perches herself on one of the high stools at the granite-topped island and I make her a bowl of oatmeal with soy milk. She pushes the spoon listlessly around in the bowl. I want to yell at her. I really should tell Bibi about the FBI coming but she said not to disturb her till noon. She hates being disturbed.

We are disrupting her life. She's not going to like it. She will get mean and say terrible things about me that I don't want Tenney to hear.

Tenney says, "Want to walk down to the Centro like we always do?"

It's the last thing in the world I want to do. I have to listen to my messages. I want to get back into bed and take an Ambien and pull the comforter up over my head.

"Eat your oatmeal and then we'll go."

Tenney swallows three unenthusiastic spoonfuls and lays down the spoon with finality.

"I need to listen to my messages," I tell her, my voice sounding strained to my own ear. "Two more spoonfuls, Tenney. Please. Then we'll go downtown."

My cell phone and laptop are in the dresser, under a pile of panties and bras, all the way in the back of the drawer. I take out my phone and turn it on. The battery is low, but not low enough to prevent me from checking my messages. There are thirty-three of them.

"*Ibrahim here. You must call me immediately.*"

"*Merryn, dahlin', this is Gordon, your mother-in-law. Ah was hoping we could talk—*" Swiftly, I push erase and cut off her lilting Southern drawl. For some reason, this gives me a feeling of satisfaction.

"*Hi, Merryn. It's Jeanne-Wallace. I know you don't want to talk to me but I need to—*" And goodbye to you too, Jeanne-Wallace. *Beep.* Message erased. And goodbye to Bucky's wife Jocelyn and her stupid tuna casserole; and the *Dallas Morning News. Beep.* Message erased.

"*Hey, babe. How's that beautiful pussy? I want to put my mouth on—*" *Beep.* Ugh. There is nothing more embarrassing than a message like that from your personal trainer, the CrossFit enthusiast, once the fire has burned out. It was a fling, nothing more. Ugh. I'm so ashamed.

Beau's mother Gordon again: *"Merryn, dahlin, we are shippin Beau home to Charleston—"* Beep. Message erased.

"Hey, babe, did you get the pic of my cock—" Beep.

I search through my texts. Yes, indeed. There it is in all its glory: *Its so hard and waiting for you.*

He can't spell. The younger they are, the more they text. Only people over forty leave voice mails anymore.

Back to voice mail.

"This is Ibrahim Ansari. There is a little trouble, a little palace coup at the office. No one is returning my calls. But, nothing to worry about. I must talk to you. Call me as soon as possible."

Ibrahim is responsible for eleven of the messages, all in this vein, nothing specific. These are the only ones I save.

After an interminable conversation with a bright and airy customer-care provider, I get her, for a measly $4.99, which will be added to this month's automatic bill pay, to block the CrossFit Nazi's number. The battery on my phone is getting dangerously low and I realize I forgot my charger. I turn the phone off and put it back in the dresser drawer.

On our way out, I notice that Bibi's shutters are still drawn. I'll tell her about the FBI when we get back.

Tenney and I step carefully on the uneven, rounded cobble-stones of the steep mountain road, heading down toward the heart of the city. Blueberry is squeezed into my purple nylon mesh bag, his head peeking out and his feet dangling through the mesh. I recall how last summer on our first trip to the Centro we felt so sunny and lighthearted. Today I am filled with gloom, though I try to appear happy and carefree for Tenney's sake.

On Sundays the artisan market is filled with campesinos,

the farmers and herders from the high desert who come in for the day with their campo wares, like nopales, pomegranate seeds, and cactus fruit, and handmade reed baskets and leather huaraches with soles cut out of old tires. We weave our way through the open space, which is enclosed by some kind of roofing held aloft by metal stanchions. Many of the weekday stalls are closed. One weathered campesino has set up bleechers of tan, handmade ostrich cowboy boots and I imagine this is probably where Doctor Handsome got his. I think about buying myself a pair but it's already too hot to be trying on boots. Tenney stops at a papier-mâché stall, where every conceivable fruit and vegetable has been reproduced in fantastic, bright, shiny detail. They hang from strings in bunches, along with giant parrots on perches.

Further down, Tenney finds the corrugated tin shack where she buys her Mexican Barbie knockoffs, dressed in sequined gowns with big, messy hair and no shoes, as if they've just been caught crawling out of some man's bed after a night of revelry. The old Chichimec saleslady remembers us from our two-week visit last summer and greets us warmly. She takes both my hands in her leathery palms and smiles. The shelves are crowded with balsa wood doll furniture of all sizes—beds, dressers, closets, even tiny microwaves. Trinkets and figurines, key chains and hand-painted wood canes hang from hooks at the front of the shack. We buy a new barefoot Mexican Barbie in a black and gold halter dress.

Soon the alley narrows, the roofing of corrugated plastic sheets arches, like in a hangar. We come to a silver shop where a reed basket on a table is filled with picture frames of different sizes. My hand wanders through the frames. *Why aren't there any photos of you or your daughter in the house?* Why would he say such a thing? Was he trying to throw me off, gain the upper hand?

Silver is cheap here in San Miguel. Some frames have carved designs of animals and stars; others are plain; others depict the Virgin of Guadalupe or nativity scenes. I find one with delicate clumps of grapes extending beyond the frame onto the glass. I hold it up. "Do you think Bibi would like this?"

Tenney considers, then nods. I buy the frame for ten dollars.

We walk to the *jardín*, the little park in the center of the square in front of the parroquia, and sit on a bench facing the extravagant Gothic spire of pink sandstone. It is just past noon and the jardín is crowded with Mexicans dressed in their Sunday finery, walking arm in arm or sitting on the wrought-iron park benches. An orchestra plays in the gazebo in the center of the park. It must be one of their myriad religious or revolutionary holidays.

Out on the street, several mariachi bands serenade the passersby in a cacophony of guitars and trumpets. The men have matching outfits and some wear sombreros with gold piping and their lamenting voices still sound hopeful, as if they know all they have to do is cry and tear their hair out and the woman will come back. The town seems empty of tourists; the heat and drought of the past few months and the bad press from the drug wars up north must have scared many of them away.

The jardín's bay laurels, pruned into spheres with rounded tops, offer respite from the battering noonday sun, but the Mexicans don't seem to mind the heat and stroll calmly in the sunshine. It's just us *gringas* melting into puddles. A hot zephyr kicks up the thin, pale dust and I know something awful is coming, an inescapable disaster.

"We need to go home, honey."

"I want a hot dog!" Tenney says, knowing full well that if she eats, I will let her stay. I know the buns from the hot dog stand are fine because Tenney shared one last summer with her grandmother when I wasn't around to stop her, and she had no reaction. And I have an EpiPen. We buy two hot dogs and return to our bench.

A little dog parks itself on its haunches about four feet in front us and pretends nonchalantly to ignore us as I eat my hot dog and wait for Tenney to take a bite of hers. The dog has big black eyes and a black nose and its fur is the color of a slab of New York concrete, stained, lusterless, filthy. In fact, it's the dirtiest little dog I've ever seen in my life. I also note that it's a she and she's pregnant, hugely pregnant, her nipples already distended on her swollen belly.

She tries to be unobtrusive, as if she's saying, *Just ignore me, I'm not really here*, but once in a while her eyes blink in our direction. This dog has turned begging into an art. While she clearly has grown to expect little kindness from humans, buried under her fathomless patience and endless experience of rejection, an ember of hope still burns. Tenney asks the dog if she's hungry, leans forward, and gives her the rounded end piece with a sliver of bun. The dog delicately inches forward and gobbles up the gift, then sits back, trying to pretend she's relaxed, no big deal, but her ears have pricked up, her body tensed. Tenney tears off another chunk and I wonder if this dog has learned to recognize tourists, the easy marks in the crowd. Tenney's entire hot dog is being gobbled up, while my skinny daughter has not taken a bite.

"Can you give her the rest of your hot dog? Please, Mom?"

I'm thinking, *Rabies*. I'm thinking, *Cholera. Fleas. Ticks. Worms. Mange. Lice.* Do dogs get lice? I hand what is left of my hot dog to Tenney, who places it on the ground before the animal.

"Be careful!" I warn, as if the dog is going to jump forward and bite her. But this is clearly not a stupid dog that is going to bite the proverbial hand that's feeding it.

"What's your name?" Tenney asks. The dog gazes at my daughter with a look that says, *Will you hurt me or will you help me?* Why is this dog able to express these feelings with one look? My heart constricts in my chest and I take in a deep breath to calm myself, to hold back some big, ugly feeling that is threatening to surface. Suddenly a wave of heat wafts up from the ground and I feel sweat pooling under my breasts and arms. I want to leave.

"Sophia is a beautiful name," Tenney says, as if the dog is speaking to her through telepathy.

"Sophia?" I say, my voice coming out with a hard edge.

"Mommy, can I get another hot dog?" The look in her eyes is as pleading as the dog's and I can't and never have been able to resist that look from my child. I hand Tenney some pesos. "May as well get a couple of them. She looks like she could use it."

Tenney's smile tenderizes my stone of a heart. She runs off to the vendor and returns with two hot dogs in buns in a Styrofoam container. She lays the open container before the animal with the hot dogs torn into chunks. The dog barely chews the food, she's in such a hurry to get it down before we have time to change our minds. A Mexican father in a somber suit and tie, the mother in a flowery, tight polyester dress, and three little girls wearing huge bows and pale pink crinoline confections are resting on the next bench. They watch all this with bland expressions, but their black eyes don't stray from the little drama unfolding before them. I know what they're thinking: *Look at those stupid gringas throwing their good money away on a mangy mutt!* I realize the dog must be thirsty too, and reach into my bag and bring out my bottle of water. I pour an inch into one side of the Styrofoam container and in two seconds the dog has lapped it up, so I pour out the rest.

"Tenney, go get a bottle of water from the hot dog man," I say, handing her more pesos, and off she goes. Now the Mexicans appear to be smirking. I don't care.

Tenney wants to stay in the jardín to watch over Sophia but we need to get back.

"It's time to go home," I patiently explain, "Bibi will be worried." And the FBI agents are coming.

All the way back up the steep hill, Tenney talks about the dog, who is following at a safe distance, as if this is simply a coincidence. How amazing, we just happen to be going in the same direction! Tenney wants to know: What's going to happen to her. Who will feed her? Where is she going to have her puppies? What if she's sick? What if she doesn't get more food today? What if she doesn't get any food or water tomorrow? What if somebody hurts her? Who would leave a dog like that all alone?

I make up answers as I go. Answers that I hope will ease Tenney's worries. But she doesn't stop.

When we get to Bibi's door, for which Marta has now given me a key, Tenney turns to the dog who is perhaps ten feet behind us, and says, "Don't worry, Sophia, I'll be back. You wait here," and I have to push her inside to close the door.

The house is quiet. No one is about.

Tenney would never mention this little episode to her grandmother since she knows that Bibi despises strays and mutts; in fact, she hates dogs of all types, and would chuckle dismissively. Bibi never wanted us to keep Arsène Lupin, the little brown dog with black spots that wandered into our gated yard in Yaoundé and killed a juvenile Gaboon viper by biting it behind the head and shaking it until its spine was severed. He charmed my dad into keeping him. Arsène Lupin was the perfect name for him, that notorious French gentleman thief. Arsène was the smartest dog I'd ever seen. But we never could break him of the habit of stealing. One time he stole a leg of lamb that was almost as big as he was right off the dining room table.

In our room, I throw myself onto the bed and cover my eyes with the crook of my arm.

"No one's here," says Tenney angrily. "I'm going back outside to get Sophia."

"*No*, Tenney."

She's taken aback by my tone. She stands completely still, aghast, and after a while throws herself onto her side of the bed, her back to me. Blueberry sits between us, his shiny eyes showing no opinion one way or the other. I reach out and lay my palm on her shoulder. She jerks away. I lie there for a long time. Tenney's breathing slows and after a while she falls asleep. The stress of these last few days has taken its toll on her too.

I tiptoe out to see if Bibi is back. It's near six p.m. and the streets are awakening after the long Sunday siesta. Music blasts from every window in the valley, carried up on waves of heat.

Bibi is having her sunset cocktail alone, out on the balcony. She says Calisto has borrowed her Mercedes to go visit his mother in Dolores Hidalgo. Bibi's eyes are glassy and slightly out of focus; she's had a drink or two already. Damn that self-righteous Doctor Handsome, now he's got me worrying about her drinking. I sit down next to her, facing the city spread out below us. She begins to complain about a new friend, a recent transplant to San Miguel from Berkeley, California, who has invited her for a potluck dinner tonight.

"Potluck!" Bibi mutters. "Whoever heard of such a thing? And can you believe, Merryn, she organizes these meetings called Brain Exchanges where they sit around discussing *ideas*.

I went to one and said, *No thank you! No more Brain Drains for me!
If I wanted to think, I would have stayed in New York. I mean,
really, Daddy would have howled.*"

I say, as calmly as possible, "The FBI is coming."

She sits up straight. "To *my* house?"

"I think so. Tonight."

"Why couldn't you have warned me earlier? What if I don't
want them in my house? Do I have to let them in? I mean,
don't they need a search warrant? And what am I going to tell
people?"

"I'm sorry."

And, abruptly, as is her wont, she changes course: "While
you were out gallivanting about town, I had a long conversation
with Faye about the news from Dallas . . ." She pauses dramatically and I suddenly feel like I'm choking. "The Dallas tabloids
are chock-full of misinformation about the whole sordid affair.
They have all the details about the girl being a waitress and her
head being under the dashboard. Though I don't think they
mention her being black. Nothing at all about this FBI nonsense. Oh, and by the way, the Huntleys are shipping Beauregard's body back to Charleston to be buried with all the other
formidable PGT Beauregard Huntleys."

I'm trying to think of something to say, something apt,
something reasonable, but I feel like I have a golf ball stuck in
my throat.

"Look at you, Merryn. You've gone all pale. Here, have a
sip." She holds out her margarita but I shake my head.

The doorbell sounds, a sharp, prolonged blast that res-
onates throughout the house. I lift my hands to my face and
cup them around my nose and mouth, trying to regulate my
breathing.

Tenney comes running across the patio from the direction of the outside door. "It's your taxi, Bibi!" she calls.

"Ah," says Bibi, putting down her drink and standing. "I'm off to *potluck*."

It takes Bibi five minutes of running hither and thither to get organized; lastly, after she's found her purse, her glasses, her wrap, and her keys, she goes to the kitchen and comes out carrying a large glass baking dish of Marta's enchiladas in green sauce. "There's another one in there for you and Tenney," she says. "Enjoy your evening, ladies. I'm sure I won't!"

The phone begins to trill as the western mountains stretch their long shadows across the valley. I don't want to answer but I know I must.

"This is Special Agent K. Warnock of the FBI," a gruff female voice states matter-of-factly. "We've been delayed by unforeseen circumstances and will be arriving late tonight in San Miguel. Is it convenient for you if we stop by first thing in the morning, say, around nine a.m.?"

I tell her that would be fine, click off, and try to set the phone back in its charger stand, my hand shaking so badly I miss the first couple of times.

Tenney pushes through the swinging kitchen door and marches toward me carrying a ball of tinfoil, a determined look on her face.

"We have to find Sophia."

I can't seem to move and stand stunned in the center of the great room, trying to think.

"Hurry up. It'll be dark soon."

I follow her out into the street. My legs feeling like they're encased in cement. Tenney starts to call, "Sophia! Sophia! Here, doggie! Here, Sophia! We've got treats for you!"

No Sophia. Our eyes travel up and down the sharply angled street.

"We have to find her," Tenney says. "It's important, Mom."

I know this is never going to happen. Sophia has given up and gone home to her flea-ridden lair, wherever that might be. But I pretend to make an effort.

"Sophia!" I call. "Sophia, here, doggie!" I clap my hands. Tenney takes off down the street, searching in the shadowy alleyways between houses where no weeds grow and little dust tornados spin in the air. The desolate ground is strewn with discarded mango pits, a fruit that the children peel back and eat like a banana. All over the ground are candy wrappers and little cellophane squares for cupcakes.

"Sophia!" Tenney calls, but I can tell by her voice she's already losing hope. Why is this upsetting me so much? I hate this. I want to go back.

"Sophia!" I call, trying for a light and airy tone. I am usually much better at faking it than this.

Tenney runs back toward me, then up, up, past Bibi's house, up the winding mountain road, disappearing around a hairpin turn. She's running toward the locked gate that is the back entrance to the Jardín Botánico el Charco del Ingenio, the botanical gardens. Fewer houses, more empty lots and discarded wrappers. A warm wind has risen and dust flies into my eyes, making them sting and water. I start running, worrying about brigands, kidnappers, and pedophiles. Shadows are lengthening quickly now, the corners growing dark.

"Sophia!" Tenney tries again. She turns and her eyes flash, wet with angry tears.

My voice so low and tight in my throat it is barely audible, I mumble, "Maybe she'll be back at the jardín tomorrow. We'll go look for her in the morning."

"Do you promise?"

"Yes, I promise."

"If you're lying to me, Mom, I am going to be really angry."

What have I done?

CHAPTER FIVE

Monday

I WAKE UP AT THREE A.M. and lie in the dark, my headache shooting up from my jaw to the top of my head and pulsating behind my ear like the woofer in a speaker. My dentist told me I clench my teeth and need to stop doing that. I've broken six tooth guards and swallowed one. *Hello?* If I could stop doing it, it wouldn't be a problem, would it?

For some reason our first Thanksgiving in Cameroon comes to mind, an uncorrupted memory, a moment that never changes, as if it were a perfect clip of film kept protected forever in a dark canister.

That first year, my parents didn't make me go to school on Thanksgiving, though it was a regular school day in Yaoundé. The US embassy had flown turkeys in from the States and we had a big feast at the ambassador's residence with the other American families. The next morning, Sister Marie-Thérèse asked me why I missed school the previous day. I told her the truth: *"C'était la fête de* Thanksgiving."

"Show me your hand," she said in French. She opened her drawer, took out her long, thin, wooden ruler, and swung it around a few times so that it made a whistling sound, then whacked me three times on the knuckles of my right hand in front of the whole, silent, fascinated class. The shame was worse than the sting. "That is for skipping school."

When I got home and Mum saw my hand, she almost turned

purple with rage. She was still in her embassy tea attire.

"Come with me," she said, and she jumped into the jeep in her high heels with me in the passenger seat, and raced back over pothole-infested streets to the school. She marched into the front office and demanded, in her perfect Sorbonne French, in an icy and condescending tone, to see Sister Marie-Thérèse. The younger nun who greeted us in the main office ran off down the hall to find my teacher. A few minutes later, Sister Marie-Thérèse came in, taking her time, looking perfectly relaxed and composed, protected, as always, behind her gigantic and terrifying habit.

"Madam," said Mum, "Thanksgiving is a national holiday in the United States, and as Americans we choose to celebrate. Inasmuch as I am the parent, and I made the decision to keep my daughter home, why not smack *my* hand with your ruler?" She lifted her long, delicate hand as if offering it for the nun to kiss. Sister Marie-Thérèse turned pale, her skin appearing gray against her starched white guimpe. We all held our breath, except Mum, who seemed perfectly calm.

"I didn't think so," Mum intoned. "Not very Christlike, is it, tormenting small children who can't defend themselves? Didn't Jesus say something about the suffering of innocents? Good thing for all of us you weren't around during the Inquisition. You can take your anger and sexual frustrations out somewhere else, madam. Not on my daughter. If you so much as rearrange a hair on her head, you will be hearing from the United States ambassador himself."

With that, my mum turned on her pointy heel and clicked her way to the front door, my rubber-soled shoes squeaking along inadequately beside her. Once the jeep had passed through the gates, Mum flicked her eyes at me and said, "I showed her who was boss and now we're going to throw a load of sugar on that vinegar. Tomorrow morning, you're going to bring that horrible bitch a beautiful bouquet of flowers." After a moment of thought Mum added, "You are much too honest, Merryn. Sometimes lying is necessary. With people like that, lying is not only necessary, but *good*. And dear, always remember, when you tell a lie, make sure you keep it as close to the truth as possible, because it will be easier to remember."

At 8:55 a.m., as I stand alone on the terrace waiting for the agents to arrive, my head is still pulsating despite six Advils and two Percocets and I feel as if I'm underwater. Bibi sent Marta off to the market with Tenney in tow and that's good—at least I won't be worrying about her while I undergo the rack. Last night I waited for Bibi to get home from her potluck party and told her that the agents were coming at nine this morning. She was a little high and I was worried she would not remember. But as soon as Marta arrived at eight a.m., Bibi enlisted her in staging an unassuming, attractive breakfast at one end of the long table—sliced cantaloupe and honeydew, mango and papaya; fresh bread and pastries; bacon, ham, and a bowl of scrambled eggs. The coffee steams in the carafe, as does the hot milk in its little pitcher.

My mouth is completely dry and the thought of food is appalling.

At nine o'clock precisely the agents arrive in their dark American business suits. The woman is tall and broad-shouldered. She hands me a business card that has a very serious-looking government seal at the center: *Special Agent K. Warnock, BS, MBA. Federal Bureau of Investigation.* I look up into her searching, opaque brown eyes and I can tell immediately she's no fool. Her partner is short, with black, brilliantined hair. He introduces himself brusquely as Theo Athas. He has a shiny black computer bag slung over his shoulder and shiny black shoes that are a little too pointy. Everything about him is shiny, pointy, and black. I stand in the great room doorway and Bibi, in a pale summer suit, hair upswept and her makeup perfect, greets the agents in the patio holding a Bloody Mary, as if she's hosting a cocktail party and they are the first guests to arrive. She leads them toward the dining area.

"You've had a long trip so I took the liberty of setting out a little breakfast," says Bibi, extending her hand toward the table. "Please, do help yourselves."

"We had breakfast at the hotel," says Agent Athas. But Special Agent Warnock is already piling a plate with fruit and trying to decide which bread or pastry to pick from the basket. She chooses a flaky bun and bites into it. She swallows and announces, "I'll have some eggs to counteract the sugar—I'm hypoglycemic."

Agent Athas watches her, seemingly trying to control the muscles in his face.

"How about a cup of coffee?" Bibi offers Agent Athas, setting her Bloody Mary on the table. Finally he nods, and Bibi pours. He sits, pulls a laptop out of his bag, and sets it on the table.

"Ma'am," says Agent Warnock to Bibi in a serious tone, "I'm going to have to ask you to give us some privacy."

"I'm off." Bibi steps out of the great room, head held high, shoulders back, and disappears up the stairs. Agent Warnock fills a coffee cup and throws in some cream and several spoonfuls of sugar.

"All right then, Mrs. Huntley," says Agent Warnock, dropping into a dining chair and taking a thin, silver laptop out of her tote bag. She pulls out a nest of wires and a little black box and begins to hook everything up, then drops to the floor and crawls around, looking for an outlet.

"And you can thank the US government for the latest in wireless technology," she says from under the table. She sets up the laptop at the head of the table with the screen facing us and in a moment, gazing at us a little myopically, there is an elderly gentleman with a thick mane of gray hair and a short, well-groomed beard.

"Hello there, Merryn," says Harvey Berger. He looks nothing like I remember.

"You understand everything your attorney Mr. Berger has told you about this conversation, and the fact that you are cooperating of your own free will in this investigation?" asks Agent Athas.

Both agents stare at me expectantly.

"Yes. But I knew nothing about Beau's business affairs."

"Wait for their questions, Merryn," says Harvery Berger from the computer screen, with a slight delay between the sound and the movement of his lips.

"Sign this," says Agent Athas, sliding a paper toward me.

"That's the proffer. Do sign it," advises Harvey Berger. I sign the document without reading it.

Agent Warnock is pale, her face muscles tight. She riffles through the documents in her file, holding them up close to her face. "You were involved in your husband's charity, Bootstraps for Dallas, is that correct?"

Her dark eyes turn to me and search my face. I feel like I have a big window right in the middle of my forehead and she can see clear inside my brain. But of course this is not possible; she can't read anything but my expression, and my expression right now is one of fear and anxiety in the face of this show of force by the powerful United States government.

"Beau asked me to help with the yearly galas. He thought I spent too much time at home with Tenney and wanted me to get more involved in the Dallas social scene. I sent out invitations to the yearly benefit, and I made phone calls. I hated doing it."

"Why is that?" asks Agent Warnock.

I tell her, "I'm not a social person. I wasn't interested in the Dallas social scene, though I was glad to help Beau with the fund-raising banquets. Bootstraps for Dallas was a great organization. Beau tried to help start-up companies that couldn't get funding by giving them free space in his buildings. But the thing I cared about most was that he was building orphanages and schools in Afghanistan. Schools where the only rule was that girls had to be allowed to attend." I'm hoping she will appreciate this detail because I certainly did.

Agent Warnock snorts. "If they built a single school or orphanage in Afghanistan, I would be amazed."

Agent Athas jumps in. "What were your financial responsibilities, if any, with the charity?"

"I . . . I . . . wasn't involved in the financial aspects of Bootstraps."

"Hmm . . . Did you ever accompany your husband to the Middle East?" he asks me as he peers down at his computer screen.

"Never. He never took me with him on business trips."

"When donors wrote checks or wired money for Bootstraps, did the checks ever come to you personally, or to Mr. Huntley?" asks Agent Warnock. She delicately lifts a spoonful of scrambled eggs to her mouth and chews, keeping her eyes on me. I couldn't eat right now if I had to. I feel sick.

"No, the checks were written out to Bootstraps. Sometimes, at the benefits, a person might hand me a check written out to Bootstraps for Dallas, and I'd give it to Beau. One time someone made a mistake and wrote the check out to Beau, and he tore it up and told the woman to write out another one to Bootstraps for Dallas."

"How much were these checks for?" asks Agent Warnock.

"The ones I saw were for a couple thousand at most. The big money usually came from corporations and private benefactors, through their foundations."

After a pause Agent Warnock asks, "Would you say you had a good marriage? Overall?"

I don't hesitate for a second: "We had a wonderful marriage." Then I choke, and tears spring to my eyes. "Until three days ago I . . . thought we had a w-wonderful marriage." I cover my face with my hands. After an appropriate lapse, I wipe my eyes and nose with a napkin. The agents' faces are pale, stolid masks. "I probably would have gone on thinking that for the rest of my life."

"You should know, Mrs. Huntley, this is a matter of national security," warns Agent Warnock.

"How well do you know Ibrahim Ansari?" Agent Athas asks.

About a year ago I got a friend request on Facebook from Rock Le Casbah. It was Ibrahim Ansari. All his photos were of himself playing polo, or golf, or drinking Crystal champagne with large-breasted women. He posted statements like, *Arab Sex is the best!* Or, *Meet the sextacular Rock!* Beau told me that back in Saudi Arabia, Ibrahim had a wife who wore the black abaya and jiddah, who followed behind him with a brood of children and never said a word. What a terrible life, I thought. I didn't want to cause any business problems for Beau, so I accepted the Facebook friend request but I blocked Rock Le Casbah's posts.

"He had a Facebook page. He called himself Rock Le Casbah," I reply.

Silence.

After a moment I offer, "Beau told me Ibrahim had a wife and children in Saudi Arabia. A silent, veiled wife."

"Well then, isn't that proof Beau traveled there?" states Agent Athas, looking at me over his shiny glasses.

"I don't know."

Agent Athas asks, "Did you ever hear your husband talking to his partner, Edward Buckingham, about an offshore account?"

Here it comes. If I were taking a polygraph, this is where the monitoring lines would start jumping all over the place. But I know how to control my face muscles and my body language. I am frowning, thinking hard.

They loved that restaurant/bar the Blue Bayou uptown and enjoyed going there on a Saturday night. I didn't like leaving Tenney with a babysitter, but sometimes Beau insisted. One night Bucky had some pills called Molly that he'd bought from the waitress LouKeesha, and Beau, Bucky, and Jocelyn teased me for being a wimp and a wet blanket. I had taken a Percocet for my headache earlier and wasn't sure it was a good idea to mix, but I swallowed one of the little white pills, innocuous looking as aspirin, with a sip of cranberry and club soda. Within twenty minutes I had a feeling of expansiveness, as if for once I could feel my outline in space and my inner being breaking out of its boundaries, floating out into the world, and I was in love with planet Earth and everyone on it. I wanted to hug everybody.

"People should feel this way all the time!" I had cried, running my hand tenderly across Beau's wide neck and shoulders. He chuckled silently, eyes smiling, glowing with the drug. Usually I was afraid to touch him unless he touched me first.

Bucky said to Beau across the table, "Why don't you take Merryn to Grand Cayman with you next weekend? It's Valentine's Day weekend. It looks better, anyway."

I had noticed for the first time how Bucky's athletic football body had gone to fat. He had three chins, and a florid look, as if his kidneys were having a hard time cleaning him out.

"She won't leave the kid," Beau said, smiling numbly, running his fingernails roughly across his face from cheekbone to chin, chin to cheekbone. He hadn't shaved because it was Saturday and the sound was strange, like his face was made of sandpaper.

"We need to move the cash into the YSL account and it has to be done now. With Ibrahim's plane . . . no travel record."

I pretended to pay no attention. They thought I was meek and shallow—that all I cared about in life was Tenney and going to the gym. As their warm, glowing faces swam in and out of focus I realized I had never felt this relaxed and content or expansive in my entire life. I hugged Beau around the neck and kissed him. He didn't resist. He did not like public displays, not even holding hands.

Later on that night, in bed, while he was still sweating and breathing hard, I asked him, "What's Bucky talking about, Beau? What's the YSL account?"

"Goddamnit," he said, pushing me away, shoving his pillow into my face, "how many fucking times do I have to tell you not to ask about my business?"

Ne lui demande pas ce qu'il fait. I'd put that Note to Self in three different places and still I couldn't resist the impulse to ask.

Agent Athas is growing impatient, waiting for my response. "Mrs. Huntley? Did you ever hear your husband discussing an offshore account with his partner?"

I turn to him. "I'm trying to remember if I ever heard them talking about something like that . . . Never."

Agent Warnock stares at me, her eyes almost predatory. "Does *YSL* mean anything to you?"

I pretend to give this some thought. "The only thing I can think of is Yves Saint Laurent."

"Yves Saint Laurent?" repeats Agent Athas, typing furiously on his laptop.

"Beau used to buy me this expensive Yves Saint Laurent perfume. He always brought it back when he traveled. It came in an Asian-looking bottle. He bought it in the duty-free shops."

"Opium," says Agent Warnock.

I look down at the table, the beautiful curving lines in the wood, and run my fingers over them.

The agents gaze at each other in heavy silence.

"Did Beau ever travel to Grand Cayman?" asks Agent Athas.

"He liked the golf there," I allow.

"Did you accompany him on any trips to Grand Cayman?" asks Agent Warnock in a softer voice.

Bibi's words of advice ring in my mind: *When you tell a lie, make sure you keep it as close to the truth as possible, because it will be easier to remember.*

"I went with him twice. The first time, we were not even engaged yet. That was more than ten years ago. I'd never flown on a private jet before. It was during winter, probably February. Beau flew from Dallas to New York in Ibrahim Ansari's Gulfstream and picked me up in a limo and we drove out to a private airport in New Jersey."

I glance at the laptop screen and notice that Harvey Berger looks unhappy. But he doesn't say anything.

"The second time I went with him was last February. Tenney was with us. It was Valentine's Day weekend. Beau told the pilot Ibrahim's plane was old and he joked that Ibrahim needed to upgrade to a G-6. The hotel was right on the beach."

We could see the cruise ships pulling in and out of port in the distance. The turquoise water lay calm and flat to the rounded horizon. Beau was lying back on a lounge chair, an umbrella drink in his hand; his foot was jiggling, jiggling. There were no palm trees, only scraggly-looking beach pines.

Tenney said, "Why don't we go on a cruise ship, Daddy?"

"One day I'm going to buy us a yacht as big as a cruise ship," he said in strange, determined tone. "That's when you know you've made it. When you have your own one hundred–meter yacht."

I looked at him and didn't say anything. I wondered for a moment if he was insane.

"Always remember this," he had said in that strange voice, "ten steps ahead. That's the secret."

Then I decided, *Oh, it's just talk.* He was a great talker, Beau. Always promising to do things, like spend two hours with his daughter on a Sunday morning playing chess. But often, just as they would be getting started, his phone would beep, some work-related emergency calling him away.

I tell Agent Warnock helpfully, "Tenney and I sat by the pool or on the beach and mostly Beau played golf."

What I don't tell her is that on Monday morning, Beau said he had to take care of some business, and went out wearing a suit. He had left a large, metallic suitcase that had a handcuff in the hotel's walk-in safe.

Agents Warnock and Athas glance meaningfully at each other.

Breaking the silence, in an aggressive tone that startles me, Agent Athas asks, "So you knew, or certainly had reason to know, that your husband and Edward Buckingham were laundering money?" He is staring at me now with the look of a man who has just won a high-stakes hand of poker.

"Calm down there, Theo," mutters Agent Warnock. "We're just talking here."

Athas, with a nasty smile, says, "Well, that was before she admitted her involvement."

"I wasn't involved!" I cry out. "I had nothing to do with it! I didn't know anything!"

Harvey slams his palm down and shouts from the laptop screen, "What is this aggressive questioning? You said she was just a witness! I won't put up with bullying!"

The two agents stare at each other. Agent Warnock finally shifts her blunt eyes to me and says in an equable, unemotional way, "Ansari is connected to some pretty nasty extremists in Afghanistan. And as for you, Mrs. Huntley, conscious avoidance, or willful blindness, is no defense of the law."

"This conversation is over!" shouts Harvey.

I can't seem to move. My fingers grip the edges of my seat, turning my knuckles white.

"Ansari's phone records indicate that he's been trying to contact you," says Agent Warnock in a gentler tone. "Is that true?"

"He left eleven messages on my voice mail. He says he needs to talk to me right away. I haven't called him back. I saved the messages, if you want to hear them."

"Oh, yes indeed, we want to hear them," says Agent Athas unpleasantly.

After a long silence, Agent Warnock nods to me as I sit stunned in my seat. "Would you mind getting your mobile phone for me, please? And also your laptop computer." She stands up and begins putting away her papers. "Mr. Berger?"

"Yes . . . yes . . . give her your phone and your laptop, Merryn."

Agent Athas packs up his own laptop.

I can't seem to get out of the chair. What if they can retrieve the voice mails and texts from the CrossFit Nazi? Or, God forbid, the *pic*— How embarrassing. But not incriminating. *I was bored*, I'll tell Agent Warnock, teary eyed. *He made me feel like I still had a modicum of control over my life.*

Finally, I pull myself to my feet by grasping the edge of the table. My fingertips leave sweat marks on the shiny, polished wood. I go into our room and take the smartphone and laptop out of the drawer. Hesitating only a moment, I open Blueberry's battery compartment and pull out the Mikimoto pearls in their black suede pouch.

Back in the great room, I hand the three items to Agent Warnock.

"What's this?" she asks, fingering the suede pouch.

"Ibrahim Ansari gave those pearls to me at the last gala for Bootstraps. If he's a terrorist, then these are blood pearls and I don't want anything to do with them."

"Hmmm," says Agent Warnock. "Write up a receipt, Athas." She tosses him the pouch.

"The phone is low on batteries," I state.

"We're leaving now, Mr. Berger," she mutters, "we'll be in touch," and she shuts off her laptop. I watch in silence as she steps away from the table, stopping to look at Tenney's chess set, which she has left in the middle of a match against herself. Agent Warnock assesses the board but doesn't say anything. Athas gives me a paper to sign that says I handed over evidence in the form of one strand of Mikimoto pearls. I sign the paper.

I walk them in heavy silence through the patio to the outside door.

CHAPTER
SIX

I RETURN TO THE GREAT ROOM to find Bibi storming
around in a fury, a Bloody Mary in one hand and a cigarette
in the other. She has changed out of her fancy suit and is
wearing a lilac, terrycloth, Caribbean-cruise, one-piece pantsuit with a hoodie and crystal buttons.

"I can't believe you've allowed this to happen—FBI agents
in my house!"

The phone rings and Bibi rushes to the table to pick it up.

"Faye! No, I'm running late. It's been a very busy morning
. . . Who told you? . . . The bitch next door? Well isn't she the
nosy one. No, no, no, they're accountants. Who said they were
FBI? . . . Well, maybe they're accountants for the FBI, how in the
world should I know? They were here to see Merryn, not me . . .
Calisto just got back from Dolores Hidalgo, he'll drive us. We'll
pick you up in twenty minutes." She puts down the phone and
turns to me with a sour look. "I am humiliated. You cause me
nothing but trouble, Merryn."

Tenney comes running out of the kitchen with a tinfoil
package in her hand. She stops short when she sees Bibi.

"Bibi . . ." I murmur.

"We'll deal with this later. I don't have time now." She says
that Faye has invited her to a hot springs spa for a jewelry-making
class followed by the cure, a bath in the steamy water and a massage, an expensive all-inclusive package that will help her relax,

which she desperately needs to do right now—she can't very well back out at the last minute.

As soon as they have left, Calisto driving Bibi's Mercedes convertible, Tenney says, "We're going back to the jardín to find Sophia."

I am too emotionally drained and too ashamed to argue.

We've been hanging around the jardín for an hour; still no Sophia. I am secretly relieved. Tenney grips her tinfoil-wrapped leftovers and the ball is beginning to look pretty squishy. I tell her the doggie surely has a good home and was just wandering around yesterday out of curiosity. She looks at me with a flat expression, her brows creased, and I know she's not buying it.

The parroquia bell strikes noon; the square is practically deserted. I'm about to suggest we head home when the little dog comes trotting around a corner and crosses the paved area in front of the church, tail up like a flag. She's heading for the jardín like a businesswoman hurrying to catch a train. Yesterday's hot dogs and water must have perked her up.

"Sophia!" Tenney jumps up from the bench and runs out of the jardín with me on her heels. The reunion is like *Doctor Zhivago*. The dog jumps up on her hind legs, licks Tenney's face, and Tenney hugs her, laughing with relief. She's going to catch something horrible, that's for certain. She offers the tinfoil package, opening it on the sidewalk before the dog—roast chicken, some rice and beans, and possibly a burrito. The dog is delighted, her tail wagging furiously.

"We need to bring her home," Tenney says in a steely tone.

Bibi is already furious at me. This is not going to end well, no question about it. I begin my litany of Reasonable Mother explanations of why this is not a good idea, but Tenney knows and I know these are all just formalities. I can see by her face she is getting ready to throw a tantrum, and I do not have the time or the patience or the resilience for a major Tenney tantrum right now.

"It'll be okay, Sophia," she tells the dog. "Don't worry. My mom's a really nice person once you get to know her."

"You know Bibi is never going to let us keep a dog."

"We'll have to sneak her in." Tenney's voice is fierce with resolve.

"All right, we'll sneak her in." Already, bile is churning up my insides and drying out my mouth. Bibi is going to feel betrayed, she's going to be apoplectic.

On the way home we pass an upscale, touristy *farmacía* and I tell Tenney to wait right outside with the dog. I go in and ask if they have insecticide shampoo. They have it. I ask if they have dog food; they don't. I buy a brush with metal bristles and a pair of hair scissors.

All the way up the steep, narrow Cuesta de San Jose, Tenney is making plans. Sophia is trotting along beside her, determined, enthusiastic even. Along the way Tenney picks up an empty cardboard box with *Tequila Herradura* printed on the side. "I'll go in first," she suggests, "and make sure no one's in our room."

"Put her down, Tenney," I whisper, and quickly shut our bedroom door, locking it. "Let me take a look." Down goes the little dog, long feathery tail wagging hopefully as her black eyes gaze up at me. Clearly this dog thinks my say will determine her fate. Little does she know there is a much greater boss over whom I hold no sway.

We put her in our bathroom sink and wash her with the insecticide shampoo. I wonder for an instant if this might harm the puppies, but in the end I know I have to do this, or she simply can't stay with us. The dog's nipples are distended and hard, her round belly stretched like a helium balloon, yet I can feel every single one of her ribs through the fur on her back. She does not resist though she looks terrified. All the while Tenney talks to her as if it's a two-way conversation. "I know," she says, "you've had a really bad time but everything is going to be okay now. We have to wash you, you see. I've had a bad time recently too. My daddy died in a car accident."

My hands stop moving. It's the first time since we left Dallas that Tenney has mentioned her father. This is a good thing. At least, I think it's good. She must think I don't want to talk about it. But I must make an effort to be available if *she* wants to talk about it. Methodically, my hands go back to massaging the soap into the little dog's fur. Tentatively, I ask, "Tenney, do you want to talk about what happened to your da—"

"No." Her tone is like the lid on a car trunk slamming shut.

I continue scrubbing the little dog. I don't even want to look at the stuff coming off of her—bugs, burs, and God knows what else. After a second washing with Tenney's baby shampoo, Sophia's fur is no longer gray but pale blond, so pale it's almost silver, with a few patches the color of sand, especially on the tips of her ears and tail.

"Tenney," I say, "your daddy loved you very much. You know that, right?" The truth is, I don't believe he loved anybody at all.

"Yes," she says. I wait, but she remains silent.

"He loved you more than anything and that is why he worked so hard. So you could have a wonderful life."

She gazes at me with her search-beam eyes and I don't flinch. Some lies are good lies.

Sophia has ticks, but only a few, and I remember how in Yaoundé my dad used to light a match and blow it out and touch the hot end to the ticks' heads to get them off Arsène Lupin.

Poor Arsène. I haven't thought about him in so long I'm amazed how sharply the memory comes back: his smell, the feel of his short hair. He had a jaunty black patch over his right eye, like a pirate. When we were given twenty-four hours to leave Cameroon, Arsène Lupin got left with the French neighbors, who were none too thrilled. Bibi was furious at us for keeping the dog in the first place. She yelled at my dad, *See what you get? See what you get? You were supposed to be Deputy Chief of Mission in Paris, not some flunky in this shit pit!*

"Did I ever tell you about Arsène Lupin?" I ask Tenney.

"Ars—what?"

"He was my dog in Cameroon."

She is curious now and wants to know so I tell her about the time my parents invited the French ambassador and his wife to dinner and Arsène jumped up and stole the leg of lamb right off the silver serving dish on the dining room table while the French ambassador and his wife were having cocktails in the next room. I stood and watched, fascinated, while my dad tried to wrestle the lamb from Arsène's jaws. Finally my dad shook the shredded leg of lamb free and put it back on the silver platter and turned it so that the best side was up, as if nothing had happened. "Don't tell your mum," he said, wiping sweat from his brow.

Tenney and I are laughing and the dog is watching us with a doubtful expression as we dry her off with one of Bibi's bath towels. It feels so good to laugh and see the light return to Tenney's face.

I find matches in the kitchen and burn the bloated, disgusting ticks off of Sophia and flush them down the toilet. She sits in Tenney's arms, quiet, impassive. It is impossible to brush the knots out of her fur, so I give her a haircut. I've never cut a dog's hair before but I'm not going for a prize at the Westminster dog show, after all.

By the time I'm finished, Sophia looks like a completely different dog. Almost like a civilized, rich lady's pet. Sophia licks my hands as I try to snip off some remaining tufts so that she doesn't look like some lunatic cut her hair. Sophia has an elegant face, now that we can see it. Thoughtful, calm black eyes, a black nose with a sharp-edged upper ridge, which gives her a dignified look, and dainty, slightly pursed, downturned black lips, which remind me of a French actress from the old black-and-white films I used to watch on TV in Cameroon.

Tenney asks me to cut a u-shaped opening into one side of the box so she can make a little bed for Sophia. She unfolds some newspapers to put on the bottom but Sophia bolts under the bed, cowering and trembling.

"You don't like newspapers? That's okay," Tenney says, and puts them away. She turns to me: "Someone hit her with newspapers."

She pulls more towels from the linen closet in the bathroom. All the towels in Bibi's house are spotless, fluffy, and white, and changed every day, like the sheets. Bibi is very careful about hygiene and demands that Allegra use bleach and the second rinse cycle on the wash at all times.

I'm worrying about germs. About worms. About rabies. How are we going to keep a dog from Bibi? The staff is bound to find out any minute, and then what? What am I going to tell her? That Tenney brought home a stray when we both know perfectly well that Bibi doesn't like dogs? The little animal keeps looking up at me with hopeful black eyes, wagging her tail. I am not always a heartless bitch. I am not going to throw a pregnant dog out into the street. Anyway, Bibi won't be home until late this afternoon and hopefully we won't even need to discuss this until tomorrow.

A knock on the bedroom door. It's Allegra, to clean the room.

"No, gracias. Estoy enferma!" I call out, telling her I'm sick.

Tenney sneaks off to scavenge in the kitchen, returning with a plate of pork burritos. I am not sure this rich food is a good idea, but who knows what Sophia has been eating. Tomorrow we'll get some kibbles.

"And you have to be quiet, Sophia," Tenney whispers earnestly, "or we'll get into big trouble."

They've made necklaces at the spa. Bibi's is of huge fresh-water pearls and amethyst drops, and while we sit at the table she keeps touching her slim collarbones where the necklace rests. Faye's is even larger, with chunky turquoise, silver, and amber beads strung in a complicated pattern, wrapped several times around her neck. I've checked Bibi's answering machine twice and Agent Warnock has not called me back and Bibi seems to have forgotten that she was furious with me this morning. Bibi and Faye apparently had a few cocktails at the spa bar before setting out for home and then their usual cocktail-hour margaritas, which Bibi has taught Calisto to make in the martini shaker. How many drinks is that today?

The roast chicken tastes too much like what it is. Tenney and I sit in tense apprehension, expecting barking to break out at any moment, but Bibi talks on and on and Faye adds her two cents and Calisto sits and broods. We left Sophia on Tenney's side of the bed in her cardboard box—so far, so good. It's amazing, the dog seems to understand the situation almost like a human being.

They're on the subject of their friend Lizzie. Originally from Houston, Texas, Lizzie caught the San Miguel bug while on vacation, shortly after her twenty-year marriage came to an end. She went back to Houston, sold her mansion, and moved to San Miguel, like so many thousands of Americans before her.

"Well, she surely isn't the first rich American lady to be seduced by your Doctor Handsome," Bibi tells Faye.

Faye acknowledges that Lizzie's sudden disappearance from the social scene does coincide with Doctor Handsome's first visit to her house several weeks ago.

"That man is nothing to write home about," Bibi says. "He's a lousy doctor."

"He's a very good doctor," Faye counters. "You don't like him because he told you to cut down on your drinking."

Bibi makes a little snorting sound of disapproval. I know that sound very well and feel strangely pleased that for once it is directed at someone else.

Faye continues, "He's trying to raise money for his free children's clinic. Maybe Lizzie is helping him."

"Well, he can keep trying to squeeze blood out of *that* stone. No one, but I mean no one, is cheaper than Lizzie Carmichael," Bibi says. "No, he was better off with that Anna James . . . but apparently it ended badly. He did *not* like being at her beck and call, I hear. Beggars should not be choosers, if you ask me."

They make an early night of it, calling Faye a cab at around nine because Calisto is too tired to get the Mercedes out again and drive her home.

"Poor Calisto," says Bibi, ruffling his hair. "He's had a long day with the ladies!"

The relief I feel when we get back to our room is like a fifty-pound weight has been lifted off my shoulders. Tenney immediately goes to the dog, who lies quietly on her side in her box, listlessly wagging her tail, as if she's simply done in. I know how she feels.

We have to sneak her out for a walk, and she follows behind us, her nails clicking on the patio flagstones. She seems to be a very well-trained and well-behaved dog. It's almost as if she

knows that any misstep could cost her everything. Just outside
the door, at the curb, she dutifully squats and her long stream
of pee runs downhill, disappearing into the spaces between the
cobblestones. She goes up a little ways and poops in one of the
dusty alleys between two big houses, then comes right back, as
if she's scared we'll lock her out.

Tuesday

Tenney is shaking me awake. I took an Ambien and am having a
hard time focusing. It's one o'clock in the morning. "Mommy!
Something's wrong with Sophia!"

The dog is lying on her side, completely listless, unable to
summon the energy to sit up. Her vagina is opening and closing,
but clearly she doesn't have any strength left to push.

"How come her bum is doing that?" Tenney asks.

"That's not her bum, honey, that's her vagina. The babies
are trying to come out."

We wait. We wait and wait some more. An hour passes and
nothing improves.

I'm sorry to cause you all this trouble, Sophia's guilty look
seems to say. It's a terrible thing to watch and I don't know what
to do. I'm reminded of when I was in labor with Tenney, lying
in the hospital, feeling utterly helpless and alone. Beau was out
of the country. He had Jeanne-Wallace send me a dozen long-
stemmed pink roses.

I don't even have my smartphone or laptop to look up on the
Internet what to do.

The digital clock on the bedside table reads 2:35 a.m. I find
Doctor Handsome's card in my wallet and dial the first of the
two numbers with a trembling hand. It rings and rings.

"Hello?" a hoarse, rusty voice. I've definitely woken him up.

"I'm sorry to call you so late, Dr. Fuller. This is Merryn

Huntley. Vivienne's daughter . . . You were here Saturday."

I hear him breathing, apparently trying to process this information.

"We have an emergency," I plow on, wondering if he might be at Lizzie Carmichael's house, and if he'll tell her and she'll tell Bibi, but I don't have time to worry about this right now.

"Is your mother all right?"

"It's not my mother, Dr. Fuller. My daughter's dog has been in labor for several hours and she's listless and unresponsive—"

"Your daughter's dog?"

"I don't know anybody in San Miguel, Dr. Fuller, we just got here from Dallas a few days ago. We need help."

"I'm not sure I . . . I'm not a vet . . ."

"Don't hang up on me. Please. This is an emergency. She's going to die."

"Let me pull myself together."

Fifteen minutes later we hear his motorcycle roaring up the mountain. I run to let him in before he can ring the bell. Still, it's a good thing Bibi's quarters are on the other side of the house and she is such a sound sleeper and the streets of San Miguel are generally so noisy. He's wearing a faded black T-shirt and black jeans and his ostrich cowboy boots and has his black nylon backpack over one shoulder. As soon as he steps into the patio, Tenney throws her arms around his waist and hugs him. He's so surprised he stands immobile, arms akimbo.

"Come quick, Doctor Handsome, this way," she whispers, pulling him by the hand.

Back in our room, he's already kneeling by Sophia's box, slipping his hands into latex gloves. "It's inertia. She's just exhausted. Probably half-starved and the puppies are too big. She doesn't look good. This a San Miguel stray?"

"Her name is Sophia," Tenney tells him. "She's had a very bad time since she was abandoned."

"I don't doubt it," says Dr. Fuller while he palpates the dog's distended belly. He pours some kind of disinfectant over his gloved hands and inserts two fingers into her vagina.

"What are you doing?" Tenney asks nervously.

"I'm trying to see what's going on."

I'm so grateful to him for not laughing at us, I feel like crying. It's probably the Ambien. The situation must seem completely absurd to him. It seems absurd to me. What have I gotten us into? What if she dies? What if she doesn't die but needs medical care, hospitalization? Are people even allowed to bring Mexican dogs back to the States?

"It's okay, Sophia, Doctor Handsome is going to take care of you," Tenney says.

"You can call me Dr. Steve." He takes a syringe out of a sealed plastic packet and fills it with liquid from a vial. "I'm going to give her something to stimulate her contractions," he explains.

"I had that; it didn't work," I say, as if this could possibly be helpful or of any interest to him.

A little while later, he reaches inside the dog and pulls out a slimy, watery balloon-like white sack that looks way too big for her opening. He tears the sack open and wipes the fluid from the tiny nose and mouth, checks for a heartbeat with his stethoscope.

"This one's dead," he says calmly, without emotion.

"No!" cries Tenney, tears sprouting from her eyes.

"More are coming," he tells her. "Let's focus on those, okay?"

The next one comes quickly. Sophia tries to lift her head to see but barely has the strength. I feel tears on my cheeks too and

I don't know why I'm crying. Dr. Fuller is holding the second puppy cupped in his hands, and he's swinging his arms up and down, up and down.

He rubs the inert thing's belly with his thumbs. "Come on," he says, "come on."

A squeak, then the tiny mouth opens and he places the squirming white hairless thing against Sophia's belly. It searches blindly for the nipple; Sophia is compliant, relieved, trying to wag her tail, sniffing and licking at the thing.

"This one's a girl."

The third one is the smallest, and after Dr. Fuller has cleared away the amniotic membrane and the mucus and severed the umbilical chord, he listens through his stethoscope and seems to have trouble finding a heartbeat. Meanwhile, I'm whispering in a tumble of words the story of how we met Sophia and how Tenney made me go back and how I just couldn't talk her out of it and how Sophia is a very well-trained dog, not wild at all, as if I'm trying to convince him. He holds the puppy cupped in his hands and swings his arms up and down, up and down again.

"What are you doing?" I ask in a whisper.

"I'm trying to clear the lungs of fluid."

Finally there's a little squeak, and he places the wriggling thing that looks like a naked mole rat next to the other one, by Sophia's belly. "This little one's a boy."

He washes Sophia's back end and legs with the disinfectant, wipes everything down, and then clears away the bloody towels. He asks if we have any clean ones to put down. Tenney runs to the bathroom.

Bibi is just going to have a whale.

He wraps the dead puppy in the folds of a soiled towel, then places the bundle carefully in his backpack.

"Thank you, Dr. Steve. Thank you," Tenney says.

"There are hundreds of strays like her all over this town," he says.

"But they're not Sophia," Tenney explains. "She's special. That one is Lola," Tenney points. "And that one is Zorro."

"Zorro?" asks Dr. Fuller.

"Sophia thinks you're Zorro, so we're naming him after you."

Dr. Fuller starts laughing, a strange, guttural, almost reluctant sound. After a long moment he says to Tenney, *"You're special."*

"How much do I owe you, Dr. Fuller?" I ask, looking around for my bag.

"Nothing," he says, "I'm not a vet."

"Well, at least let us donate to your children's clinic." I hand him a hundred-dollar bill. He thanks me solemnly, then folds the bill and slips it into the back pocket of his jeans. We sit quietly for a while, watching the two puppies nurse. Sophia seems to be regaining some of her aplomb.

"If you need help at your clinic, Dr. Fuller, I have nothing but time. I have no medical experience, but I could do other things," I offer. "I used to teach English as a second language, maybe I could do something for the kids?" What am I doing? I must be high as a kite on this Ambien. I don't even like children, except Tenney, and she's like an old person in a child's body.

He glances at me in surprise. "I always need help."

Dr. Fuller tells us we need to feed Sophia very well for the next few weeks. *The next few weeks!* We're probably not even going to get through tomorrow. He says we need to take her to a vet to make sure she's all right and check for worms and giardia.

Tenney makes up a bed for herself on the floor next to the box, and as soon as she curls herself around the box and puts her head down on the pillow, she's asleep. I ask Dr. Fuller if he'd like me to bring him a drink. He says he doesn't drink. How about coffee? He says he'll take a rain check. I walk him back out through the patio. The birds are starting to chirp though the sky is still dark. They sense the coming of dawn even though it feels to me like the middle of the night.

"My mother hates dogs," I whisper to him. "She doesn't know about this yet. I had a dog once, in Cameroon, when I was a little girl. Arsène Lupin. We had to leave him with the neighbors and I haven't had a dog since." I'm babbling again, and I don't know why. I never babble. I'm Miss You-Will-Never-Know-Anything-About-Me. "I didn't want to bring this dog home but Tenney just wouldn't let it go. I couldn't force her to walk away." I feel like a fool. Why do I keep trying to make excuses to him?

At the door he turns and places a hand on my arm. "I'm glad you called me," he says, a reluctant smile stretching his lips. "I don't often get to feel like Zorro."

He straddles the seat and kickstarts his motorcycle with his beat-up cowboy boot. I watch as the taillight recedes down the street's steep incline and disappears around the corner. I keep listening for a long time while the roar of the engine wanes in the distance and finally becomes indistinct, merging with the chattering of birds.

CHAPTER
SEVEN

AWAKEN SWEATY AND STRANGELY STIRRED from a dream about Dr. Fuller's motorcycle. Ambien usually stops me from dreaming so I am a little surprised. I look around the room; Tenney is already up and gone. I roll over to her side of the bed to check on the dog. The puppies are nursing and Sophia looks up at me, her tail thumping hollowly against the cardboard box.

"Hi," I say. She's taking their suckling very well, with that seemingly bottomless patience of hers. She thinks she's safe with us now, which makes my stomach churn with apprehension.

I stumble into the large, cerulean green–tiled bathroom and wash my face with cold water. There are no signs on the mirror to remind me of what I'm supposed to say and do. What am I supposed to say and do? I can't remember and suddenly the side of my head is pounding again. Wincing, I inspect my reflection closely in the mirror, turning my face from side to side. My skin is marred by freckles—face, neck, shoulders, arms. Even my legs. I'm not inordinately pale to have so many freckles. *It's that damn Scottish blood of your father's*, Bibi used to say. When I was a child and someone would mention how pretty I was, she would say, *Well, she's certainly Celtic looking.*

Suddenly I catch a whiff of Beau's Clive Christian manly man cologne that makes me spin around every time. A realization strikes me like a fist between the eyes: I hate that cologne.

Just as I am sniffing furiously at a pair of clean black yoga pants trying to determine if they smell like Beau, Tenney rushes in carrying a plate of bacon. While Sophia gobbles it up, Tenney jumps on the bed with her sudoku book and starts a new puzzle.

"You need to eat some bacon too," I say, feeling like a nag.

"I did," she replies indifferently. I think she's lying. "Want to do a puzzle with me?"

I swallow a Percocet with a sip of water from the glass on the bedside table. I can't even complete a "Light and Easy" puzzle in forty minutes. Tenney takes fifteen to complete a hard one. I think small, square by square. Tenney thinks big and sees the whole nine squares at once. That's probably why she is so good at chess too.

Tenney explains how a certain number goes in a certain place, but my aching brain is riding the hamster wheel again. I am going to have to grovel at Bibi's feet. That's okay, I'm used to groveling. But what if she says no? Where will we take Sophia? Allegra knocks again, wanting to clean. To make up for missing yesterday, today she intends to start with us, bright and early. The longer I wait to tell Bibi about the dogs, the worse it's going to be.

"I have to go talk to Bibi," I mumble, getting to my feet. I feel like I have the flu. My knees and voice are wobbly. I really need to cut back on that Ambien.

"I'm coming with you," Tenney says, resolutely putting down her book. She takes my hand and squeezes it tightly. I should face this alone. But perhaps there is power in numbers. Bibi has trouble resisting Tenney, though she has absolutely no trouble resisting me.

Outside the door, Allegra is standing with her mop and bucket. I quietly shut the door behind us, blocking her path.

"*Espera cinco minutos, por favor.*" I ask her to wait five minutes.

"La pobrecita," she says softly, and shakes her head. Poor little thing. Is she speaking about the dog? I am aghast. How could she possibly know already? I give her a nervous, uncertain smile.

Tenney and I cross the patio and find Bibi at the dining table, where, thank God, she is alone, browsing the bilingual weekly paper, *Atención San Miguel*. She's wearing her shimmery crimson robe with plum-colored piping. She doesn't acknowledge us and already my gut is clenching; I'm sure she is going to berate me soundly.

"Bibi," I start tentatively, "Tenney and I need to speak with you."

Suddenly she's completely attentive, a tiny worry line trying without success to form a crease in her brow. Is it possible she uses Botox too? Bibi?

"What is it? What happened?"

"It's my fault," Tenney blurts, and bursts into tears, shoulders quivering, big sobs wracking her body.

"My goodness!" says Bibi, pushing her chair back and opening her arms. Tenney rushes around the table and Bibi pulls the sobbing child onto her lap. "There, there, now. What in the world, Tenney? There, there. Dear me, don't snivel all over my gown!"

"Actually, it's my fault," I say. "I'm the parent and I'm responsible—"

"Yet sometimes I truly wonder about that," Bibi spits out. She's not angry at Tenney; that's good, we're 50 percent there.

"I made Mommy bring home a . . ." A renewed outburst of sobs and tears.

"There, there," says Bibi. "Whatever it is, it can't be that bad. Bibi can fix it." She's glaring at me accusingly. I collapse into a chair on the opposite side of the table.

"Last night we brought home a dog and she had puppies in the middle of the night," I say.

"She almost died!" Tenney blubbers. "We had to call Doctor Handsome."

"You called Doctor Handsome to come deliver puppies in the middle of the night?" Bibi is so amazed that she's forgotten to be angry, and bursts into her high, ringing laugh. "Ahahahaha! That is too precious! *Calisto!*" she calls over her shoulder, and her voice carries out the French doors and across the patio. "Ahahaha!" She picks up her cordless phone and hits a speed-dial button. "Faye! Pick up the phone!"

A wave of itchy heat rises from my chest to my face and I can't swallow it down. What the heck is wrong with me? I should be relieved. When she's done laughing, she wipes her eyes on her napkin and turns her attention back to Tenney, who is so startled she has stopped sobbing.

Bibi says, "So let's see these dogs."

Tenney jumps up and leads her across the patio to our door, with me on their heels. The patient Allegra is still standing there with her bucket and mop. Bibi tells her surreptitiously to start with the upstairs bedrooms, flings the door open, and flicks on the light. Tenney rushes to the box and stands beside it like a bodyguard, tense and ready to defend. Sophia picks up on this and springs to her feet expectantly, tentatively wagging her tail at Bibi.

"Oh dear," says Bibi, stopping short. "Is that one of my towels?"

"I'm sorry," I mumble, suddenly exhausted. "There was nothing else."

She turns and glides back to the family room, her crimson and plum satin peep-toed mules with a little nest of matching ostrich feathers on top clicking on the flagstones.

Tenney and I stare at each other.

"I cried really well, didn't I, Mommy?"

"Very well," I say. "And you may need to cry again in a couple of minutes."

She glares at me, her eyes like laser beams. "Why are you so scared of her?"

Unnerved, I tell her to keep an eye on the dogs; I am going to go talk to Bibi.

And why hasn't Agent Warnock called me back? Maybe she found the pics and sexts and is having a good laugh. I feel sick.

"I know you think I'm a heartless bitch," Bibi says indignantly when I sit across from her at the dining table.

I pour myself a cup of coffee; lifting the cup with a trembling hand, I try to swallow some down. The black, rich, earthy coffee helps. In a moment I feel revived.

"Are you listening to me?" says Bibi. "What on earth is the matter with you?"

"It all happened so suddenly," I try to explain, though it was not nearly so sudden. My tongue is like glue, sticking to the roof of my mouth. "You were out. I thought . . . Tenney has been through so much."

"You are such a pushover, Merryn. You always were. Just like your father."

"I know you don't like dogs . . ."

"It's not that I don't *like* them, they're just so obsequious!"

I feel lightheaded, as if I'm going to faint. But the Percocet has eased the migraine. I suddenly remember the fight my parents had in Cameroon when I was a child and I begged them to keep Arsène Lupin. *I'm not a heartless bitch, Henry, even though you think I am. She wants a dog, she wants a dog. Of course she wants a dog! She's a child! God only knows how long we'll last here in this shit pit.*

It was the one time that I can remember where he overrode her. And she did not let him forget it.

I sip from my cup. Bibi pours herself a second Bloody Mary. The disruption to her routine must be causing her to drink more than usual. She's used to a certain order in her life, to certain patterns, and we've completely shattered that. I need to ask for a reprieve on Sophia's behalf. Bibi always says, *Compliments only work if they are exceptionally well delivered. Obsequious fawning only makes people recalcitrant.*

"You have always been the kindest and most generous person I've ever known," I begin, "and I know you have our best interests at heart and always do—"

"That goes without saying," Bibi interrupts, but I can tell she's pleased from the slight blush rising in her cheeks.

"And I know we've caused a terrible upheaval in your life and I'm very sorry for it. I have a hard time saying no to Tenney, she can be so persuasive. Bibi, if you could just let her have some time with the dogs—"

"Listen," she murmurs quickly, leaning across the table, "I hope you haven't told Calisto your age."

I am dumbfounded. The man hasn't said two words to me since we arrived.

"He thinks I had you very young—at twenty—and you had Tenney in your early twenties; so please don't disabuse him of this notion."

"It wouldn't cross my mind. But Bibi, what about the—"

"Yes, yes, all right," she cuts me off impatiently. "A little while, a week at the very most. You do realize you're probably going to prison. Once the FBI gets ahold of you, they never let go. You are a total nitwit, bringing dogs into the mix. Ah, I hear Calisto coming."

I get up and stagger toward the kitchen, I need to stick my head in the freezer for a minute. I need to cool the heat in my face and chest. Calisto saunters in, sleepy-eyed, hair uncombed.

"Calisto," I hear Bibi's voice echoing as I pass through the kitchen door, "you won't believe what we missed last night!"

Marta is busy stirring a pot on the stove.

So it appears we've made some kind of a deal, I reassure myself as I breathe in the icy air. I have bought us a week. I hear Bibi talking to Pedro in the great room, already dispatching him to find the dogs a home among his connections. There is always the campo, Pedro assures her, where good *perros pastores* are in demand. Sophia is not well suited for the task of shepherd, but it will surely be a step up from what she had before. Sophia must have been a house pet. What kind of people put a dog out in the street? Visitors who are leaving after a nice long vacation, that's who. I hate people.

When I close the freezer, Marta is standing behind me, holding a blue ceramic bowl in her soft, clean hands—oatmeal mixed with honey and milk, the honey's sweet earthiness rising in the steam.

"*Avena para la perrita,*" oatmeal for the little dog, she whispers. "*Es saludable.*" Good for her health. She thrusts the bowl into my hands and turns away swiftly, as if it never happened.

"*Muchas gracias,* Marta," I murmur to her back as she busily hunches over the sink.

When I tell Tenney the dogs can only stay for a little while, she is inconsolable.

"But what's going to happen to them then? What if—?"

No matter what I give her, she always wants more. I snap at her, despite my best intentions: "Stop, now!"

"You're not going to let that happen, I know it . . ."

Both child and dog gaze at me with forlorn expressions, and I am assailed once again by a feeling of breathlessness. The best recourse when I feel this way is to take action, to do something useful.

I return to the kitchen and ask Marta about vets. The only one she knows is off lower Canal Street. She looks up the number for me in the local phone book. We make an appointment for right now. Then, lightly, almost as an afterthought, I ask Marta if she has the key to the outside lock on our bedroom door. I tell her I'm concerned about my possessions, since so many strangers are constantly coming and going through the patio. She pulls a ring of keys out of a drawer and removes a small gold one and holds it out to me. She says not to lose it, it is the only one.

I open the battery compartment on Blueberry and draw out two hundred-dollar bills. We load Sophia, and the two puppies in their box, into the backseat of the Honda beside Tenney, who tries to explain to them that everything will be fine.

The veterinary hospital is also an SPA, *Sociedad Protectora de Animales*, and there are dozens upon dozens of abandoned animals in cages, stacked on makeshift shelves under a mansard roof, barking and meowing their heads off. In the waiting room, Sophia is trembling despite Tenney's best efforts to reassure her.

The lady vet who examines Sophia tells us it's a miracle she survived; Sophia is between one and one and a half and weighs nine pounds (she's very skinny) and this is probably her first litter. The vet checks out the puppies, clips their tiny nails, and while she's cleaning Sophia's ears, she tells us all the things we're going to need to do over the next few months. *No, no, no,* I want to say, *you don't understand*—but she keeps on talking, explaining that Sophia will clean up after her pups for the first several weeks; they can't expel on their own without their mother's stimulation. There will be no mess. Well, this is a relief.

Once the pups are weaned, at around eight weeks, the doctor says, Sophia can be spayed. *Eight weeks!* Not a chance in hell. Right now, though, we need to feed her vitamin-enhanced puppy food and vitamin supplements.

In a little alcove, leashes and collars and animal toys hang from pegs. Some are quite fancy. Tenney goes right to a pink collar encrusted with rhinestones and a matching pink leash. Hardly the look for a future campo shepherd; I tell her no. Tenney says yes. "Sophia's a princess and should have a princess collar."

The woeful barking from the abandoned dogs disturbs Sophia, who thinks she's going to be left here. I lift her into my arms. Her shaking subsides somewhat as Tenney buckles the new collar around her neck. While I'm paying for our visit and the extra items, I ask the bored girl behind the counter if the hospital accepts donations for the abandoned animals' care. Of course, she says, as if I'm an idiot. I give her a hundred-dollar bill. She looks like the kind of girl who might see nothing wrong with taking the cash to buy herself a nice new dress, so I ask her to log it in while I'm standing here.

Back home, when we let Sophia loose on the patio, she scampers and jumps about. She must feel like a condemned person given a stay of execution.

Tenney places a bowl of vitamin-enhanced puppy kibbles with a spoonful of wet food before Sophia and she sniffs at it suspiciously, unimpressed. But she eats every last morsel, not one to look a gift horse in the mouth. She crawls back into the box with mincing steps and lies back, the puppies squealing as they search blindly for her teats.

Allegra knocks on the open bedroom door. La señora wants

to talk to me in the great room. My heart pounding again, I cross the patio that is white with sunlight and enter the great room, eyes squinting to adjust to the dimness. Bibi is reclining on the sofa with her head on Calisto's lap, an icepack over her eyes. He is massaging her temples and I feel like an intruder and begin to back away, until my backside encounters the doorframe.

"I spoke to Harvey Berger while you were out being a PETA activist," she intones. I stand frozen at attention. Calisto lights a cigarette and sits back, apparently thinking deep thoughts that have nothing to do with me. "Harvey has been trying to reach you for hours. What is the matter with you? I knew you never were the brightest bulb in the chandelier, but really. You're signing your own death warrant. Harvey has been 'haggling,' as he says, with the FBI since yesterday. They want you to fly back to Dallas immediately. You need to turn on your damn phone, Merryn. I'm not your secretary and this is *my* phone. I am a very important person here in San Miguel and people can't get ahold of me with you taking up all the space on my answering machine. My God, you're acting like this is all a big joke. I just hope that when you're sent to prison, I'll be able to get legal custody of Tenney . . ."

But I don't have my phone, I want to say, yet I stand in the doorframe, shaking as if from cold while the heat of the sun bakes my back.

"Sorry, I don't feel well." I turn and flee, barely making it back to our bathroom. There's nothing in my stomach but bile. Kneeling with my face in the toilet bowl, I feel something wet on my ankle. It's Sophia licking me, her tail tucked between her legs and her steps mincing and tentative, as if she doesn't quite know what to do. Tenney stands behind her in the doorway, both of them wearing the same concerned look.

"What's wrong, Mom?"

I tell Tenney I probably ate something bad. "You're being careful about not drinking the water, aren't you, Tenney?"

"Of course," she says. "Even Sophia gets the cooler water."

In a while the comida bell gongs. Stretched horizontally across the bed, I try to get up but feel as if I have weights attached to my limbs. I send Tenney out, promising to be right there . . . As long as Marta is the one cooking, Tenney will be safe . . . I seem to be slipping into a black, bottomless sleep despite my efforts to stay awake and vigilant. I must be vigilant and watch out for my child . . .

Bibi and Beau were drinking martinis in our Dallas condo living room, sitting on the very same couch I will be sitting on when the policemen bring the news of Beau's demise. I was not partaking and they teased me for being such a square, even though I was seven and a half months pregnant. Bibi had flown up from San Miguel for the February sales, and silvery shopping bags stood all around her like devoted courtiers. I'd had a strange pain since morning just below my left ribs and now, at cocktail hour, I announced that I didn't feel well and needed to lie down. As I waddled away, passing the room that would soon be Tenney's nursery, I heard Bibi tell Beau, "She's such a hypochondriac. Can you believe what I've had to put up with all my life?" And they started to laugh. I continued on my way, certain that I must have invented the pain, remembering how Bibi said I always pretended to be sick to get her attention when I was little.

I am covered in sweat. I feel as if a red-hot screw is being hammered into my jaw on the right side, the pain almost unbearable. In this twilight state, this short segment of film runs through my mind over and over and I can't seem to stop it. I sit bolt-upright in the king-size bed in Bibi's guest room in San Miguel with the shutters closed and the fan turning overhead and a headache splitting my brain in two, realizing that the pain below my left ribs was probably the beginning of the placental abruption that almost killed me. But I ignored it, convinced that Bibi was right because Bibi is always right.

I stumble into the bathroom and take two ibuprofen tablets and a Percocet. I need to take action. I need to call Harvey Berger.

I tiptoe across the patio. I hear Tenney's laughter and the sound of splashing water rising on the hot air, bouncing off the patio's walls. I enter the kitchen from the outside door. No one is about. Harvey Berger's card is right in the middle of the corkboard by the wall phone, pierced with a red pushpin, curling at the corners and yellowing with age. I take the card and hurry back to my room. I pick up the phone on the bedside table and dial 001 and then the New York office number of Farragut, Berger and Dewaitt, LLC.

An assistant tells me Mr. Berger will be in court for the rest of day, but he left a message for me. "It says here . . . *tu tu tu* . . ." Why do people make that weird sound when they're looking for something? "Mr. Berger said to wait to hear from him. He will call you this evening on the landline."

His message doesn't seem angry or panicked at all. Maybe Bibi is more stressed out by all of this than I thought?

I thank the woman and click off.

Tenney runs in soaking wet from her swim in the pool and, feeling revived from my medication, I tell her to get dressed, we're going to walk back down the hill to the Garza Spanish School on San Francisco Street. No point sitting here biting my nails, waiting for Agent Warnock to call.

Tenney has studied at the Garza School before, when we

were here last summer. It's an immersion program. This will be good for her; it will get her out of the house. I lock the door so that Sophia will be left in peace.

The Garza School is like Spanish summer camp. They have two hours of Spanish, then teachers take the children on excursions: to the Tuesday market, or the papier-mâché factory, or the recycled glass factory. Sometimes a guitarist in a sombrero comes to the school and serenades the children with Mexican songs. The *maestra*, Señora Garza, is not at her usual place behind the office desk, and we are greeted by an elegant gentleman with graying temples in a sharp black, tropical-wool suit and light blue tie, who approaches from one of the rooms off the patio.

"*Buenas tardes,*" I say, "we are looking for Maestra Garza."

"I am Ernesto Garza, the maestra's husband. I am sorry. *Mi esposa ha muerto.*" My wife has died. He holds his hands out, palms up, and on his face is an expression of astonishment, as if he still can't believe it himself.

"*Mi papa ha muerto tambien,*" my daddy has died too, Tenney replies. Her Spanish has gotten quite good—between school and San Miguel, she is almost fluent. Her statement seems to take Señor Garza aback and he looks at us with a different expression, one of sudden recognition. I tell him how much we liked Maestra Garza and how kind she was to Tenney when we were here last summer. My mother lives here, I tell him, up on Montitlán; my voice finally trails off.

In English, Señor Garza adds, "We were married thirty-five years. Three niños, all grown up and gone now. I am lost."

"How long has it been, Señor Garza?" I ask gently.

"Six months only. She had the breast cancer many years ago. It was gone a long time but then . . ."

"My daddy died in a car accident," Tenney tells him, and

looks at him almost fiercely, as if she's expecting him to contradict this statement. And I'm oddly relieved that she does not add, *Five days ago*.

"And you are so young," Señor Garza murmurs, looking me solemnly in the eyes, "a calamity."

"Yes," I nod, and suddenly my eyes fill with tears—for him, for his terrible loss, his heartbroken face—to love someone the way Señor Garza loved his wife—that is something. Señor Garza takes both my hands in his for a moment, then pulls the little white handkerchief out of his suit coat's breast pocket, gives it a shake, and hands it to me. I always feel uncomfortable when men do this. I wipe my eyes and crumple it in my hand.

The three of us stand in the hot courtyard, a quiet, shared moment of companionship passing between us. I think Señor Garza is going to start crying too, but he takes a deep breath, pulls himself up, straightening his shoulders. "The last thing she said to me was, *Ernesto, do not close the school*. But May is very quiet in San Miguel. We have only a few students. *Mañana*, nine o'clock, your daughter can start?"

"Yes, yes, of course," I murmur.

Then, to my surprise, Señor Garza invites us to have a coffee with him down the street.

It's a small, peaceful café that you'd walk right by if you didn't know it was there, through an arching entryway that leads to a small patio with a few wrought-iron tables and chairs, set out among potted ficus trees and palms. A little stone fountain gurgles in the far stucco wall while some colorful parakeets squawk at us from a large, ornate cage. A wonderful smell of fresh-baked breads and pastries emanates from the little *panadería* within and Tenney asks if she can have a look inside; I nod and she runs off.

Just as Señor Garza is officiously pulling out my chair for

me, Dr. Fuller walks through the entryway with Lizzie Carmichael, whom I've only met once at one of Mum's cocktail parties. For some reason I feel myself blushing, as if I've been caught in a compromising position. My pulse quickens—a totally inappropriate reaction. I avert my eyes, pretending I haven't seen them. Tenney, coming out of the panadería, yells, "Dr. Steve!" and runs to him. He waves to me and so does Lizzie Carmichael as they approach the table. Señor Garza is standing stiffly, his hands on the back of my chair. I jump up and introduce everyone. The men shake hands.

Lizzie Carmichael has an outdoorsy, horse-woman kind of look, the lined, leathery face of someone who has spent too much time in sun and wind. Her nails are short, unpainted, and her hair is bobbed and silvery-blond. She has large, innocent-looking blue eyes and wears a Native American choker with a chunk of turquoise that is just slightly darker and more opaque than her eyes. It's hard to tell her age, but she's at least twenty years older than Dr. Fuller. I gather this is not a problem for him.

"How's Sophia?" he asks Tenney.

"Sophia is doing really great, thank you. And so are Zorro and Lola! We went to the vet this morning." As Tenney fills him in on the details, Lizzie follows the exchange with a little questioning wrinkle on her forehead and I feel inordinately happy that she apparently hasn't been filled in on his late-night adventure.

"And how did Vivienne take the news?" he asks me, his eyes merrier than usual in his somber face, a smile parting his lips. I tell him we have a week to find the dogs a home.

"I'll ask around; we'll find them a home," he promises.

"They already have a home," Tenney says, an angry frown crossing her thick brows.

After a slightly awkward moment where no one can think of

what to say next, they go into the café and Señor Garza, Tenney, and I sit down. I say to Señor Garza in my best Spanish, so that there is no confusion, "*My hija tiene alergia a la leche de vaca, puede causarla la muerte. Su comida no puede incluir ningún especie de leche de vaca.*" I have said this sentence many, many times over the years: My daughter has a serious allergy to cow's milk and could die. Her food cannot contain any type of cow's milk. He nods thoughtfully.

It seems like a month goes by while we sit in silence— Mexicans are better at companionable silences than we are— and finally Dr. Fuller and Lizzie Carmichael come out of the café holding to-go cups. They wave goodbye as they head out through the arched passageway to the street.

The young waitress in a blue apron finally deigns to saunter over. Señor Garza asks the cranky girl to bring an assortment of pastries and a *café negro* for himself, and for you? *Café negro muy caliente* for me and a glass of *limonada* for Tenney. Tenney wants a piece of cake covered in icing and sprinkles but she can't have it. She wouldn't eat it anyway; she'd take one bite and say she's full and we'd spend the night in the hospital. Señor Garza asks the girl if the pastries in the panadería contain butter or milk. She has no idea. Señor Garza gets up and asks Tenney to come with him into the shop to talk to the baker.

In a few minutes they return, Tenney holding a lollipop the size of a Frisbee, a swirling helix of psychedelic primary colors. Tenney is delighted, her lips and chin already stained purple.

"Only sugar and water and food dye," he reassures me as they sit down. "And the pastries, all of the pastries, are made with vegetable oil, no butter, no milk."

The pastry basket arrives, and Señor Garza points to the different delectable goodies—*galletas, conchas, cuernos*, and *empanadas de piña.*

Tenney doesn't want to try the pastries; she's happy with her lollipop. I wish she'd eat a pastry. She needs the calories. But at the same time, I didn't expect to be sitting in a café and so I rummage through my mesh bag to make sure I have an EpiPen, just in case. Of course, I have several.

"An afternoon café always makes the day pass better," Señor Garza says with a sad smile. He tells us he has received dozens of prayer cards from his wife's former students and admirers, and even a condolence card from one of the priests at the Basílica de Nuestra Señora de Guadalupe where his wife went on pilgrimage last December and prayed on her knees to the Mother of Jesus to cure her. She so much wanted to see her grandchildren grow up. He tells us he was only eighteen when they married; he has never been on his own, never loved anyone else. He has felt so alone the last six months. He has not sensed her presence.

After a long moment of silence he asks, "Was your loss recent?"

"Very . . ." I look down at my lap, unable to hold his wide-open, friendly gaze.

I tell him I am not doing so well myself and that yoga seems to help me more than anything. I ask him if he knows of a good yoga school in San Miguel.

"Ah, yes," he says, nodding. "There is a man—he is from El Salvador's Pipil tribe—who came here with a priest some years ago. He is a maestro of yoga but also a healer with the true gift. He made my wife's pain go away, though of course he could do nothing for the cancer. His name is Alberto Zaldaña. Tomorrow you will go to him and say Ernesto Garza sent you." He reaches across the table and gently pats my hand. "I see that you are suffering as I am. But it will get better. It must."

I nod, not knowing what else to do, and stick a piece of dry, warm, sugar-coated cuerno in my mouth. The dusty flour crumbles against my tongue and I struggle to swallow. Mexican pastries always smell so much better than they taste.

CHAPTER
EIGHT

ENNEY AND I ARRIVE HOME LATE from coffee with Señor Garza and cocktail hour is already in full swing on the balcony. The sun takes its final bow, sinking quickly behind the mountains. Bibi is delighted, shouting,"Bravo!" and clapping as if she's got loge seats at the opera and this particular tenor has truly outdone himself. The phone beside her rings and she puts the receiver to her ear, annoyed at the interruption.

"It's for you," she tells me, "your new *veterinarian!*" She and Calisto giggle and snort through their noses and I feel that strange, uncomfortable heat rising to my face.

"Hello" is all he says, and then I hear his breath in the phone. It seems so intimate that I'm suddenly frightened of the rapid beating of my heart. Can Bibi sense this?

"Hi, Dr. Fuller," I say, attempting to sound neutral. "How nice of you to check in on us." I can feel Bibi's keen interest in the heat of her eyes upon my back.

A moment of baffled silence, then he clears his throat. "I'm going up to the Charco—the botanical gardens—tomorrow morning. I wondered if you and Tenney would like to come. I have a key to the back gate."

I glance over at Bibi and Calisto who are in deep conversation. To avoid disrupting them, and for a little privacy, I take the phone and walk through the great room and out to the north terrace. Behind me I hear them giggling again. Darkness descends like a blue ink stain upon the mountains and the reservoir below.

"It'll be just me. Tenney's starting at the Garza School at nine," I say quietly into the receiver. "And I'm waiting for an important call. If I can't make it, I'll call you."

"If I don't hear from you, I'll pick you up at the Garza School."

I don't want Señor Garza to see me taking off with Doctor Handsome like some young chippie. I tell Dr. Fuller I'll meet him on the corner of Cuesta de San Jose and Calzada de la Presa at 9:10 a.m.

I return to our room to recuperate before cena, when I hear the phone trilling again, all through the house, different ringers going off. It rings in the kitchen and downstairs by the pool and in the great room and wherever Bibi has the cordless receiver. I've turned the ringer off on the phone in our room, or it would be an incessant strain on my nerves. I wait to see if it's Harvey Berger, though Bibi doesn't call to me. It must be one of her friends. But I don't hear her laughing and talking. Something nags at me. I step over to the phone and carefully lift the receiver from the cradle.

"I don't know where she is, Harvey. You'll have to call back later."

Why would she tell him this?

"Well . . . aahh . . . Vivienne, dear, please have her call me as soon as she can." His sonorous voice is calm and benign and not remotely angry, at least it doesn't seem so to me.

"Hello?" I say, as if I just heard the phone ringing and picked up.

"Ah, well, there she is," says Bibi, her tone prickly.

"You can hang up now, Bibi," I say, and wait, a bloom of heat spreading in my chest. In the background I hear Calisto talking in Spanish but can't make out his words. Finally, a loud click, then silence.

"I'm so sorry I didn't call you back, Harvey, the FBI lady took my phone and when I checked Bibi's answering machine, you hadn't called. Your assistant said—"

"No worries. The feds are delighted that Ansari seems so desperate to talk to you. I think I've got you a deal, Merryn." He sounds quite pleased with himself. "They're . . . aahh . . . waiting for a wiretap order to be handed down for Ansari's cell phone. Ansari's in New York, which is good because he has no clue what's going on. This is all very hush-hush. They apparently haven't been able to find Edward Buckingham."

"What do you want me to do?" I choke up at my own help-lessness.

"You may need to fly back to Dallas on short notice. I am going to fix this, Merryn. Your father and I were great friends . . . great friends . . ." His voice trails off. "I am . . . ah . . . I'm going to get there as soon as I can. Agent Warnock will ask you to sign a consent form, so they can record your conversations with An-sari. Sign it, and sit tight. I'll have more news for you, possibly as early as tomorrow morning."

Wednesday

Suddenly I'm wide awake, covered in sweat, my heart fluttering inside my rib cage. The bedside digital clock reads 3:07 a.m. My jaw is clenched so tight the pain shoots up the right side of my head as if a torturer heated a nail in a brazier and hammered it into my jaw joint.

I don't know if I was dreaming or remembering . . .

The horse chestnut trees along the quai de Conti were covered in white blooms. I was heading across the Pont Neuf on the way back to my mansard maid's room on the Right Bank from the Sorbonne where I was taking classes as a foreign exchange student. An elderly man and woman, elegantly dressed and walking a little brown dog with black spots, ambled toward me across the bridge. They were about twenty feet away, and just as they passed the bronze statue of Henri IV on his horse, the dog bounded away from them, pulling the leash right out of the lady's hand. Like a torpedo the dog headed for me. I stood frozen; I didn't know what to do. They started shouting. But the little dog's tail was wagging and he lifted his front paws up onto my jeans, mouth in a wide grin. He had a black patch over his right eye, and some teeth missing, like an old pirate. He tried to jump up to lick my face, but he was too arthritic now to make that familiar basketball player's flying leap. The hairs around his muzzle were white, as if he'd stuck his nose in a bowl of sugar.

"Arsène!" the woman yelled. "Arsène! *Arrête ça!*"

I dropped to my knees on the sidewalk in the middle of the bridge.

"Arsène? *C'est toi*, Arsène?" But how did he know me? How did he know me after all these years? Tears stung my eyes as the elderly couple approached—they were the French neighbors from Yaoundé. They were as amazed as I. They never would have known me, they both said, they would have walked right by. They kept the dog, Madame de Villeneuve explained, because he was so charming, even though he was a consummate thief.

"You had no problem bringing him out of Cameroon?" I asked.

"No, of course not," said Monsieur de Villeneuve. "Your parents gave him all his shots. And you know how it is with diplomats: the customs people just let us through."

"Your mother didn't want him, that's all," his wife added. To them, this was a simple fact; to me, it was the end of the world.

But he was mine! I wanted to shout. And the way I had cried when we had to leave him. I had cried for days and days. No, they must be wrong.

Arsène could not come home with me to my little maid's room in the *deuxième arrondissement*. After all, he'd been with the Villeneuves much longer than he ever was with me. He was not mine anymore. We said goodbye as he licked the tears from my face. They went on their way, Arsène pulling at the leash and the French couple making exaggerated motions of exasperation as they smiled back at me, but he kept craning his head to look over his shoulder, until they finally disappeared, sinking beneath the curve of the bridge.

I'd like these nasty bats to fly back into their dark cave. I don't want them. And why do they assail me now, at three in the morning?

Beside me, Tenney sleeps soundly, undisturbed. I lean over the edge of the bed to check on the dogs. The two little ones are pressed up against their mother in a pile, sound asleep, peaceful and safe in their box. Sophia is awake, as if she has sensed my distress. She lifts her head and stares at me, her eyes glittering in the green glow of the digital clock. I quietly throw back the sheet.

"You want to come?"

She seems to be thinking this over. Rising slowly, careful not to step on her sleeping babies, she follows me toward the door.

Sophia and I go out into the dark and silent patio and make our way to the balcony that overlooks the city. It must be a religious holiday because the churches and basilicas are all lit up, shining and golden like welcoming fairy-tale castles. The royal-blue sky is filled with silvery stars. I sit on one of the lounge chairs and Sophia jumps onto my lap. She's warm and smells of milk and puppies. I can feel her heart beating against my hands as I stroke her chest. My hand slides further along her stomach and I check on the little nipples, which feel hard, but the surrounding tissue is soft and vulnerable and feminine. Her fur is silky, not coarse like Arsène's. I could put Arsène into a complete trance just by scratching his chest like this. His eyes would half close and go out of focus and not even the thought of catching a snake could disrupt him in this exalted state. These are dogs that refused to succumb to fear and neuroses and retained their faith in human beings, which, given their horrendous circumstances, is an amazing thing.

"You remind me of Arsène Lupin," I whisper to Sophia. "He was a prince too. A prince fallen on hard times."

Her head cocks to the side and her ears go up, as if she's making an effort to understand what I'm saying.

"What are we going to do, Sophia?"

Her head cocks the other way. Her tail wags; she licks my jaw, and I imagine her saying: *I don't care who you are. I don't care if you're a liar. I'm on your side, and I'll watch out for you, just as you watched out for me.*

At a quarter to nine, Harvey Berger still hasn't called and neither has Agent Warnock, so I walk Tenney down the mountain to the Garza School. Señor Garza comes out from behind the desk to greet me, warmly taking both my hands in his like an old friend. He asks me if I'd like someone to bring Tenney back to the house by taxi, but I tell him I'll come fetch her myself at one p.m.

I walk north down the hill toward Cuesta de San Jose. Dr. Fuller is already there, straddling his idling motorcycle with one battered cowboy boot up on the sidewalk. I can see why they call him Doctor Handsome. No one that good looking is good news. He gazes at me as I approach and I have no idea what he's thinking. I'm wearing a fifties-style, black-and-white polka dot halter-top dress. Why did I wear a sundress? At least I'm wearing my fisherman sandals. Good, no-nonsense walking shoes.

"Hop on," he says, handing me a helmet. He's wearing his black nylon backpack in front, like a BabyBjörn. I eye the motorcycle suspiciously. It is tall and thin, with deeply grooved tires and a yellow gas tank that says *Yamaha*.

I swing my leg over the seat, primly gathering in one hand the hem of my sundress. I tuck the dress under my legs so it won't fly up.

"Careful you don't burn your calves," he says. What was I thinking? I should've worn pants.

Through the thin fabric of my dress I can feel the taut muscles of his . . . ass? butt? gluteus maximus? pressing against the insides of my thighs. He is much less hefty than Beau. All that muscle and heft . . . sometimes I felt like I was wrapping my arms and legs around a refrigerator.

I put on the helmet. My arms encircle his torso and he takes off, the sudden rush thrusting me away from and then into his back. I hold him more tightly, acutely aware of the two layers of fabric that separate my breasts from his warm skin and hard muscles. Something weird is going on. God, this feels so good. The engine is vibrating beneath me. I haven't felt this good in a long time. He goes over a bump and it feels wonderful. His skin smells fresh and earthy, a little like a muddy field of lavender. When we fly past Bibi's house, the dark windows seem like accusing eyes and I turn my face away.

He pulls to a stop in front of the locked gate, the back entrance to the Charco del Ingenio, and turns off the engine. I'm out of breath and have broken into a sweat. I have to pull myself together. He fools with things, I don't know what—the saddle-bags, the key, the kickstand.

"Are you all right? Not scared of motorcycles?" His voice sounds strangely low. I shake my head, deciding I'm better off not talking right now.

Probably one of his rich old ladies, maybe even Lizzie Carmichael, gave him a key to the private gate. A brisk morning breeze is blowing and the sun, strong and golden, is like a splash of paint across the canyon and the glittering mercury river below. He tells me members get to have a key and he's had a membership to the botanical gardens for a year.

"Where's Lizzie today?" I finally ask, trying for a light tone though my voice comes out a little strained.

He glances back at me, his expression unreadable. "I have no idea," he says.

The path is worn smooth and on both sides unfriendly-looking cacti and other succulents with spiny leaves grow stubbornly from the arid ground. Every leaf and flower is covered with that ubiquitous pale dust, giving the place an extraterrestrial look. Some of the plants have bright flowers that send off a sweet, almost imperceptibly delicate scent, as if they're thumbing their noses at the heat and dust. Scraggly patches of wildflowers of various colors attract fat bees and other insects. Their buzzing seems to be coming from inside my own head. I feel his presence like a magnetic field.

He strolls down the path toward the river and the dam. I notice how thin he is, muscular but thin, how his Levi's are loose on his hips and worn paler in the seat. The murky river is so low that the old concrete dam, which is usually almost totally submerged, is now exposed. There is a hand railing all along the cement platform at the top so people can walk across. He says the flowers are not as beautiful this spring because of the intense heat and drought. I tell him they look beautiful to me.

He takes my hand and leads me across the top of the dam, and with my other hand I hold on tight to the flimsy railing. On the other side are the ruins of an ancient water mill. We hike up and up, away from the river. The path is narrow and rocky and sometimes it goes straight up an incline, other times it's flat and deep with dust. The terrain is wild and unfamiliar. We walk for a long time in the hot, buzzing air. We've passed no one on this side of the river. I secretly admire the back of his head where his short, dark hair meets his neck and jaw. This is a spot that can tell you a lot about a man's character. Well, Beau had a lovely, strong, trustworthy jaw line too . . .

Dr. Fuller stops and out of his backpack pulls a bottle of water and offers it to me. I take a swig and pass it back. My heart knocks around frantically as I watch his lips circling the top of the bottle where my mouth just was.

"Lizzie Carmichael is gay," he says, as if I've asked. "I've slept with her—well, her and her partner. They like it with a guy sometimes. But I'm not involved with her. With them."

"Oh," I respond. I am slightly shocked that he says this as easily as he might if he were talking about a weekend soccer league or something.

He gazes out over the countryside with a serious expression. "I liked the dry goods a little too much and got into trouble in the States. My mother was Mexican; I'm fluent in Spanish. So I came here and took the exams. I haven't been able to stop thinking about you."

"Dry goods?" I ask.

"Prescription drugs."

A junkie! But what high horse am I sitting on? And what in

the world does that non sequitur mean, *I haven't been able to stop thinking about you?*

"It's your freckles," he says, his voice hoarse. "They're like constellations. And you're so reserved." Then, as if this were a perfectly normal, everyday occurrence, he begins to recite:

*"Déjame que te hable también con tu silencio
claro como una lámpara, simple como un anillo.
Eres como la noche, callada y constelada.
Tu silencio es de estrella, tan lejano y sencillo."*

"Neruda," I eek out, the word stuck somewhere in the back of my throat. And now I am slavering in that most private of places, even though I know, I just *know*, that he's roping me in with his magic golden lasso that he has used so many times he's totally perfected his technique.

"Wow. You know the poem." He switches into English:

*"And let me talk to you with your silence
that is bright as a lamp, simple as a ring.
You are like the night, with its stillness and constellations.
Your silence is that of a star, as remote and candid.*

"Not nearly as good in English, right?"
"Right."

We come upon a ruin, some kind of ancient structure. The outside layer of stucco has worn off in patches, exposing an infrastructure of adobe bricks. Above the doorway are strange, snakelike designs carved in the stone, probably by a native mason. The doorway leads into a small, roofless room. I run my hand over the rough adobe bricks, the mortar crumbling like sand under my fingertips. Suddenly he's standing behind me, his hands pressed into the wall on either side of my shoulders, his nose against my neck.

"I've wanted so bad to kiss you here," he murmurs, his lips grazing my shoulder, his voice low and gravely.

I turn around, facing him, palms to his pectorals, as if to push him away, but my resistance is perfunctory. His mouth is wet and mine is completely dry as our lips and tongues meet. The force of him lifts me up against the wall.

He pulls away, slides his T-shirt up over his head, and lays it down flat on the packed earth. On our knees, he unties the halter of my dress and buries his face between my breasts. Off come the boots, the jeans. He's wearing white gym socks. He pulls off my panties and I'm so wet his gentle thumb slides easily over my folds, sending electric shocks up through my spine.

"I don't have any protection," he mumbles. What could he possibly catch from a pair of lesbians? I'm wondering. No, this is ridiculous. He's probably got every damn STD in the book.

"I can't get pregnant," I say. "I had complications with Tenney and—"

He lifts me onto his hips and we've barely begun and already I'm imploding, trying to hold back from crying out. All this and we're not even on a first-name basis.

This is really atrocious behavior on my part. I am a terrible person. He pulls up in front of Bibi's house at 12:25 p.m.; I barely have time to take a shower before I must collect Tenney. At a loss as to what I should say, I hand him back his helmet without looking at him. He gently takes hold of my hand, thumb against my palm, stopping me from turning away.

"Will you bring Tenney over to see my clinic? It's in the *casita* in front of my house. It's on 20 de Enero Street in Colonia San Antonio. The indigo house."

"When?" That's the best I can do right now. Bibi will surely be inside, with Calisto and maybe Faye. I'm going to try to sneak by them.

"Just call my mobile." He locks eyes with me and I feel a jolt run through me. What am I doing? Where to start, when I can't even recognize a lie from the truth?

He drives off, the motorcycle roaring. The key turns quietly and the big wooden door barely squeaks as I press it forward. Coming toward me through the stone archway in the shadows are Bibi, Calisto, Faye, and her old friend Maurice, the gentleman who was beaten with his own cane by Faye's former young Mexican boyfriend. They're talking again about Lizzie Carmichael and Doctor Handsome.

"He'll sleep with anyone with a checkbook!" Bibi chortles.

And even ones without a checkbook, I'm thinking. They're so busy talking they practically run into me. Bibi wears a Mexican cowboy hat of straw with a large brim and a red scarf tied around the crown, and folded over her shoulder is her red and gold, hand-spun silk rebozo that she has informed me cost three thousand pesos.

"Today I'm blending in," Bibi says, then her expression suddenly changes to displeasure. "You look a sight, Merryn. Don't you know it's not good to be out exercising in the noonday sun? 'Mad Dogs and Englishmen,' remember that song? You're completely flushed. Isn't she flushed, Calisto?"

Calisto looks me up and down as if I'm some kind of unwanted plant dropped off by an overly friendly neighbor.

"And you're not even dressed for exercise," says Bibi. "How did you get so dirty? You didn't fall, did you? My goodness, you have the common sense of a five-year-old. Take a nice cold shower, that will help. Well, we're off to comida! We may take a house tour later."

She passes me without a backward glance, and her three friends file out behind her. Faye and Maurice smile at me a little nervously. People often seem to wear that slightly guilty look when they witness a conversation between Bibi and me, and I can never figure out why.

In the shower I take Bibi's advice and don't turn on the hot water; hopefully the cold will shock me out of my fiery madness. I read a book once about women's sexual issues and it stated that women have some kind of chemical that is released during sex that makes them feel the need to cling. I've worked my whole life to not be the kind of person who clings. Why is it so much easier for men not to cling? For Doctor Handsome, *who can't keep his pants on*. It was easy for me not to cling to Beau, he was like Teflon. But the picture looked so good! And for the most part he left me alone, was not interested in Tenney's and my daily activities.

Standing wrapped in a towel before the mirror, I remember the feel of Doctor Handsome's lips on the back of my neck and I break into a sweat all over again. Then I get another whiff of Beau's unpleasantly bracing cologne and practically jump out of my skin. How many weeks will it take for the last traces of that scent to dissipate?

Honeymoon in Kauai, Hawaii, where neither of us had ever been. We stayed in a lovely white cabana. Wide glass doors with gauzy white curtains opened onto a grove of palm trees and the aquamarine ocean beyond. There was an outdoor bar with a thatched roof, and by the second day Beau knew all the bartenders' names and where they were from. Snorkeling, catamaran tours, golfing (not me, him), socializing at the outdoor bar and pool—we never spent a minute alone in our honeymoon cabana, except when it was time for bed. Lying in a chair by the pool, even though I'd been in the water twice, I realized my skin and hair smelled of Beau's cologne.

When I come out of the bathroom wrapped in my towel, I hear whimpering and rush around to the other side of the bed. Sophia is having a nightmare, her short legs kicking out as if she's trying to run away from something. Her puppies are completely oblivious to her discomfort. I crouch, put my hand on her ribs, and softly say, "Wake up, Sophia, wake up. It's okay. You're safe now."

She startles awake, looks at me with confusion, then recognizes me, licks my hand, and settles back down. Arsène used to dream he was catching snakes, so I know dogs dream, just like people.

"I'll be right back," I tell her, scratching behind her ears. "Then we'll go for a walk."

She wags her tail slowly, her shiny black eyes looking into mine as if she understands every word.

Cleaned, scrubbed, dressed in light black linen cargo pants and a thin cotton Mexican peasant top with wide sleeves and my trusty, sensible fisherman sandals, I rush down the hill to the Garza School to collect Tenney.

Señor Garza is waiting for me in the courtyard. He says he has an astonishing story to tell me. The children's Spanish teacher, Señorita Maria, took the three niños to Parque Juárez for some local color. In the recreational area, a sunken arena with basketball nets, the two little American boys became engaged in a children's soccer game. Tenney wandered over to a couple of old men sitting on the cement bleachers, playing *una partida de ajedrez*, a game of chess, on a portable board. She stood for a long time in silence watching their match. Señorita Maria tried to get Tenney to come play with the other niños but she was entranced. Tenney asked the *ajedrecistas* if she could play the winner. They chuckled good-naturedly, thought it was adorable, and laughingly agreed.

Twenty minutes into Tenney's match against the winner, the *viejo* started grumbling. He told his friend to watch out, next the little girl would beat him too. A small crowd began to form, including some of the older basketball players, and people who didn't even understand the rules, curious because a tiny niña was beating a viejo who considered himself quite a good ajedrecista. Tenney checkmated him and the viejo asked for a rematch but Señorita Maria had to insist they leave, because it was growing close to one p.m. The viejo told Tenney they did not usually play here, but they would return tomorrow, if she would come back.

"Did you know this about your daughter?" Señor Garza asks me.

"Yes. She's ranked second in her grade in the state of Texas." Her chess master, Mr. Khlebnikov, wanted Tenney to go on a national chess tour, but I thought she was too young and didn't want to put that kind of pressure on her.

"That is very interesting," he replies. "Is it good for you if they go back tomorrow after class? I do not mind because the school is so quiet in May. If she wants to play that is fine."

I think this is a good plan and tell him so. When Tenney comes out of her classroom, Señor Garza walks us to the outside door and tells me he's phoned the yoga maestro he mentioned yesterday. He explains how to get to the studio, which is all the way at the north end of Hidalgo Street by Calzada de la Luz, down past the edge of the Centro. He tells me Alberto Zaldaña is expecting me and there is a yoga class at five p.m. today. I thank Señor Garza for his kindness and Tenney and I head out into the startling hot sunlight.

"Perhaps a café tomorrow?" he calls after us hopefully.

"With pleasure, Señor Garza," I call back. Am I giving this lovely man the wrong impression?

Tenney doesn't want to have a bite in the Centro. She doesn't want to do anything but get home to Sophia and the puppies. For some reason she is anxious.

"There's nothing to worry about," I tell her. "I locked the door."

She looks at me with her hazel eyes as if she understands something I do not; what it is, though, I have no idea.

We climb the steep and unevenly cobbled Cuesta de San Jose, which just hours ago I flew up on the back of Dr. Fuller's motorcycle.

We leash up Sophia for a short walk and as we're coming around the corner of a dusty lot up the street, we see Agent Warnock huffing up Montitlán toward us. She has changed out of her suit and wears a white button-down shirt with the sleeves rolled up, blue jeans, and brand-new pale leather huaraches, which she must have bought in the artisan market. The strap of her black satchel bag is strung across her front like a bandolier.

"Phew!" she says, wiping sweat from her brow with a handkerchief. "That is one heck of a climb."

"Where's Agent Athas?" I ask.

"Went back to Dallas. I have the paper for you to sign."

"Please come in."

The house is quiet and sleepy under the weight of the afternoon sun. The world seems struck dumb by the heat. Cicadas are buzzing in the heavy air. The kitchen is cool and quiet and I ask Agent Warnock if she'd like a glass of water or limonada.

"Water," she says, her breath coming in short, wheezing rasps. I fill a glass at the water cooler and hand it to her. She drinks it down in three seconds and holds it out again. Tenney hurries to refill the glass.

"I am staying at Casa Schuck. It's nearby and if you can't get me on my phone for some reason, you can leave a message there."

I ask Tenney to take Sophia back to our room and make sure her water bowl is full. She leaves reluctantly, followed by the dog.

Agent Warnock produces the document I am to sign. It is very basic, a couple of sentences indicating that I consent to have all of my conversations (telephone or otherwise) with Ibrahim Ansari and Edward Buckingham recorded.

"Bucky too?" I ask the agent.

"He's got himself one of those disposable phones and he's been leaving you messages. He's still in Houston, probably wondering what on earth is going on. It'll take us a day or two to find him. And that's really all I can say right now."

I sign the document without a word.

"Good." Agent Warnock slips the paper into her large tote bag, then lays my smartphone and laptop on the polished granite island, along with a new charger. "Keep your phone charged, and keep it with you. Don't answer unless it's me or your lawyer." Then she turns and heads for the door that leads to the patio. "I can find my way, thanks," she says. But I walk her out to the front door anyway.

I take my smartphone out to the north terrace where there is no direct sun, but a hot wind blows up from the reservoir, carrying the scent of the Charco and images of Dr. Fuller. I push them away. The reservoir today looks like liquid lead. A red-tailed hawk rises on a hot current of air about twenty feet from the retaining wall, its wings extended so that I can see every detail of its black-tipped feathers, its bright rust-colored tail spread out like a fan. Each wing feather has tigerlike stripes, a beautiful pattern of dark lines against a tawny background. Red-tailed hawks are territorial. This is probably the male, searching for prey while the female sits on their eggs in a well-protected nest high up on some rock ledge. He will bring food back to her and protect her till the hatchlings leave the nest.

The hawk rises and rises until it is only a dark speck in the great pale-blue expanse. I sit down at the glass-topped table to check my messages. I have thirteen. Three are from Jeanne-Wallace, who is still sitting in the Dallas office, unaware that she is being watched by the FBI. She wants to know what to tell Beau and Bucky's worried clients. Two are from Gordon, my mother-in-law, who wouldn't sound frantic if her house were on fire. Three are from Bucky: *"Ah know you're goin' through hell, Merryn, and Beau acted bad. Real bad . . . Ah'm worried that the feds are lookin into our business . . . If the feds question you, you tell em you don't know a thing. And that's the truth. You hear me? You don't know a thing."*

Five are from Ibrahim.

"I thought we were friends . . . Are we not friends, Merryn?"

"We must keep the funding coming for our school in Kabul."

"You would not want suddenly for your child to be without funds, without support, without a mother?"

"I am growing concerned now, Merryn."

"I am sending someone to your apartment."

I'm not scared of you, I think. But my hand is shaking so badly the phone rattles against the glass tabletop as I set it down.

CHAPTER
NINE

I LEAVE TENNEY WITH HER SUDOKU and her *Harry Potter and the Order of the Phoenix* and her EpiPens, and Sophia and her pups, since Allegra and Marta are back in the kitchen preparing the evening meal and will keep an eye on them. Marta always makes a little separate dish for Tenney when she's cooking with cheese or milk, so I don't worry. In my yoga pants and tank top, I head out, carrying my mat over my shoulder in its cylindrical case. Bibi has not returned yet from her comida in the Centro. I fear they probably had a great number of cocktails during the house tour and dinner will be another chaotic affair.

The streets are waking after the long, hot afternoon. I walk through the artisan market, since it is on the way and ends at Calzada de la Luz. On a shelf in one of the shops stands a tin mariachi band of skeletons, four feet tall, and miniature hand-crafted skeleton figurines: a skeleton bride and groom; a skeleton doctor examining a skeleton woman; a skeleton dentist leaning over a skeleton patient with terrified eyes and a wide-open, bloody mouth. They come from Chiapas, the saleslady tells me. In a closed glass case stand an array of halved walnut shells, with minuscule nativity scenes inside, and still other tiny skeleton families performing mundane tasks.

"What do the skeletons mean?" I want to know.

They mean, she explains in Spanish, that no matter what

you do all day long in your life, one day you will die. This is very funny to Mexicans.

The yoga studio is in a nondescript two-story house with a weathered wooden door and small sign outside on the coral-painted stucco wall that reads, *A. Zaldaña*. Up a flight of creaking wooden stairs, I smell jasmine incense burning and enter a large, joyful, indigo-blue room with a shiny wooden floor. On the walls hang religious icons—crosses of carved wood, silver, and tin, some are painted by hand, others show Jesus in his agony; representations of the Virgin de Guadalupe, and other saints I don't recognize.

From a door at the far end a copper-skinned man with beautifully sculpted deltoids and biceps approaches, his arm around an ancient woman with an injured wrist in a sling. He has thick, straight black hair cut short and layered so that it sticks out around his head, and high, flat cheekbones and a sharp-edged Mayan nose. It is impossible to determine his age. He could be thirty or fifty. This must be Alberto Zaldaña. He smiles at me, still leading the old woman forward, all the while murmuring soothingly in her ear. She says something to him about *el té* that is *saludable* and he replies that the only thing that will be saludable is if she leaves her husband and goes to the center for battered women. He will make sure there is a bed for her. "They will protect you," he says. Suddenly there's a thundering racket and a group of children pour through the doorway, followed by two younger women. They look with questioning, concerned expressions at Alberto Zaldaña, who shakes his head. "She doesn't want to go to the center."

One of the young women tries to press a handful of bills into Zaldaña's hand but he will not accept the money. No one argues with the old lady, they simply take her by her good arm and lead her toward the stairs in silence. I notice as she passes me that she is not old at all. She is stooped as if a crushing weight were pressing down on her fragile shoulders. I realize with horror that she is probably close to my age, probably no more than forty.

He turns his attention to me and I note how black his irises are, but the whites of his eyes are so clear they seem like porcelain.

I say in Spanish that I'm Merryn and Señor Garza recommended his yoga school to me.

"I speak English," he says, his hand extended. It is large, the muscles strong but the skin surprisingly soft. "Señor Garza telephoned to me. He said you are a special friend and to take good care of you."

For some reason I feel myself blushing. He says to call him Alberto.

"Is that lady going to be all right?" I ask, not knowing quite what to say.

"Her husband broke her arm. She will not leave him. One day he will kill her," he says simply, as if this is so commonplace in his experience there is no reason to get excited.

A little startled, I ask if there is a five o'clock yoga class. He says he thinks it will be just us today; May is very quiet. He asks if I have any physical ailments or complaints. I say no. Then, reconsidering, I explain that I've been practicing yoga for years but it doesn't seem to help my TMJ. I point to the right side of my jaw.

"Yes, the teeth clenching," he says. "I know this."

He comes around so that he's standing behind me, and gently presses a thumb into my right trapezius muscle. I cringe under the unexpected pressure, letting out a small cry.

"The problem starts here," he states. "Since you are right-handed, the right side is worse. Do you wake up from sleep?"

"Yes," I allow, astonished. Sensing my discomfort, he backs away and with an open hand, indicates the open floor space. I take my Jade mat out of its case and unroll it.

Alberto starts the class with five minutes of pranayama breathing. Then he leads me through a series of Surya Namaskaras, not exactly the ones I practice, but similar. I push too hard. He holds the downward dog pose a long time, much too long for me, and soon my arms are trembling and I'm dripping sweat onto the floor and mat. As I'm straining, my palms shoulder-width apart pressing into the mat, he comes over and turns my upper arms inward, toward each other, pressing lightly on my biceps.

"Do you feel a release in your neck and shoulders?"

My arms and back muscles are about to collapse; I can't hold the downward dog much longer. He lifts me up by the shoulders with surprising strength and eases me back down to a sitting position on the mat.

"More than yoga, you need a massage," says Alberto. "Whatever it is that is making you so tight, you must let go."

Sitting back on my heels, I tell him I don't have time for a massage. I must get home to my little girl. He continues the class, with many Warrior poses, which don't give me any trouble.

After final relaxation, he asks me if I will permit him to feel my chi.

"My chi?"

"I won't touch you," he adds with a smile, his palms open at his sides.

I nod. He approaches and kneels before me, placing both palms parallel to my head, about six inches away from my ears, as I sit cross-legged on the mat. Alberto waits, and after a moment moves his hands down to my shoulders, then six inches from my chest and six inches from my back, so that my upper torso is sandwiched between his palms. He stops there, and I feel a strange heat radiating from his hands.

"Your lung meridian is out of balance," he says.

"My . . . what?"

His voice is gentle, unobtrusive, calm, as if he's complimenting me on a job well done. "You have breathing issues? And maybe you wake up at three o'clock in the morning? If you wake at two, you fall quickly back to sleep. But, I think, if you wake at three, you do not fall back to sleep."

I am reluctant to admit this. It seems too personal. I am suddenly quite ready to leave. "I have to go now."

He smiles and nods as if I've said something profound. "Yes. Of course." He hops lightly to his feet and floats toward the door at the back of the room. "I will give you some tea that will help you sleep." In a moment he returns with a little satchel, which he places in my palm.

"Three a.m. is the anger meridian," he says.

"The anger meridian?" I sniff at the pouch. The tea smells like flowers, fresh and complicated.

"It is the time of the twenty-four-hour cycle that anger is the strongest and that the problems with the lungs occur."

"What is this tea?"

"Chamomile and lavender, bergamot with a little pear blossom. Please, come back tomorrow. I will not charge you for the massage."

I try to hand him a twenty-dollar bill but he pushes it away.

"The first class is free," he says. I lay the bill down on the desk. "When I was a child I was rescued from the war in El Salvador by American Catholic missionaries. They taught me to read and write and speak English. They were good people. But the war left me badly scarred." He searches my eyes with a penetrating, compassionate look. "I see how much you are suffering." He takes my hand in his. His palms are soft and warm and comforting.

"My husband just died . . ." I look away from his painfully piercing gaze.

"This pain is older," he says. "Tomorrow I will have a class at twelve and a class at five. I hope you will come back."

The sidewalks are high and narrow and every time a person approaches, one of us has to step off into the street, where the cobblestones are rounded and uneven. The afternoon shadows are already long and in the west the sun has disappeared behind a threatening bank of purple clouds; the air is suddenly heavy with moisture, so thick it feels like chicken broth. I walk up, up, up through the city, my yoga pants and tank top soaked with sweat as if I've been caught in a downpour. Alberto Zaldaña's words toll in my head like the bells in these church towers that call people to prayer. The faithful come and they pray on their knees before dead saints and icons, to cure their cancer, to help their children, to save their crops. Poor Señora Garza crawled on her knees to the Virgin of Guadalupe. And that old lady who is only forty who goes to Alberto Zaldaña for help but then will not take his advice. Why do people do that, keep going back to the same place over and over again, expecting help, expecting salvation, expecting the impossible? I realize I'm gritting my teeth and the pain shooting from my jaw up into my head startles me all over again.

When I get back, the house is deserted and silent even though it's cocktail hour. There will be no sunset today; the low-hanging clouds have rolled in from the mountains in the west and the entire sky seems like a dark bruise, the air tinged with a greenish hue. Still, Bibi must have had a long day if she's missing cocktail hour and taking a nap before dinner.

In our room, the fan turns overhead and the air is not so humid. Tenney crouches on the tile floor, talking to Sophia while cupping one of the tiny pups in her hands. The little thing is actually starting to look like a dog. Sophia greets me, her tail wagging joyfully. Her nails click on the smooth gray tiles as her back end contorts from side to side. I throw myself onto the bed and ask Tenney if she'll get me a cold washcloth.

"What's wrong, Mom? Are you okay?"

"Just a headache; it's so hot!"

She brings me a dripping washcloth—she never squeezes the water out and I forgot to tell her again. Sophia jumps up on the bed and stands with her front paws on my chest, looking into my face like a concerned nurse. She smells my breath and then tries to lick my mouth. I turn away, saying, "Yech!" and scratch her ears.

"Zorro and Lola grew so much already in two days!"

"That's very good." My voice sounds tired. Water drips onto the silvery bedcover where it beads up, but I don't have the energy to get up and wring the cloth out. I remember I have to clip the puppies' tiny nails in the next few days to protect Sophia's nipples and I'm not looking forward to it. "Pretty soon their eyes will open. The vet told me it takes about a week."

"That's going to be so cool," Tenney says.

On the bedside table on her side I spy the silver frame that I bought for Bibi in the artisan market on our first day. Tenney has put a photo inside, taken last year at Disney's Animal Kingdom by a professional photographer. Behind us is the faux Mount Everest with its faux snowcapped peak. We're in shorts and T-shirts, standing on a little bridge. Marring the otherwise pristine vista are the roller coaster's black tracks that look like the sutures on Frankenstein's monster.

A knock on the bedroom door. Sophia scurries to her box.

"*Adelante*," I call, sitting up.

It's Pedro. He looks sheepish, his shoulders hunched, his large, calloused hands curled into fists by his sides. He says he is here to take the dogs.

Tenney takes up a defensive position in front of the box. "No!"

I clamber to the foot of the bed and stand, my head spinning. My Spanish is not up to this. "*Porque ahora?*" Why now?

He moves a few steps into the room and Sophia, on her feet behind Tenney, starts to growl, the sound low and threatening and unfamiliar. He says he has found the perros a home in the campo, at a goat farm, and la Señora Bibienne wants them gone by nightfall.

Tenney starts to wail. She turns to me, her face contorted, red and splotchy, and screams, "They're our family now! This is our *family!* It's just *us* now. You can't let them do this!"

"*No es posible*," I tell Pedro, my voice trembling. I'm not sure if this means it is impossible, or simply, *You can't.* I have no idea.

Pedro steps back, arms extended. He says la Señora Bibienne is sleeping, we must quiet down; we must not disturb her. It is a good place, he says without much conviction. I must let him take the perros or la Señora Bibienne *se va a enojar;* she will be angry.

Tenney is mumbling, "Mommy, Mommy," between choking sobs.

There must be some mistake. He must have misunderstood.

"*Ahora no es posible, Pedro*," I repeat shakily. "*Los perros son nuestros.*" Now is not possible. The dogs are ours. "*Se quedan con nosotros.*" They're staying with us.

With three females standing against him, he slowly backs out of the room, shoulders tight. I can see he's angry; maybe his pride is hurt. I realize I'm still gripping the washcloth and throw it through the bathroom door, completely missing the sink.

"I'm going to go talk to Bibi," I tell Tenney. "Stay here with Sophia. Lock the door."

But when I step outside, I find Pedro blocking the path that leads to the stairs. He will not let me pass.

I say I need to speak with my mother.

He says she does not want to be disturbed and asked him to take the dogs as soon as possible to the campo. He won't move out of the way. I look up at Bibi's bedroom windows but the shutters are closed.

She has planned this, I realize, and I'm overtaken by a wave of nausea. I'm trembling, as if from fever. I try to take deep breaths but I can't seem to get enough air into my lungs. I hurry back to our room; the door is locked. "Let me in, Tenney!"

She quickly unlatches the lock; she's been standing right on the other side, waiting.

I sit on the floor by Sophia's box. Sophia looks at me expectantly. I have to think this through. Bibi can't just take the dogs away from us; I have a say in this. I can stop this. I am an adult. So why do I feel like a small, bad child? The ceiling seems to be caving in. I cup my hands tight around my mouth and nose and breathe in slowly. I reach for the landline phone and try Dr. Fuller's number, my hand trembling so badly I misdial and have to start again. He picks up after two rings.

"I'm glad to hear from you."

"Could you take Sophia and her puppies, just for tonight, or maybe a few nights?" My voice is strained.

"Of course. What's wrong, Merryn?"

"Bibi wants them out of here by nightfall. I don't know what else to do."

"Your mother is a bitch," he says, his voice tight and low.

"Well, but it's her house—" I jump to her defense.

"She's a bitch."

"I've really put her out." He doesn't know her that well; he won't feel this way when he gets to know her better.

After a pause he says, "I have a waiting room full of patients and can't come get them right now. Can you bring them over?"

"Thank you, Dr. Fuller—"

"Please, Merryn, we've . . . we're past that now. Call me Steve."

"Thank you. We're on our way." I hang up and turn to Tenney. "Put the leash on Sophia. We're taking them to Dr. Steve's. Quickly." Like a revolutionary standing before a firing squad while the soldiers cock their rifles, I want to scream, *Viva la revolución!* But I also want to fall to my knees and beg the general for mercy.

No. I'm overreacting. When I was little Bibi used to tell me when I couldn't sleep or worried incessantly over a small detail that I was hysterical and needed to get a grip on myself. I'm certain it's not that Bibi wants the dogs necessarily to go to the campo; surely she just wants the disruption to end. It's her house, after all. We've caused her enough grief. When we get back from Dr. Steve's I will explain calmly why I could not let Pedro take them to the campo.

Tenney leads the way, with Sophia on her leash and the kibbles and vitamins in a plastic bag gripped by her other hand. I follow carrying the box with the puppies inside and Blueberry squeezed under my arm. Sophia nervously turns and cranes her neck to make sure I'm behind her. Bibi's shutters are open now and the lamps send a watery, yellow light into the garden. The sconces at the entryway beyond the arch have also been lit, turning the stone to gold. Bruise-colored clouds hang low in the sky. A long shadow crosses the flagstone path amidst the jungle of plants. I stop short. Bibi has stepped out of her doorway and is standing at the top of the outside stairs, her hair uncombed and hanging loosely around her face. She looks tired and slightly haggard. I never see her like this; this is not her public face.

"But . . . where are you going?" She sounds very upset.

Tenney and Sophia have made it to the garage door, just beyond the archway.

"Pedro said you wanted the dogs out by nightfall, so we're taking them to Dr. Fuller's." I sound guilty—apologetic. This is my role. This is who I am. The bad child. The annoying child.

"I worked very hard to find them a good home in the campo," she says, gliding down the stairs in her high-heeled slippers, gripping the banister. On the ground her shadow moves toward me, then splits into several shadows of varying shades, which rotate around me slowly as she descends. I feel rooted in place, as if stuck in cement. I know I have to move. It's insane but I have a terrible feeling she is going to yell for Pedro to come and wrest the box from my hands.

"Yes," I say, my voice quaking because I'm a coward and my will is no match for hers. "Thank you for doing all that, Bibi. And I'm sorry for the disruption. I know I've been imposing terribly on your generosity. But Bibi, Tenney is not ready to give them up. She's lost so much already . . . At least at Dr. Fuller's she'll be able to see them."

No answer. I wait. She crosses her arms.

"After all I've done for you," she finally replies, "you have to embarrass me in front of strangers. That man hates me already and now you are making me look like . . . like some kind of monster. I can't believe how ungrateful you are. I just can't understand how you are kin of mine."

Her words reverberate off the stones and finally shatter and disperse somewhere in the thick air above us. But there is an equation here that is not adding up. To give the dogs away will hurt my daughter; and yet, by protecting my daughter and Sophia, I am doing the wrong thing. I am a bad daughter. I've never doubted her opinion of me.

I am barely able to unglue my tongue from the roof of my mouth. But I have to do this. I have to. "We'll be back later, Bibi. Go ahead and have dinner without us." My voice sounds strange, wooden to my own ear.

No response, but her silence is louder than any words she could utter. What am I waiting for?

Finally, I step with jellied knees through her thin shadow, which stands immobile now, and head for the archway and the garage door beyond it. Tenney rushes to open the door for me; thank God it is not locked. She steps aside to let me through with the box.

I glance back for a moment. Bibi is still standing rigid in front of the fountain at the center of her patio garden, staring at us with a stricken expression, as if we're thieves who've broken in and robbed her. She looks as if she might call the police. I feel like I belong in prison. It takes all the energy I have to step into the garage. The Mercedes is gone, which means Calisto must have taken it again to visit his mother in Dolores Hidalgo. I open the Honda's back door and deposit the box and Blueberry in the backseat, press the garage door opener on the wall, and hurry around and slip in behind the wheel. Tenney sits in back, seat belt fastened, with Sophia on her lap and one hand gripping the top of the box. I start the engine but am unable to proceed. A memory assails me.

Early one morning in Yaoundé, I was awakened by the loud squawking of birds. They did that to chase away snakes that were after their eggs. I got out of bed and went into the kitchen to get a glass of water and there was Mum, frantically opening and closing cabinets.

"I can't find a goddamn thing in this house!" she cried, then inexplicably burst into tears. She sat down at the little Formica table and wept into her hands. I crept closer, until I was only inches away. Her dark hair was in disarray, hanging over her face, and her shoulders shook and I didn't recognize the childish wailing voice that was coming out of her. I put my hand on her back. "Poor Mum. Poor Mummy." She threw her arms around me and wept harder with her face pressed into my hip.

"I expected so much . . . so much . . . but nothing has turned out right."

I don't know how long I stood there or what happened next. What I remember is asking her, sometime later, maybe the next day, "Why were you crying, Mummy?"

"What on earth are you talking about, Merryn?" she replied with icy calm. "You must have had another nightmare."

Now, with the car engine running, every muscle and sinew and synapse in my body screams to turn back, to grovel, to beg for her forgiveness. How bad could life be for Sophia in the campo?

"Drive, Mommy," Tenney says in a low voice, leaning forward between the front seats, and I remember why I can't give in. I can't give in because I don't want Tenney to grow up and remember today as the day her mother acted like a coward and betrayed her. I'm in a cold sweat, feeling sick, as if I have the flu.

I put the gearshift in drive and step on the gas.

Tenney has the map and is giving me directions by the glow of a little flashlight I keep in the glove compartment. Sophia stands on her hind legs, alert, ears cocked, her front paws on the door, watching the road with her nose pressed to the window. Even though night has fallen and the sky is black with clouds, it is not difficult to find Dr. Steve's house on 20 de Enero Norte in Colonia San Antonio, a neighborhood beyond the Centro that is completely deserted at this hour, and ill-lit. The street slants upward, though most of Colonia San Antonio is in the bowl of the valley. Above the doorway of the indigo-blue wall shines a lamp in the shape of a smiling sun. The top of the outside wall has colorful broken glass embedded in the cement to keep out thieves, but the outer door is wide open, inviting anyone to walk in. I leave the Honda as close as I can to his front door.

I carry the puppy box inside. Tenney is holding her bear by the hand and he hangs there like a recalcitrant child.

To the left is the casita with the door wide open, Dr. Steve's waiting room; beyond must be the examining rooms. A young woman in a patched frock and unraveling huaraches sits holding a sick infant on her lap. An old man also waits, his cotton pants so faded they have no color and his face so dark and lined it looks like a walnut shell. Straight ahead is a courtyard with, on the left, a chicken-wire fence and a hut on stilts and maybe a dozen chickens and one self-important, prancing rooster milling about, pecking at the ground. On the other side is another pen that holds two little brown goats; they also have a wooden hut standing on cement bricks with a slanting roof and a little ramp.

"Oh, wow!" Tenney says, moving down the path between the enclosures, Sophia straining at her leash.

Dr. Steve appears in the doorway of the casita. "My patients keep bringing me animals, even though I ask them not to. Know anyone who needs two baby goats?" He laughs soundlessly.

He leads us down the brick path to the front door of the indigo house. Off to the side is a domed, slightly scraggly frangipani tree in bloom, the orange and yellow flowers filling the air with their delicate scent.

The interior walls are a warm adobe-red, and to the left is an open kitchen, with a long countertop and three tall hand-painted stools. I wonder who painted them. Straight ahead is a staircase and to the right, the living room. It feels like he sort of threw the furniture together—the mission-style chairs with oak armrests and two wicker couches with flowery cushion seats and a battered oak coffee table—but somehow everything fits. The colors are mostly clay-red and earth-toned, with a floor of large, polished brown tiles. There are bookshelves crowded with big, thick medical textbooks and many paperbacks with cracked spines, and a fireplace at the far end.

I put the box down on the floor. Tenney lets Sophia off her leash. Sophia busily sniffs and licks her babies, making sure everything is in order. I'm the one who is traumatized. I've crossed some boundary, some line with Bibi, and I have no idea what is going to happen next. I feel unmoored.

I realize I must look a fright, still in my yoga pants and tank top and my hair wild from the humidity. I push a strand back off my face.

"I'll be back in a little while," says Dr. Steve. "There are some bowls in the kitchen cabinet for Sophia." He opens the front door and looks up at the sky. "We may get a freak storm tonight." He goes out and the door clicks shut behind him.

Tenney says, "We could marry Dr. Steve. Then our family would have a dad."

I am so stunned I don't know what to say. "I know you miss your daddy, Tenney."

"How can I miss my daddy when my daddy was never there?" she shouts at me. "What if something happens to *you*? Then what? Then what will happen to *me*? Bibi is crazy. I can't live with a crazy person."

I collapse onto the closest chair and fold over, practically in two.

On the table, just in front of me, a paperback—*Obstetrics in Remote Settings: Practical Guide for Nonspecialized Health Care Professionals*.

"Why are you so scared of her?" Tenney asks, hands on hips. "What can she do to you? You're a grown-up."

A bolt of lightning strikes nearby, immediately followed by a clap of thunder that causes the windows to rattle. Tenney and I jump. Dr. Steve steps through the front door. Another lightning strike, and the electricity flickers, then goes out. He pulls a tall hurricane lamp out of a cabinet and flicks it on. The long tubular fluorescent lights make a loud buzzing sound and send out a strange, artificial white glow. Sophia is whimpering, hiding in her box with her pups. Tenney takes a blanket off the back of the couch and spreads it on the Aztec-patterned rug and lies down, hugging the box, telling Sophia things could be much worse. She could be in the campo right now. The thought of Sophia trembling under a tree or some makeshift lean-to makes my bones ache.

Dr. Steve puts a kettle on the stove for tea.

He leaves the room, then returns after nearly ten minutes with three cups and sets them down on the low table. Tenney and Sophia have fallen asleep. I sip the fragrant tea, which has spices floating through it and is sweetened with honey. Dr. Steve unfolds another knitted blanket and covers my child, tucking the corners in under her shoulders and feet.

"Normally the rains don't start till the middle of the month," he says.

The deluge that follows makes me think of dams breaking. It beats down on the roof like a Napoleonic cavalry charge, the thunder like cannon fire. Tenney must be exhausted because she doesn't wake.

"Bibi will be worried," I say uncertainly.

"Your *Bibi* is not thinking about you." His tone has turned cold, tight like it was on the phone earlier.

"What?"

"I'm sure she wouldn't want you driving in this mess," he says, softening. "I saw her Mexican boyfriend—"

"He's not her boyfriend, he's her protégé."

Dr. Steve looks at me quite strangely, as if suddenly he doesn't recognize me. "He was driving around Colonia San Antonio in her Mercedes last Sunday. He had the top down and the music blasting. And two girls with him in the front seat."

"They must be his cousins. Sometimes he takes Bibi's car to visit his family."

"There's a name for guys like him around here. *Vividor*."

"Vividor?"

"It means scrounger."

A bolt of lightning turns night to day beyond the windows, followed moments later by an ear-shattering crash of thunder.

"Jesus," he says, "it's right on top of us. I hope the animals are okay." He goes to the window and looks out.

I cross the room and lean in beside him, squinting into the downpour. The light touch of his cotton button-down shirt against my bare arm sends a charge up my spine. The street beyond the outside door has turned into a raging river. I fear the cars are going to float away down the street.

"We'd better go. Bibi is going to be flipping out."

"The roads are flooded," he says. "It's not safe to drive right now. It should calm down in a little while."

In a flash the world lights up to day again; one of the baby goats is standing in the rain, the water rising rapidly, already up to its belly. Then, complete darkness.

"I should've locked them in. What was I thinking about? I

was thinking about you, that's what," he mutters. "They're so dopey they break my heart. I have to go out there."

In the kitchen he grabs a flashlight and I follow him to the door. He steps out into the teeming rain. The water in the courtyard is already halfway up his calves. The drainage system must be blocked; drains never seem to work properly in San Miguel. He struggles to open the latch to the pen but it's stuck. He needs help. I run out, the water drenching me in seconds. I take the flashlight for him and train the beam onto the gate's latch. The latch gives, but he has to struggle to push it open against the mass of water. He shoulders his way in and lifts up the kid in both arms and, cradling the little bleating thing, carries it into the hut, where the second kid is crying for its companion.

"All right, you guys. Sleep tight." He pushes the plank up so that it blocks the hut's entrance, and now they're safely tucked in for the night. A crack of lightning splits the sky in two, a jagged vertical line that seems to reach the earth somewhere close by.

We stumble into the house, dripping puddles onto the tile floor. In the living room Tenney has not moved, she's still sleeping soundly on the blanket on the rug, her body wrapped around Sophia's box.

"I'll get you some dry clothes," he says, and bounds up the stairs. In a moment he's back with a soft towel and a pair of sweatpants and an aged blue flannel shirt that smells like him. I peel off my soaking-wet clothes and his flannel shirt feels strangely intimate against my bare skin.

Water runs from the gutters as if from open faucets and even the house seems to be hunkering down under the weight of the onslaught. I collapse on the couch. He boils more water and we drink tea, sitting quietly, listening to the rain.

"My father was an alcoholic," Dr. Steve says suddenly, his

voice tight. "I left as soon as I could and never looked back. I got all kinds of scholarships to college and med school. I never drank, but I had a little problem with the dry goods."

"Steve . . ."

"I lost my medical license in the States." He sits forward, tense, elbows on his knees. I reach out and take his hand. The room is completely dark. Do I need to reciprocate now? Do I need to tell him something intimate and personal that no one knows?

"I had an affair with my CrossFit trainer."

He looks at me, his eyes shining in the darkness.

"You know about this *sexting* thing? Oh my god. These youngsters! He sent me pictures of his—"

Dr. Steve starts to laugh. Soon I'm laughing too and I don't know why.

"Stop!" he says, holding his stomach with both arms as if his guts are about to spill out. "You're killing me." As I'm trying to contain my laughter, snorting air out my nose, I'm thinking, *Wow, he's not jealous at all.*

CHAPTER TEN

A HORRIBLE SHRIEK tears through the deep black lake of sleep. I open my eyes to the glare of the overhead light buzzing and sputtering, dimming then brightening. I'm lying on the couch alongside Tenney, who is still asleep on the floor. I sit bolt upright, remembering where I am.

That murderous shriek splits the silence again and I realize it's the rooster. He must be completely insane. Outside the bare windows there is no hint of dawn, but the courtyard lights are ablaze. We never switched them off when the electricity went out during the storm.

"I'm going to wring that rooster's neck," Dr. Steve murmurs from the armchair. "He does this every fucking night."

Tenney stirs, rolls over, and blinks up at me. Her hand is under the couch. She seems to be tugging on something. She pulls out her hand and hanging from the crook of her finger is a bright pink, lacy thong. She looks at the strange thing dangling there like a boy who's amazed to have caught a fish.

Steve frowns, reaches forward, takes the flimsy garment, crumples it in his fist, and throws it across the room to the wastebasket, but it falls just short and lies in a hot-pink knot on the floor, made only brighter by the mirror effect of the metal pail.

Does this belong to one of the lesbians? Or are there others?

"Merryn," he says. "Listen—"

"I have to get home. Come on, Tenney. Get up, we have to go now." Where are my yoga pants and tank top? "Where are my clothes?"

"They're not dry yet."

"I have to go," I mumble, refusing to look at him. He sighs, but steps out of the way.

"Merryn." He's right behind me. "It's probably been there for ages."

He goes into the kitchen where he takes a coffee filter from a cabinet and places it in the coffee maker. "How about a cup of coffee?" he suggests as if this is nothing. "I have some excellent dark roast."

I find this man and his constant offering of hot beverages suddenly very irritating. And irritating too is the fact that he's even more handsome with rumpled hair and stubble. It all seems so easy for him. How could I have let down my guard so completely? I feel like crying.

In the living room, Tenney is in no hurry. Still half asleep, she pets Sophia who has also awakened and seems to be wondering what's going on. The hurricane lamp has gone out but all the lights are blazing. They dim and brighten all at once, as if the guys at the electric plant are turning some giant dial but can't quite get the voltage right.

"Tenney!" I holler. "We have to get back to Bibi's before she wakes up and has a fit."

She looks up at me, blinking. Sophia jumps to the floor, wagging her tail and glancing up at me expectantly. Tenney stands and looks around as if her mind isn't quite processing yet. Sophia follows us as I lead Tenney toward the door.

"Stay," I tell Sophia. The hopeful look in her black eyes and her wagging tail make me want to cry even more. I kneel and pull her to my chest. She makes a sighing sound, just like a child. Swallowing hard, I put her back on her feet on the floor, stand and turn away, grasping the door handle.

"She'll be fine," Dr. Steve says behind me. He follows us out. The air carries the slightly metallic, battery-spark smell of ozone, and the rich and damp humus of decomposing plants. The pale blooms of the frangipani tree lie spread out on the ground like fallen butterflies. He follows us down the path to the front gate. In the glistening courtyard the rooster is strutting around his enclosure, glancing at us with his little hysterical eyes, his coxcomb hanging over the top of his forehead like the crooked crown on some demented king.

"Did it rain?" Tenney asks dazedly.

"It sure did," says Dr. Steve.

I help her into the backseat of the Honda and as I'm shutting the door, I feel his hand on my arm. "You need to relax," he murmurs. "Everything is good."

Nothing is good! What the hell is he talking about?

I don't know what to say, so I slip in behind the wheel, busying myself with my seat belt. He's standing in the doorway watching us. I don't wave, but focus hard on the road, my eyes stinging. The streets are deserted, shining like oil in the depressions where puddles have formed.

At Bibi's, the outside lights are on. I leave the car running in the street with the headlights off and sneak inside to open the garage. The Mercedes is not back and I'm relieved because it means Calisto also got stranded in the storm. I press the garage opener, watch the door slide up, and duck back out to the idling car. Tenney is asleep in the backseat, rolled up in a ball on her side.

I turn off all the outdoor lights and we tiptoe, holding hands, through the quiet patio, the house a black shape backlit by a deep, royal-blue sky, like a velvet curtain hanging over a stage lit from the bottom by muted floor lamps. The birds are starting to stir but the patio is dark and silent, the fountain still. Even the fish are sleeping. Bibi's bedroom windows are dark.

I open our bedroom door. The bedside digital clock reads 4:35. I pull down the silver bedcover and Tenney and I collapse on the king-size bed with Blueberry between us.

The dogs are gone, the storm is over, we're back where we're supposed to be, and it's as if none of this ever happened, as if we never left at all.

I lie awake for a long time, thinking about an African boy in Yaoundé. We were both twelve. He kissed me in an alleyway between two buildings on our way home from school. He wore a white shirt and blue trousers and his irises were so black I couldn't see his pupils, and he sighed and told me in French that his heart felt swollen with love. It was a dusty alleyway only a few feet wide, a place no one would look at twice, but to me it became the entrance to a world filled with magic and possibility that stood outside of time. Every day I would pass the spot on my way home and relive our luxurious, secret kiss. No one knew—certainly, the world outside would never have allowed us, neither me nor the boy, to display this romance in public—and I was scared of it, scared of his passion and of how I felt. He often asked me if he could walk me home after that, but I said no. I loved him, yet I said no.

Bibi would not have minded that he was black; but in her extreme boredom and restlessness, she would have turned our romance into a funny story with which to entertain the other restless diplomats' wives. She would have torn it to shreds. I was much safer being the boring person she thought I was. Sometimes I think about that boy and where he might be now. All my life I've wanted to tell him I'm sorry.

Eight a.m., Tenney and I, in an exhausted stupor, enter the great room. Bibi sits at the dining table in her crimson silk negligee, sipping a Bloody Mary and smoking, deep in thought. My heart quickens. Bibi doesn't even glance up until Tenney and I are standing right on the other side of the table. She turns her focus to tamping out her cigarette but does not speak.

"Hi, Bibi," Tenney says tentatively.

"Good morning, Tenney," says her grandmother in a clipped tone.

"How are you feeling today?" I ask, sitting down as if the day is perfectly normal.

Nothing. She is freezing me out.

I busy myself by filling my cup but clearly no amount of coffee is going to help me today. Tenney flops into the seat next to mine and reaches for the pitcher of orange juice. It looks too heavy, so I grab the curving glass handle and pour for her. The phone trills loudly, making me jump in my seat and spill. I quickly wipe up the juice with my napkin.

"Ah, there you are, Calisto," Bibi says in her warm, honeyed tone. She listens intently, nodding. "Well, I'm just happy you didn't try to drive back in that mess . . . Can't you hear me?" She bangs the receiver against the tabletop and brings it back to her ear. "Damn it, we've been cut off." She places the receiver on the table and says to no one in particular, "Poor Calisto got stuck in Dolores Hidalgo. He says the roads are still a mess and he won't be able to get back until late this afternoon."

The roads are perfectly fine but I'm not going to be the one to tell her. Bibi's eyebrows are trying to frown and I realize she has definitely been getting Botox injections, despite the fact

that she swears she is "completely natural." Marta arrives with
our eggs, which she places before us, but I can't eat. I turn to
Tenney and tell her to eat her eggs. I drink another cup of coffee
while Bibi puffs away at a fresh cigarette. My eyes float off toward the mountains to the east, which seem to have had exploded
green overnight.

"I've made an important decision," Bibi says with a long
exhale of smoke. "I've been thinking this over for quite some
time. I've decided to make Calisto executor of my estate. I'm
going to leave him everything and let him decide how to divvy
it up. I just don't trust you, Merryn. You are so mercurial and
intemperate."

I'm suddenly trembling, as if from a fever. What am I without Bibi? What will become of us if we no longer have this shel-
ter? I will be orphaned, abandoned, without kin.

"What is *mercurial and intemperate*?" Tenney asks me, not Bibi.

And I remember that I am the parent, I am responsible for
this child, not just myself. How could my own mother talk to me
like this in front of my daughter?

"So Doctor Handsome took in the mangy stray," Bibi says in
a pinched tone. "You don't have a clue about life, Merryn. I just
don't understand you." She turns her shiny eyes to Tenney. "*You*
are more like me than your mother. When she was little I used to
tell her the stork made a mistake."

I spent endless hours trying to imagine that very child the
stork dropped off at the wrong address, the one that belonged to
Bibi, a perfect, dark-haired, quiet child who made no mistakes.
Not a lumbering, slow-to-read, self-conscious, humorless,
dreamy child like me who was neither American, nor French,
nor white African. How could I change? What could I do to
please her? To be more like her? These questions preoccupied
and tormented me.

At my shattered core I feel that sharp-toothed, slithery thing start to uncoil, as if her words, these blows, have loosed it from the rubble that is all that is left of the fortress that was my love for her.

"I don't want to be like you," says Tenney to her grandmother, standing and taking my hand, her eggs untouched. For a moment Bibi looks shocked, as if Tenney just reached over the table and slapped her. I feel heat spreading from my chest to my extremities, a kind of victorious elation.

I shove my chair back and the legs screech on the tiles. Bibi winces but then her phone trills again. This time she lets it ring, her eyes trained on me like cocked arrows. "You should leave. As soon as possible."

"We're grateful for your kindness and hospitality," I say, my voice tight. "As soon as I talk to Agent Warnock, we'll be out of your way."

"Where are we going? I have to finish my chess matches!" Tenney protests.

"You can finish your chess matches." My voice sounds off to my own ear. I turn away, feeling the heat of Bibi's eyes on my back. I have a lot to do before we can leave. A lot to do.

I am in a kind of stupor as we dress, as if I'm standing just outside myself, one step off, one step behind. I realize we'll need a place to stay tonight, or perhaps a few nights. I'm not sure what Agent Warnock has in mind. She will want me to return to Dallas, perhaps tomorrow. As I close and lock the bedroom door I see Blueberry sitting on the bed, his back against the pillows like some kind of resting pasha, without a care in the world.

On the way down the hill I call Agent Warnock and leave a message to call me as soon as possible. Surely we can stay with Dr.

Steve for a night or two. I have to get a health certificate for the dogs so we can take them back to Texas. I must go back and pack our bags.

Señor Garza meets us in the courtyard and announces that he will be accompanying the children himself to Parque Juárez this morning, as he is curious to see this chess. He asks me if I'd like to come along. A few hours away from Bibi will surely help calm her mood and mine, so I nod to Señor Garza, and Tenney and the two tow-headed little American boys, Señorita Maria, and I head toward the Centro.

We walk down San Francisco, passing the jardín and the parroquia on our left and the main police station on our right. The air still has a crisp, clean feel from the rain and the bay laurels in the jardín seem refreshed. The cobblestones exude a slight dampness, but within an hour the sun will have baked all the moisture from the stones and the earth and the heat will be back with stunning force.

Down the hill the sidewalks narrow, and the unadorned but colorful stucco walls of the houses facing the public street give no hint of the depth or the beauty that lie beyond them. The bright sunlight sparkles off the mica in the cobblestones, forcing me to squint.

The recreational area in Parque Juárez is a sunken cement court surrounded on two sides by perpendicular hewn-stone walls, above which stretch rows of cement bleachers, painted an earthy clay tone. Down on the courts there are more of these bleachers with a clear, hard plastic rain awning above. Although it's fairly early in the morning on a weekday, small children kick a soccer ball around in one corner, while young men in groups crowd around various basketball nets. The two viejos sit on the top bleacher under the awning, their portable board between them. They're smoking and waiting for their new opponent.

"Buenos dias señores," Tenney says with great solemnity in her high, little-girl voice, and the two old men break into gap-toothed smiles. One of them slides back along the bleacher and she takes his place across from the other, who slowly, deliberately, lights a fresh cigarette from the smoldering tip of his old butt. Señorita Maria follows the two American brothers down to the court and they join in the soccer game. The old man who is not playing tells Tenney he teaches ajedrez to children at the Casa de la Cultura up the hill on Saturday mornings and would she like to be his assistant? The littler children, he explains, shrugging unhappily, are afraid of him.

"Why are they afraid of you?" she asks, as if the mere thought is absurd. Tenney seems at ease, focused on her chess pieces and smiling secretively from time to time as she moves her army around without trepidation. The old man sitting across from her grumbles. She wins the first match but it's pretty close. As her second match begins against the second viejo, I glance over my shoulder and there is Agent Warnock, her arms crossed, immobile and silent, standing at the edge of the wall above the bleachers. She wears sunglasses, and a new straw cowboy hat, and a silver pendant, a scorpion encased in amber, which she must have bought in one of the artisan market stalls. I jump to my feet, intending to go talk to her, but she turns and stalks off, disappearing among the trees.

Bibi is sitting on the north terrace, an ice bucket and bottles of tequila and tonic water on the table before her. Tequila? She hasn't changed out of her crimson dressing gown. This, for her, is unheard of. We sneak by, and as soon as I push the bedroom door open, Tenney throws herself on the bed. Blueberry is not there on the bed.

"Where's Blueberry?" I ask.

"I don't know. He was right here before."

"You didn't take him out of the room?"

"No."

"Tenney, did you tell anybody about the money?" I try to keep my tone light because if I sound frantic, she will not tell me.

"Well . . ." She stares up at the ceiling as if deep in thought. "This was awhile ago . . . Bibi asked me if we had any money and I told her that before we left Dallas we put $19,500 in Blueberry's battery compartment."

I collapse into the armchair.

"Bibi said she was having a heart attack worrying about us because we didn't have any money, so I told her. Are you mad at me?"

"No, sweetheart. Of course not." My voice sounds hollow despite my best efforts. A few minutes pass while I try to regain my equilibrium. Taking our money is a power play. She has taken control. Without the money, I am helpless.

I must go talk to her. I rise to my feet but my entire body feels lethargic, as if I'm trying to wade through chest-high water. Tenney looks exhausted too. I would like her to sleep. I lie down beside her, just for a moment, so she'll let herself rest. I can feel her delicate bones through the thin cotton of her lavender T-shirt, and her heart beating, which to me is the most comforting feeling in the world . . .

I open my eyes, alert and fearful. Tenney is gone. I throw my legs over the side of the bed and walk barefoot out to the patio, the soles of my feet soaking up the heat of the flagstones. No one is about. It must be four o'clock by now, and the staff seems to have left for the day. Through the glass walls of the great room I see Bibi and Tenney sitting at the outside table. As I'm crossing the great room I see that Tenney's mouth is wide open and she is about to bite into a piece of golden cake sprinkled with powdered sugar and cinnamon, which fall over her hands and shirt like the Sandman's golden dust.

"Now don't go getting fat on me, Tenney," says Bibi.

"Stop! Tenney!" I shout, and break into a run.

She looks up at me, stunned, and suddenly blushes. "Bibi said it was okay."

"It's just cake," Bibi says, vaguely waving around a hand that holds a Virginia Slim.

"The dough could be made with butter, and the icing could have cream in it," I mutter, trying to find my composure, to still my heart. "Put it down, Tenney. Come wash your hands."

For a moment the cake remains suspended in front of her mouth, and I'm sure she's going to bite into it, and I'm getting ready to run for an EpiPen, but slowly, reluctantly, she puts it down on a napkin on the glass tabletop.

I grab the napkin and cake and carry them to the kitchen and drop them in the trash. I see a pastry box on the counter, the string cut.

"Please come here, Tenney," I call over my shoulder. Does my voice sound firm enough? I'm quaking inside, too upset to even cry. What if she won't come? What if she takes Bibi's side against me? What will I do? My hands are trembling. It seems like an eternity passes before I feel her behind me.

"Mommy?" she says tentatively. Relief floods through me.

I lead her by the shoulder back to our room and we stand over the bathroom sink, and I soap up her small, thin hands while tears of relief stream from my eyes.

"I'm sorry, Mommy. I'm sorry. I didn't eat any, I promise."

I shake my head, swallowing back sobs. But the tears keep streaming. I thought Tenney would be safe here. But she was safer in Dallas. "You don't understand, Tenney. You don't re-member the last time you ate something that had cow's milk in it. You got so sick I had to rush you to the emergency room. Your throat closed up and you couldn't breathe. You just don't remember."

"I do remember. But Bibi says it's all in your head."

Frantic now, tears still falling, I pull our suitcases out of the deep closet and tell Tenney to start packing. In the bathroom I gather up our toiletries and EpiPens. I wipe my eyes with the back of my hand, pull some toilet paper from the roll, and dab at my face, blow my nose. But the tears won't stop. Once I've filled both suitcases, I realize I've been putting off the inevitable.

"You stay here."

"Don't go," she says, looking up at me in the mirror with a worried expression.

"I'll be right back." I try for a reassuring, motherly voice, but the words catch in my throat. "Check around for anything we may have forgotten."

I close the bedroom door, walk across the patio and through the French doors. Bibi is still sitting at the wrought-iron table, pretending to relax, pretending to admire the view. She must sense me standing behind her because her shoulders tense. She gazes proprietarily at the rounded mountains bathed in golden light. A red-tailed hawk rises from the canyon, and hangs sev-eral hundred feet above the reservoir but parallel to the terrace, perhaps thirty feet away in the still air, like a kite fluttering at the end of a string. My mind seems to lift from my body and rise on a hot zephyr to join him in flight. What a lovely way to see the world, looking down at the silent panorama, the stranger sitting at a wrought-iron table with a drink in her hand.

"Where is Tenney's bear?" I ask the back of her head, try-ing to keep my voice steady. Before yesterday I had never fought back, never disagreed with her. When confronted by her wrath, I am naked, exposed. I am not myself.

"I have no idea what you're talking about," she says crisply, pulling me back down into myself. I realize she is drunk. "You are a spoiled, selfish girl." She stands, carefully lifting herself out of the chair by grasping the armrests, and walks unsteadily in her high-heeled crimson- and pink-feathered mules to the stone parapet that runs along the edge of the terrace. She sets her ashtray down on the coping and flicks her ash, but misses by several inches. "I've done nothing but help you." She takes a deep pull on the cigarette, lifts her chin, and blows smoke into the air.

Is all this happening because I would not let Pedro take Sophia? I am not tracking properly. I have the sense of a noose tightening around my neck, not enough air getting through.

"Mum, you have to give me back that money. It's my money. Our being here has stressed you out." I know I shouldn't try to talk to her right now. I should leave, but I can't seem to move.

"I don't know what you're talking about," she says, sitting, swaying, crossing her legs. The negligee slides open, revealing a long and well-chiseled thigh. Her body wobbles slightly, as if she's sitting in a little boat. It's a two hundred–foot drop to the first natural shelf in the ravine.

"Mum, you'd better come back and sit over here."

"I tried to give you every advantage in life," she enunciates carefully, her voice low, "just like Daddy gave me." She points a finger in my direction. "I always gave you money when you needed it. The sad truth is . . . the sad truth is . . . I never liked you. And I know you don't like me."

The ground seems to be shifting, the floor dropping out from beneath my feet.

"I even found you a husband and you had to fuck that up too.

You've turned Tenney into a complete neurotic. You're not capable of raising a child." Her words slam into me like a blow to the solar plexus. I feel sick with guilt—or is this shame?—but then I feel the sharp-toothed monster uncoiling, raising its ugly head.

There is no justice in this world. People like you don't deserve to get away with such brutality. But you always do. I swallow the words back with difficulty.

"The truth is . . . the *Truth* is . . ." Bibi seems to lose track of what she was planning to say. I'm steeling myself for the next blow. Her words will slice right through me, as if I have no armor at all. "You're insane," she says. "I talked to Harvey Berger and I'm suing you for custody of Tenney."

My air seems to be cut off completely and my vision closes in, as if I'm looking down a dark tunnel. Hot blood pounds behind my eyes, beating like some wild tribal drum.

The phone trills on the wrought-iron table. Bibi stands, seemingly in slow motion. Everything appears to be slow, as if we're moving underwater. The heel of her mule seems to be caught in the hem of her gown. She is trying to kick herself free. She stumbles, totters at the edge of the parapet. The picture is not clear, not sharp. In the blue expanse the red-tailed hawk tips his wings, his feathers ruffling lightly in a mild puff of air. He floats suspended above us, waiting, watching. This must be the hour the hunt begins, when the voles and mice and rabbits come out of their holes.

Oh, to be free like that. I want to be free like that.

I step toward her and the look on her face is one I don't recognize—then, yes, I see she is afraid. My vision closes in, turning black as the circle of light shrinks until, like on an old-fashioned television screen when you turn it off, there is nothing left but one bright spot of light at the center. Then, blackness.

PART TWO

"Doomed enterprises divide lives forever
into the then and now."
—Cormac McCarthy, *The Crossing*

PART TWO

CHAPTER ELEVEN

T HE DAMN PHONE WON'T STOP RINGING. I'm sitting on the flagstones with my back up against the parapet, trying to get my bearings. The sun has vanished around the corner of the house but the terrace is still bathed in crimson light. Through the great room I see Tenney approaching, Blueberry in the crook of her arm; she runs toward me through the open doorway. I stand on shaky legs and take hold of her, blocking her way. The ravine and the valley and the reservoir below lie in deep shadow.

"B-Bibi took him," she says. "He was on her desk upstairs. The money's still there . . ." Her voice trails off as our eyes lock, then Tenney turns to see Bibi's one shoe, tipped on its side and lying some six feet away, the ostrich feathers trembling as if in their last throes. There is a large spider-shaped crack in one of the windowpanes, where the heel must have smacked into the glass.

"Bibi's had an accident," I say, wrapping my arms around her shoulders.

On the top of the stone parapet is Bibi's ashtray. The bottles of tequila and tonic stand on the wrought-iron table, three-quarters empty, the blue handblown glass ice bucket beside them, as if still waiting, along with a tumbler that holds a few fingers of liquid. The portable phone is lying there too, finally silent. Condensation has formed a puddle on the glass tabletop under the bucket, and one chair is pushed back at an angle, as if Bibi just got up to get something. Time still seems to be passing in slow motion.

I have to call the police. I don't know how to call the police in Mexico.

I lower myself into the chair opposite Bibi's and take hold of Tenney's cold hands. Her tawny eyes stare into mine, showing the lower crescents of white. She's got one arm around Blueberry's neck in a chokehold. I take deep breaths, trying to slow my heart.

"Bibi was very drunk. She was sitting on the parapet yelling at me and then she just . . . fell backward." I call Faye who is #1 on speed dial and Faye says she will call the police. Then I call Dr. Steve and he says he'll be here in ten minutes.

"Mom," says Tenney soberly, "you need to tell them you were with me the whole time. That you weren't here at all. That's what you need to tell them."

"I—"

The doorbell sounds but I can't move. Tenney disengages herself from my grasp and runs off through the great room to answer the door. Within moments, dozens of policemen— perhaps the entire police force of San Miguel—pour into the house. They're in short-sleeved, dark-blue uniforms and they spread out and run through the patio garden and into the great room and kitchen as if in hot pursuit of a murdering thief.

I rise from the chair as Tenney runs back to me and throws her arms around my waist, burying her face in my stomach. My Spanish isn't up to this. They don't even look like real policemen, more like boys playing. An older one in a rumpled gray suit brings up the rear. He walks self-confidently across the patio, followed by another man, also in a suit, but darker, perhaps blue. The boss looks like someone who wouldn't brook fools easily. In his midfifties, he has a deeply lined, tanned face and a graying buzz cut that looks like a shoe brush.

The two detectives approach as we remain in the doorframe that leads to the terrace; then the older one walks to the parapet and leans over, fingertips pressing into the stone coping as he stares with great intensity down into the ravine. He looks at the ashtray, then at the table, then at Bibi's shoe, then up at the spider-shaped crack in the windowpane, and finally at us. A young uniformed cop runs up with a pair of binoculars, which he hands to the second, younger detective, who then hands them to the boss. The boss looks through the lenses toward the bottom of the ravine for what seems like a long time. He says something and hands the binoculars back to the younger detective.

Soon there is a crowd of policemen at the parapet. After a moment the head detective gives some orders to his companion, who charges off with purpose and four officers directly behind him. The boss in his rumpled, shiny gray suit approaches.

"I am Detective Sanchez-Berilla."

I nod. My mouth feels gummy and dry. I need to unglue my tongue from the roof of my mouth. I probably look pale, ashen even. But I feel myself coming unhinged, as if I'm floating off, watching the scene from ten feet above.

Detective Sanchez-Berilla says, "*Con permiso*," then passes me and enters the great room and begins to inspect everything slowly and intensely. He seems especially fascinated by the array of photographs. The policemen are downstairs at the base of the house, attempting to climb down into the ravine from the pool level. For some reason they're blowing their whistles, as if the house were on fire. Detective Sanchez-Berilla stands by the fireplace, lifting frames and staring down at the faces of dignitaries. I notice that the silver frame with the photo of Tenney and me at Disney World is on the side table by the couch. How did it get there? The detective lifts the picture and gazes at it awhile.

The younger detective returns with a grave look and says something to Detective Sanchez-Berilla in a quiet voice. I can understand enough. The second detective says it looks like la señora's neck is broken and it's going to be very difficult to get down there and they will have to drive down into Colonia Azteca, the next neighborhood, and try to get to her from the end of Moctezuma Street, which is unpaved, then follow a path on foot through the undergrowth. Sanchez-Berilla says hurry up but if she is *muerta* don't touch the body and wait for the *perito de* something to arrive. Some kind of satellite phone or radio with an antenna crackles loudly in the younger detective's hand and he yells into it with importance.

Detective Sanchez-Berilla approaches the crack in the windowpane, which is just slightly higher than the top of his head, then bends down to pick up a piece of glass lying on the tile floor. Finally he turns to me as I continue to stand in the doorway between the terrace and the great room. "When was the last time you saw Señora Alderman?" he asks.

I give this some thought. "I . . . I came out to the terrace to talk to her—"

"What time?" Detective Sanchez-Berilla interrupts.

"I'm not sure," I murmur thickly.

"Right around three," says Tenney with certainty. "We came back from the Centro, then we saw Bibi, and then me and Mommy took a nap."

"You didn't heard nothing?"

Tenney shakes her head with that same vehement seriousness. I realize I'm shaking my head as well, because Tenney isn't telling things right.

"Where is your room?"

"On the other side of the patio, on the street side," I say quickly.

"And you," he bores into me with his black irises, "you came back after?"

I stand rooted in place, my mouth opening to respond, when Tenney says, "Mommy and I fell asleep and then I woke up and read by myself when Mommy was sleeping and then we got up and came out here to see Bibi, but she was already gone."

She knows this isn't true. I catch myself staring at her and turn back to the detective. "My . . . my mother has been having trouble lately with dizziness and sinus problems."

"Dr. Steve even came to see her," adds Tenney.

"Dr. Steve," the detective repeats. He has moved on to Tenney's chess board, which lies at the center of the antique wood game table. It appears the board was abandoned in the middle of a game.

"Bibi—she calls him Doctor Handsome," Tenney explains.

"*Ah, el doctor americano.*"

"Sí," Tenney replies.

"You call your *abuela* Bibi?"

"Sí," Tenney says. "She told me to call her Bibi. She says she's too young to be a grandmother."

He almost smiles, just a little twitch at the corner of his mouth. "Who is playing this chess?" he asks.

"Me," Tenney says. "I play by myself sometimes. The viejos, *los jugadores de ajedrez* in the Parque Juárez, they owe me fifty pesos. But I'm going to give them a chance tomorrow to win it back."

I stare at her, stunned.

"So you are the niña who beat my old *Tío* Diego. The whole family is talking about it. *Cuántos años tienes?*" he asks Tenney.

"*Tengo nueve años,*" she responds proudly.

"You are playing this game here against yourself?"

"Sí," she says. "I pretend I am both, and both want to win. I pretend it's the world championship."

"*Dios mío*," he murmurs.

I never learned past the rudimentary moves. Bibi always said Tenney got it from Bibi's own daddy, who could beat anyone, even a professional Russian. Beau was a good player. He always told her to watch out for every possible contingency . . . *Think ten steps ahead.*

Why is my mind floating off like this?

Detective Sanchez-Berilla nods thoughtfully, as if somehow Tenney's age and talent for chess is an important factor in this investigation.

"Please, sit down," the detective offers. He spreads his arm out toward the big, soft, coral-hued sofa.

Suddenly a deep, piercing bellow cuts through the air. We all turn to find Marta standing on the far end of the terrace by the kitchen door, twisting a bulging red mesh grocery bag in her hands.

"Excuse me," says Detective Sanchez-Berilla, and goes to talk to her. Their conversation is muted and I can't make out what they're saying, but Marta is nodding, explaining something.

I sit on the edge of the sofa. I feel like I'm going to fall asleep. This is not normal. After a few moments the detective returns. I drag myself out of my stupor and ask him if he'd like a glass of juice or water. He shakes his head. Tenney presses her body into mine as if for comfort but I know she believes she's comforting *me*. Detective Sanchez-Berilla doesn't suggest she leave us.

"It will grow dark soon," he observes.

Marta shuffles in carrying a coffee tray with several cups, which she puts down on the low glass table. Tears continue to drop from her eyes.

There is shouting from the patio and Calisto storms in, followed by four policemen who seem at a loss what to do. The detective turns to him and asks him who he is. Calisto, insulted, looks down his thin nose at the shorter man and says, *"Soy Calisto Rivera, el protegido de la Señora Bibienne."*

The protégé. The most brilliant philosophy student at the university; so brilliant he doesn't need to study or attend classes and spends his days brooding and moping around the house.

There's a name for guys like him around here. Vividor.

Calisto shouts at the detective, gesticulating wildly. I can't understand what he's saying. Detective Sanchez-Berilla responds calmly, but in rapid-fire Spanish. Suddenly Calisto makes a run for the terrace through the other set of doors, reaching the parapet where he seems about to jump, lifting one leg over so that he has to be restrained by two cops while Detective Sanchez-Berilla stands back and watches, arms crossed, a bemused expression on his face.

Calisto turns and yells at me over his shoulder: "This is your fault! You cause estress for Bibienne ever since you arrive! She say you are a bad daughter!" And he bursts into a flood of tears, collapsing in a heap into the terrace chair that Bibi pulled back from the table earlier this afternoon.

My first reaction is to shout back: *You think I don't know you take her car to drive your novia around town?* But I remain silent.

I have to call Harvey Berger . . . is it really possible he would try to help Bibi wrest Tenney away from me? What if she already changed her will?

Detective Sanchez-Berilla asks Calisto when he saw Señora Bibienne last. What a difficult name to have in Mexico, *Vivienne*, I'm thinking. Calisto is blubbering that he took Bibienne's car to visit his mother in Dolores Hidalgo and got caught in the storm. Normally, he says, he goes to Dolores Hidalgo on Sundays to see her, but last night he went because she isn't feeling well.

Faye and Dr. Steve step in through the doors at the far end of the great room. He has brought Sophia and her puppies. He sets the box on the floor by his feet. Sophia is straining at her leash. He unclips her and she bounds across the tile floor toward Tenney and me.

"Sophia!" Tenney shouts. The little dog jumps up into her lap, twisting and turning this way and that, her tail wagging, then she shifts to me and starts licking my face. That anyone would be so happy to see me still utterly stuns me.

Dr. Steve approaches, his hand out. He tells Detective Sanchez-Berilla he's la señora's doctor. His Spanish is flawless. Mrs. Alderman has been suffering from fainting spells and shortness of breath, as well as an inflammation of the sinuses, which could easily have caused her to lose her balance. Not to mention her prodigious drinking. He opens his hand, indicating the three-quarters-empty bottle of tequila on the terrace table.

He says: "She is an alcoholic."

Now that's going too far.

"Well, I don't know if she's an *alcoholic*, per se," Faye intercedes indignantly. "She likes her cocktails, just as I do."

"Why your suitcases are packed?" Detective Sanchez-Berilla asks me suddenly.

How does he know this? The policemen must have searched our room.

"I have to . . . we have to return to Dallas."

The younger detective gallops in, out of breath, his suit pants covered in that fine, powdery dust, his expression grave as he marches up to Detective Sanchez-Berilla; they converse in low tones. The detective comes toward me and I stand on quaking legs as he shakes his head. "It's not good," he says. "It is just as we feared."

Apparently I've been gripping Tenney's hand because she tries to gently unclench my fingers from her palm. "Is Bibi dead?" Tenney asks, looking up at me with somber eyes.

"Yes."

Agent Warnock, in her blue suit, enters and says with booming authority, "What the heck is going on here?"

Detective Sanchez-Berilla approaches her with an officious air. The top of his head barely reaches her chin. She pulls out her FBI badge and flashes it in front of his face.

"Mrs. Huntley is returning to Dallas with me today," Agent Warnock states.

"I am sorry, but this is now the investigation of a suspicious death. Mrs. Huntley cannot leave San Miguel," says the detective.

"What? But that's crazy. My mother was drunk and had an accident! How can you even suggest—" My throat constricts, and I start to sob.

"Don't worry, Mommy." Tenney squeezes my hand. "I'm here. Everything is going to be all right."

CHAPTER TWELVE

SOMEONE IS BANGING on the bedroom door, waking me from a sleep so deep I feel like I'm emerging from the bottom of a dark lake.

"Señora Merryn!" shouts Allegra through the door.

I blink at the bedside clock trying to bring the numbers into focus. My God, it's past ten a.m.; I haven't slept till ten a.m. since . . . I've never slept till ten a.m. in my life. Last night after everyone left, when I was finally alone and scared I'd never fall asleep, I put a few spoonfuls of Alberto Zaldaña's loose tea into a teapot, boiled water, and let it steep for ten minutes, then drank four cups. His witch's brew must have knocked me out cold.

The fingertips of my left hand crawl across the covers and feel my girl, still sound asleep. She's getting some rest, at least.

"Señora Merryn!" Allegra calls again. *"El Señor Garza esta aquí."*

"Momento por favor!" Señor Garza? *"Vengo ahorita."*

Just as I'm sitting up Sophia jumps onto the bed, tail wagging tentatively, assessing. She must still feel uncertain every morning, waking up warm, clean, dry, belly full, babies safe—and thinking this good thing can't possibly last.

I throw my legs over the side and stand, grabbing hold of the bathroom door as I brace for the red-hot poker of pain just below my right ear.

No pain.

I carefully palpate my jaw hinge and the back of my head. I prod and poke, but I can't find it. My TMJ is gone.

Where did it go?

Suddenly my body feels light as air. I must be in shock.

In the bathroom I scrub my face with a cool washcloth and brush my teeth, slip on clean panties and the yellow sundress with tiny red flowers. Catching my reflection in the full-length bathroom mirror, I realize I look like a woman on her way to a summer picnic. I pull the dress off and throw it onto the bed and choose instead a charcoal-gray linen shift with an uneven hem from Eileen Fisher. Slip on sandals and I'm ready to face Señor Garza.

He stands on the west balcony, both hands behind his back, holding the brim of a white Panama hat with an elegant black ribbon, gazing down at the city.

"Buenos dias, Señor Garza." I approach him with my hand out.

"Oh my," he says, clasping his hat to his chest, "I cannot believe it." He throws the hat onto a chair and jogs toward me, clasps my hand in both of his, shaking his head. "It is terrible."

"Terrible."

Marta approaches with the coffee tray.

"Señor Garza, please sit with me, have a café."

"Call me Ernesto, I insist."

I lean over to adjust the canvas armchairs to an upright position.

"*Lo que es una tragedia*," he says. A tragedy.

"Una tragedia," Marta agrees, her dark eyes spilling tears. She sets the tray down on the side table and pulls a large, red-checked cloth out of her apron pocket and wipes her eyes.

"Señor Garza, my Spanish is not so good, would you please tell Marta that everything will stay the same here at the house for the time being? I will find out everything in the next few days but they must not worry. They will be paid as usual—today and every Friday—and I will make sure they are taken care of."

He nods once and turns to Marta and repeats what I just said, the three of us standing as if in the greeting queue at a formal reception. Her face wears that impassive, granite mask and I have no idea what she is thinking.

She shuffles off and I open my hand toward the armchairs. Señor Garza picks up his hat and sits with it on his knees, very upright, and I sit and pour the coffee into thick Mexican ceramic mugs with colorful winglike designs around the blue rim.

"Was your mother ill a long time?" he asks gently, his face lined with compassion.

Like a lightning strike suddenly illuminating a completely dark landscape, I see a flash of silver from her rings as her fingers grasp at the air.

"She . . . did not like to ask . . . for help," I manage to say.

He leans forward quickly and pats my hand. "Please, do not estress yourself!"

"She was seeing Dr. Fuller." Just saying his name causes my heart to flutter.

"El doctor americano. All the American ladies love him." After a longish pause, Señor Garza coughs politely into his fist and says, "I came myself today to offer you my essupport. You met Detective Sanchez-Berilla, yes? He is the cousin of Maestra Garza, my wife, God rest her soul. Very intelligent people in that family. We are lucky in San Miguel to have a detective of that caliber. My wife, God rest her, was very fond of him and he of her. Sometimes, Señora Huntley, the Mexican way is very complicated in such matters. I—"

"Please, you must call me Merryn."

"Sí. *Muy bien.* Señora Merryn, you will need someone to

help you. Someone who knows how to . . . *como se dice* . . . how to manage the Mexican way. I will be that person."

"Thank you so much, Señor Garza. This is a foreign land—a foreign place to me."

He nods. We sip our coffees in silence.

"But, my God, this is a view," he says, indicating with a sweep of his hand the city sprawled out before us.

"Yes. My mother watched the sunset from here every day. She loved this view."

"I am so sorry for your loss."

"Thank you," I murmur. Yet it is not loss I feel, but . . . something. I have to have some time by myself to figure out what happened. Maybe if I focus very hard I will remember . . .

"You seem perturbed . . . yes? Correct? It is a terrible thing." After a moment he adds, "The Mexican authorities can be difficult. But Detective Sanchez-Berilla is family. He is very thorough. If you will allow me to accompany you to the authorities, or to the . . . ah . . . the place of the bodies . . . if and when it is necessary, it would be my honor."

"Thank you, Señor Garza."

"Ernesto, please."

We sip from our cups and gaze out at the view.

"For the moment, you will be staying here, no?"

I nod.

"I must go to the eschool," he announces, rising.

"Thank you, Señor . . . Ernesto, for taking the time to come see me."

On my way back through the patio after escorting him to the door, I glance up at Bibi's bedroom windows to see if there is any movement, but the shutters are still closed.

In the kitchen Marta is busy making tortillas. Her hands expertly shape the corn flour into rounds, flattening and patting and then dropping them onto the cast-iron griddle. It seems so strange that life goes on so normally, as if nothing has happened . . .

I ask her if she's seen Calisto. She indicates with a flick of her eyes that he is still upstairs.

I climb the outdoor stairs, noticing how the slabs of pale stone are worn down slightly from the weight of countless feet. I knock on the door.

"Calisto, would you please open the door?"

No answer.

"I know this is a terrible time for you too, Calisto. When you feel up to it, we need to talk." I wait. No response, not a sound.

I return to the great room and press Harvey Berger's speed dial number on the cordless phone. While the line rings, I enter the kitchen and stick my head in the freezer and take long, deep breaths. Marta is still at the stove flipping her corn tortillas.

Harvey Berger's secretary puts me through immediately. "Harvey . . ." I sigh deeply. "Harvey, my mother has passed away."

"What's that? But I just spoke to her—"

"She fell. She's been having dizzy spells. She fell off the terrace into the ravine."

Silence.

"Well, I'm . . . aahh . . . so terribly sorry, Merryn . . ." His voice trails off; then, a deep and sonorous sigh.

"And now they're telling me I can't leave Mexico. The police want me to stay here until this investigation is over."

"What investigation?"

"It was an accident but they have to do an inquest of some kind. And an autopsy."

"All right. I'll try to wrap this case up today and get there by tomorrow afternoon. It's such a long damn trip from New York. Lovely place, though, San Miguel. First time I visited was in . . .

oh . . . must've been February 1968, when Neal Cassady died on the railroad tracks outside of town and Allen Ginsberg asked me to . . . aahh, but that's a long story."

Jack Kerouac's Neal Cassady? And Allen Ginsberg, the poet? At my dad's funeral, I remember Harvey Berger wore a dark Savile Row three-piece suit complete with gold pocket watch and chain and Phi Beta Kappa key, the epitome of the prosperous, conservative corporate lawyer. He knew Neal Cassady? I read the story somewhere, of how Neal Cassady, drunk after a wedding, decided to count the railroad ties between two Mexican towns and died of hypothermia on the way. But I had no idea one of the towns was San Miguel de Allende.

"Are you holding up all right, Merryn?" Harvey asks.

"I think so," I reply, struggling to stay focused and on point.

A little while later the outdoor bell rings again and I call to Marta that I'll get it. It's Dr. Steve, helmet in hand, in a different guayabera shirt, pale blue this time, with white piping in two columns down the front. He looks so . . . not like a doctor. Not like someone I know and have . . . We appraise each other warily.

"You all right, Merryn?" he asks, like the concerned doctor he is.

"Did you know that Neal Cassady died in San Miguel?" I ask him.

He searches my face, my eyes, for something more, and I look away. I have been fooled once again, this time by a man who has pink thongs under his couch, but I will not let him in again. After a pause he replies evenly, "I did hear that."

I move aside, making it clear that he is welcome to step through the doorway. Suddenly Sophia is at his feet, jumping up, tail waving like a battle flag as she tries to paw his leg.

"Down, Sophia!" I say. He dutifully crouches, pets and

scratches her, and then, as we're walking across the patio, Tenney comes out of our room wearing her Tinkerbell nightgown.

"Dr. Steve!" she shouts, runs forward, and propels herself into his body, almost knocking him off his feet. That's exactly what my unbridled reaction might be, but I will not let down my guard. I shake my head, dislodging the thought. He seems slightly stunned by Tenney's enthusiastic welcome but he reciprocates with a squeeze across her shoulders. We settle in the great room, shady at this hour and still cool, while the hills bake nakedly beyond the glass wall. Marta arrives with a pitcher of limonada on a tray. I ask her for more coffee. Dr. Steve drinks a whole glass of limonada down without pausing for air. Tenney drains hers through a straw, making an unpleasant gurgling sound.

"Tenney, how many times have I told you not to do that? It's extremely annoying."

"Sorry," she mumbles.

"I was thinking . . ." Dr. Steve begins, and I stiffen, having no idea what he's been thinking. "My research assistant quit last week. Went back to Mexico City to finish med school . . ."

He's not using a gender-specific pronoun. Perhaps she is the owner of the pink thong, and suddenly I feel myself blushing, my face turning hot and the muscles in my jaw tightening at the same time. My head should be pounding right now. Where's my headache? I turn my chin from side to side; then up, and down.

"Headache again?" asks Dr. Steve.

"Yes." What am I supposed to say? That it's gone for the first time in twenty years? I am so used to being in pain that I don't know how to be without it.

"Do you want me to prescribe a painkiller for you? It used to be you could walk into any farmacía and order them over the counter. Not anymore."

"No thanks, I'm all right."

He turns to Tenney. "I was thinking maybe you could help me, Tenney. Have you ever looked at bacteria through a microscope? When patients come to see me and they have a sore throat, or some other kind of infection, I take a swab and I look at it through my microscope. When we grow the germ we call it a culture, and cultures have to be sent out to a lab, but with a microscope I can identify a lot of different things quickly."

"You have your own microscope?"

"Yes, it's an old American Optical from the early seventies that I bought at an estate sale. It's kind of complicated at first, but you're very smart and I could teach you how to—"

"Yes!" she shouts. "Can we go now?" She turns to me, her eyes filled with expectation.

Dr. Steve shifts his serious gaze to me. "You're welcome to come too, Merryn. The lab is in the back of the casita and my nurse and nurse's aid will be there. I thought maybe you might need some time to yourself, but you're welcome to come too, stay until Tenney feels comfortable—"

"I feel comfortable now," Tenney points out. She doesn't understand why a mother might not care to leave a child alone with a man she's known for less than a week. He's definitely a sex addict, but his tastes most certainly run to the adult variety of female, perhaps even the mature female adult—lesbian or not, it's probably all the same to him.

"Is it dangerous?" I ask, realizing how silly this sounds. "I mean, the germs."

But Dr. Steve doesn't laugh. "We're very careful. We wear latex gloves, and face masks when we need to."

I say okay, not quite convincingly, and tell Tenney to go change her clothes. I check on Sophia, who is back in her box nursing her puppies that squeal helplessly every time they lose the nipple.

"We'll be back soon," I tell the dog. Her head cocks to the side, feathery ears up, as if she understands exactly what I'm saying.

But I don't trust that Pedro. He might get it into his head to take them to the campo out of spite, or some twisted sense of duty toward his former employer. So when Tenney is ready, I lock the door behind us, and just to make sure, I stick my head in through the patio kitchen door and tell Marta to tell Pedro that if he goes near the dogs, he will never be allowed back in this house.

Marta nods once and says, "No se preocupa."

We get into the Honda and follow Dr. Steve's motorcycle down the mountain.

Dr. Steve's waiting room is clean and tidy, the floors recently mopped and all the toys put away in plastic bins. Several mothers are already waiting, with their still faces and endless patience, their quietly suffering children on their laps. Through a door to the right is a hallway with a gray tile floor and three closed doors. The casita is bigger than it looks from the outside, like most structures in San Miguel. His nurse comes out of the room on the right and I spy a well-lit, cell-like space with an examination table covered with white paper, and in the far corner, a small white desk and two folding chairs.

At the end of the short hallway on the left is the lab. The door has a padlock, unlatched. The room is around twelve feet square with two barred windows, bright desk lamps on each counter surface, and an overhead bulb hanging down from the middle of the ceiling. There are file cabinets and a large refrigerator and beakers and burners and other equipment. Under a counter is what appears to be a generator. This must be for when the lights go out. There is a deep stainless-steel sink with two thin, parallel metal bars suspended over the edges. The solid and stately battleship-gray microscope is a little scratched up, like his cowboy boots and his motorcycle. Dr. Steve comes in wearing a white lab coat and hands a smaller one to Tenney, which has the name *Maria* embroidered over the heart. He helps her into it and rolls up the sleeves.

Maria, a pink-thong girl all the way.

He leaves the door open and his nurse passes by, shuffling back and forth in her own lab coat that says, *Dolores*, carrying manila folders, gowns, towels. Dolores is short and thick, matronly, probably not a pink-thong girl. The industrial metal stools beneath the counter have round adjustable wooden seats. He offers me a stool and turns another seat as high as it will go for Tenney, and proceeds to identify the different parts of the microscope.

"First I'm going to show you a bunch of old slides," he says. "Then we're going to do a Gram stain. I'm going to show you how to prepare the iodine dye, and then how to rinse it. This is so we can see the germs better. We have to go through all these messy chemical steps. These bacteria are really, really small, and there are basically two types. There are Gram-negative bacteria and Gram-positive bacteria. When we find out what kind of bacteria it is, we know which medicine to give the patient."

"Okay . . ." Tenney says uncertainly.

"We do a Gram stain. A lot of people who come to see me have bacterial infections or parasitical infections. Some are serious and some aren't so serious. But you can die from some Gram-negative infections. They move really fast, so it's important to get the medicine right away."

He is a stranger to me, this man in his intimidating white lab coat. I think of all the TV doctors that I and every other straight woman and gay man have had a crush on over the years;

he could give them a run for their money. *I hate him. Why does he make me feel this way?*

"Some bacteria are so distinctive that they shout to you through the eyepieces." He puts a slide on the stage and adjusts the knobs. "Here, take a look at this one. It's called *Diplococcus pneumoniae*. It's instantly recognizable—it's a Gram-positive bacillus that shows up in pairs. *Diplo* means double—I bet you didn't know that."

"I did too," Tenney says. "And I bet it's what gives people pneumonia!"

"I get a lot of patients with pneumonia, especially during the winter."

She rises to her knees on the stool and, hunching down, looks through the eyepieces. Dr. Steve shows her how to adjust the knobs, how to find the right spot, talking her through the process.

"You see it?"

"Wait! Wait! Oh, wow! Oh, *wow!* I see it! This is awesome, Dr. Steve. Mom, come look at this!"

I approach and squint through the eyepieces and see nothing. Dr. Steve stands close behind me—I can feel his breath on my neck—and slides the eyepieces further apart. Finally, I see tiny dark spots paired in twos in a sea of pale purple.

"Amazing," I say, attempting to shake away the frisson I feel being so close to him.

"Are you ready to do a Gram stain?" Dr. Steve asks.

Tenney nods with a big smile. She is so focused on the little slides he's slipping under the microscope that she seems to have at least temporarily put yesterday aside. This was a good idea.

"First thing we have to do is fire up the burner. We have to set the specimen with heat. We pass it over the burner like this

... This part you can't do by yourself yet, because it's dangerous. You could burn yourself."

"I'm not a baby, Dr. Steve," Tenney says.

"You are definitely not a baby. After we set the slide, it's a four-step procedure, but it's really important to be exact." He points to a series of plastic bottles lined up above one of the sinks. "Each step has to be done for the exact right amount of time. Do you know how to tell time?"

"Dr. Steve, I've been able to tell time since I was three."

"Sorry. I'm not used to being around brilliant nine-year-olds."

They move over to the sink, and he drags Tenney's stool behind him.

I need some air. "I'm going to go for a walk," I tell them, but their focus doesn't waver from the petri dish they're admiring.

"Okay, Mom." Tenney doesn't even look up.

He walks me out into the hall. "If it's all right with you, I might let her observe a couple of consults. But she'll have plenty to do with the slides, it looks like." He steps closer, takes me into his arms, and holds me so close I can smell his earthy scent, and my heart starts to race. I pull away suddenly and he looks confused.

He holds onto my elbows for a moment. "I want to be your friend," he says.

My friend? My goddamn friend? I nod and back away, knocking my shoulder into the wall as I flee.

CHAPTER THIRTEEN

I MUST HAVE BEEN WALKING FOR A WHILE because I notice the sun has passed its zenith and the shadows of the houses have begun to stretch across the narrow street. But it's not yet siesta time, the shops are still open. I don't recognize the neighborhood but I'm down in the bowl of the city, to the north. I pass a store with colorful hats hanging from hooks on a grille on the outside door. The single window has been set up like a stage and there are rows and rows of San Miguel sandals. Just like in Mum's closet. A shiver passes through me.

Many of the hats have little nests of berries and flowers and bows, bursts of color that draw my eye. As I'm standing outside on the narrow sidewalk blocking pedestrian traffic, a tall lady with a long silver side braid hanging almost to her waist and a coral cloche hat with feathers steps out the door and asks me in perfect English if I'd like to try on a hat.

I stand frozen by indecision, feeling the urge to explain that I can't be trying on hats, I'm in mourning. But this lady doesn't know me. She doesn't know that I am not a hat person and have never owned a hat in my life, or that my TMJ is gone for the first time in twenty years.

But why shouldn't I try on a hat? I am permitted to try on a hat, even if I am in mourning and deep shock. I step inside the store, which is steeped in shadow, and my eyes take a moment to adjust. On the wall to my left hang dozens and dozens of exotic hats—narrow-brimmed, soft bucket hats; wide-brimmed sun hats; cowboy hats; cloches, so finely woven they seem like they're made of angels' wings; and strange straw hats with bits of straw extending from the edges of the brims, giving the impression of a bird's nest—all decorated with individual detail, some with flowers, some with fruit, some with feathers pinned to shiny satin hatbands. I touch a soft pale lilac cloche with a downturned, wide brim, a cluster of lilac blooms and green leaves as a trim. The lady lifts it off its hook. Three white butterflies made of some kind of paper-thin gossamer seem to be flitting around the flowers, attached to the material by clear plastic filaments that give them the semblance of flight.

"This is a sinamay hat," she explains in a tremulous voice. "It's a natural weave made from the abaca plant. I have all the materials shipped to Laredo, Texas, and then we have a private van that carts the US mail to San Miguel."

"You made all these yourself?" I ask, amazed.

"Oh no, not all of them. Here, try it on," says the lady, placing the cloche on my head.

"You're American," I state.

"From Massachusetts, originally. I came down here on vacation with a friend after my husband died, and I caught the San Miguel bug. I just fell in love with the place! I knew right away I wanted to live here. So I sold my business in Boston and just up and moved." This is a story you hear over and over again in San Miguel, Americans catching the San Miguel bug and uprooting themselves for good.

She gently urges me toward a long, narrow mirror hanging on the back wall. What an elegant hat. I turn to the side, admiring it. A shadow passes behind me, across the mirror. *You look ridiculous! Ha-ha-ha! What in the world, Merryn!*

I turn and stare at the door, a prickly warmth rising from my chest to my face, my heart beginning to pound; but it is only an elderly couple, a husband and wife in matching khaki Bermudas, and she's chastising him for something—for wearing the wrong shoes. Silently he plods along, inured to her criticism.

"This hat needs someone with a big personality," I say to the lady, removing it and passing it back with a shaky hand. "I could never wear it."

"Hmmm," she says, her untended brows furrowing as she gives this statement some thought. "What about this one?"

She places on my crown a pale, cerulean-green summer hat of a fine, supple paper weave, which, she tells me, comes from China. The front is turned jauntily downward over one eyebrow while the opposite side curves upward and around to the back. On the downturned side is a bouquet of small, white silk roses and sprigs of lilies of the valley. A delicate little ladybug with black spots sits perched among the soft green silk leaves.

"Oh," says the lady, leaning back with her hands clasped to her chest. "Now that is a hat."

I stare at myself in the mirror, turning my face from side to side.

"Ladybugs are good luck," she says.

I feel a lightness within me as I realize that there is no one in the world left to stop me from wearing this hat. The ones who would have laughed, who would have made some snarky comment, are gone.

"How much?" I ask. She says if I pay her in cash she will knock 20 percent off the price. Forty dollars even.

I walk out into the street wearing my new hat, a spring in my step. The brim offers much-needed protection from the blinding sun, and a feeling of being protected overcomes me.

But the farther I get from the store, the more I sense that people are staring at me strangely. As if they're thinking, *That*

woman's mother died yesterday and here she is, out buying hats!
Maybe it's too much of a statement, this hat. Walking along a
wider thoroughfare, out of the corner of my eye I spy an elegant
woman in a similar hat strolling toward me in the opposite direction. What an attractive, self-possessed woman, I think—*she*
can get away with wearing such a hat. But then I realize I'm passing a standing mirror outside a clothing store, and the woman
is myself. I'm so startled I stop and stare. There is a little
wooden bench and I collapse onto it and close my eyes. I feel as
if I can't breathe and my heart is pumping too hard. I hear no
other sound but that wild blood drumbeat in my head. I see a
flash of Bibi's white face, her eyes and mouth three distinct Os.

I cup my hands around my nose and mouth and try to
breathe slowly. When I finally pull myself together I notice a
café across the street, with little round tables lined up outside
on the sidewalk. At one table sits Agent Warnock, with a news-
paper and an espresso. She wears a khaki-colored safari shirt
with dozens of pockets, jeans, and her straw cowboy hat. She has
tied a thin scarf around the band, the ends trailing down her
back. Is she following me?

"Care to join me?" she asks. She seems to be staring at my
new hat.

"Well, I can stop for a minute." I walk across the narrow
street.

"Nice hat. New?"

I shake my head as if it's just some old thing I grabbed off
the closet shelf. This is a mistake. But it's a smaller mistake than
admitting to being out buying festive hats the day after such a
calamity.

"Every store I pass I want to buy something," she says. But I
know what she's thinking; she's thinking, *A woman who just lost
her mother in a horrible accident should not be out shopping.*

"We're making progress on catching that associate of your husband's, Edward Buckingham. He's a scared little mouse, isn't he, our Edward, for such a big fat guy?" She snorts with disdain. "These privileged white-collar dudes, they think the rules don't apply to them. Why is he calling you, though? I thought they locked you out of their business decisions. Does he think you know something?" She gazes at me, her opaque brown eyes divulging nothing.

"He hasn't called me today, I've been checking," I say, good girl that I am. "What could he possibly want from me?"

"My question exactly. And I intend to find out."

I don't feel well. As if I've remembered something important, I mumble that I have to run, and turn back the way I've come.

My mind slowly clears and I find myself walking along another street, when I realize I'm standing outside a familiar door. It's Alberto Zaldaña's yoga studio, but I've come to it from a different direction. I really should ask him for more of that tea—I haven't slept through a whole night in years. I climb the creaky wooden stairs and enter the large blue room. Alberto is upside down in Pincha Mayurasana, a forearm stand, in the middle of the floor. He remains completely still, undisturbed by my arrival.

There is a large coffee can on the desk and taped on it is a washed-out color photo of the abused woman I saw the last time. In the photo she is much younger and smiling and missing an incisor. Stepping toward the can, I see peso bills stuffed inside.

"Hello," says Alberto, still holding his stand with no effort.

"What happened to the lady with the broken arm?"

"He beat her again. She is in the hospital with a broken jaw. We are trying to raise money for her."

I reach into my purse for my wallet and pull out a hundred-dollar bill, feeling guilty that I just spent forty dollars on a stupid hat.

Alberto brings his legs down like a lever, slow and straight. After resting for a minute with his forehead on the mat, he looks up at me. His eyes pause for several moments on my new hat. Should I have taken it off and hidden it somewhere before coming up?

"Where did you get such a beautiful hat? You have a perfect face for such a hat."

"Thank you. I came to ask you if I could buy more of that tea. I slept very well for the first time in years."

"It is good that you are able to sleep. I am sorry to hear about your mother. Señor Garza told me." He approaches, hands out. "May I feel your chi?"

"All right."

He leads me to a mat, where I sit cross-legged, and he kneels before me with his open hands encircling my head about six inches away. He moves them up and down around my body, exuding that strange, electric warmth.

"Hmmm," he says. "Amazing." He says *amayssing*.

What is amazing? I'm afraid to ask.

"Your chi is clear today."

"You should put that tea on the market," I say. "That's some incredible tea."

"It is not the tea. Your head pain is gone too, no?"

I stare at him, eyes wide, mouth agape. I don't know what to say. He watches me impassively and I feel like I'm standing naked in a brightly lit window. "Why do so many people refuse freedom, even when it is offered to them? I will tell you why. It is because the cage is a much safer place."

"I . . . just came to get more tea."

He jumps lightly to his feet and floats into the back room,

returning in a moment with a pouch of tea. I try to press twenty dollars into his hand but he shakes his head. "You gave for my friend, the least I can do is give you some tea. It is nothing."

"Thank you." I turn toward the doorway.

Alberto calls after me, "Please come tomorrow."

When Tenney and I return from Dr. Steve's, I take off my new hat and slide it onto an upper shelf in the closet of our room. I just want to lie down and go to sleep but Sophia is wagging her tail and prancing from one paw to the other, expecting her walk. Tenney leashes her up and we trudge up the road toward the Charco. I'm so exhausted I feel as if I'm walking three paces behind myself, like a shadow. The sun is about to dip behind the hazy blue mountains to the west that from here look like a low-lying bank of storm clouds. Down in the heart of the city the parroquia's whimsical steeple and the four smaller ones that surround it gleam like pink icing on an elaborate *quinceañera* birthday cake.

"If we marry Doctor Handsome," Tenney suddenly says, "we will have a dad again."

"Tenney! I barely know him."

"But he really likes you."

He doesn't know me. I shut my eyes for a moment and in the sunset glare an image appears behind my eyelids of Bibi's ten fingers splayed out, her silver rings flashing. I double over, unable to breathe.

"Mom! . . . Mommy?"

In the gutter just a foot from my face I spy a disgusting dead centipede. I focus all my attention on it, counting slowly as I inhale through my nose. "This is a very interesting dead bug. Look at this bug, Tenney."

She kneels and examines it, ready with a baggy already

covering her hand, just as she does to pick up Sophia's poop.

"Be careful, it might be poisonous."

"Look!" She holds it up to my face and I cringe. The ugly brown thing is about four inches long and has many blue-tinged legs and creepy antennae and it's hard to tell head from tail. "Look how many legs it has!"

"I think it's a centipede," I manage to say.

"I'm going to take it to Dr. Steve's tomorrow to look at under the microscope."

"Sweetie," I say, my voice tentative and weak, "why did you lie to the detectives?"

She turns her eyes to me, serious and seemingly unperturbed. "Because it was the best thing to do."

"But . . . but . . . I didn't hurt Bibi, I was trying—"

"Look at this!" Tenney says, her voice rising unnaturally, as she points to a sad little weed with scraggly yellow flowers protruding from a crack in a stucco-covered wall. "Why did that weed grow here, all by itself, and nowhere else? Did you ever wonder about that?" She tears a thin strand off the stem, careful not to harm the flowers. "I need another baggie," she says. She holds the weed up to her nose, her eyes almost crossed. "If you look at things really close up, like through the microscope, you can understand so much about the world."

If only it were possible to examine one's deepest hidden emotions under a microscope and understand what they are and how to deal with them.

She says, her words coming out quickly, "Did you know there was a scientist called Dr. Gram, and he's the one who figured out how to tell different bacteria apart under a microscope? He was super intelligent. He thought *outside the box*."

Air seems to be passing more freely through my throat and chest. I nod, listening, trying to recover my balance.

"Dr. Steve let me watch one of his consultations," she says, her face animated. "It was a mom with a baby with an eye infection. He took a swab and then he let me help him while he made the Gram stain. And guess what it was? Guess!"

"Was it conjunctivitis?" I know this illness because Tenney had it as an infant.

"*Streptococcal* conjunctivitis! They're Gram-positive bacteria shaped like a sphere—I *saw* them, Mommy. And we gave the lady eye drops, and also liquid antibiotics. She was so poor she couldn't pay and she kept saying, *No, no, no medicine*, and Dr. Steve kept saying, *Es gratis—it's free, it's free.* And then the lady started crying and she kissed his hand . . ." After a pause she adds, "I've decided something."

"What's that, my angel?"

"I'm going to be a doctor when I grow up. I want to go to Africa and cure poor people."

Suddenly tears are spilling from my eyes. I crouch and hug her to my chest. But it's okay. I'm going to change everything. For her I'm going to become a better person than I've ever been. And once this is over, I'll never lie again.

"You are going to be free to do whatever you want with your life. Isn't that wonderful?"

"It is," she says solemnly.

"I'll make you a scientist's kit. I'll lend you my little scissors and maybe some tweezers so you don't have to touch all these gross things."

Her face lights up as if a lamp has been turned on behind her eyes. "Can I take a sample of Sophia's poop?"

I laugh. "Maybe we should ask Dr. Steve about that first."

"Tell me about Africa, Mommy. Tell me about was it was like in Cameroon when you were little."

Way in the back of the highest shelf of the closet of my mind lies that locked jewel box. *Simplice*. I haven't said his name aloud in close to thirty years.

"In my school in Yaoundé there was an African boy. His name was Simplice. His skin was so black it looked blue in the sunlight."

"Did you love him, Mommy?"

I am caught off guard by her question. I almost want to re-treat, to push her away by becoming icy, like my mum would do. The sky above the parroquia has turned a glowing red, as if someone just kicked over a bucket of hot coals on heaven's floor.

"Yes," I tell her. "I loved him."

Then I tell her about being afraid of what my mum would say, of how big and out of control the feelings were. I describe to her in great detail that little alleyway where he first kissed me, and why I never went back.

CHAPTER
FOURTEEN

THE DINING TABLE IS SET FOR BREAKFAST, with three place mats, in a lovely semblance of domesticity, even though Calisto is still locked upstairs in Mum's quarters and has avoided me since Thursday. I am up early; I set the alarm for eight o'clock because I can't be sleeping till ten a.m. like some princess on vacation. But I'm letting Tenney sleep in. Last night before bed I only drank two cups of Alberto Zaldaña's tea but I had another night of dreamless, uninterrupted sleep. Now I sit sipping my second cup of coffee, dressed in a loose T-shirt and comfortable black yoga pants, in case Calisto deigns to grace us with his presence. He must have come down to eat at some point yesterday, but when I asked Marta about it, she simply shrugged.

The outside bell gongs. A minute later Detective Sanchez-Berilla and his younger partner appear amidst the patio's greenery, which they expertly sidestep like jungle explorers. They enter the great room's dining area and I stand and offer them a cup of coffee but both refuse. Detective Sanchez-Berilla looks over the three place settings with his penetrating black eyes.

I am grateful to Marta for going through the motions, for giving the house the semblance of normalcy, even though nothing is normal.

"Where is Calisto Rivera?" barks Detective Sanchez-Berilla,

remaining standing as he plucks a little spiral notebook out of his jacket pocket and begins to thumb through the pages. I fear the ruckus will wake Tenney and I want to ask them to lower their voices.

"He's upstairs in my mother's quarters," I murmur softly in the hopes that they will follow by example. "He is very upset."

Detective Sanchez-Berilla turns to the younger detective and says a few words in Spanish and the other man bounds up the outside stairs and starts pounding on Bibi's door. He is officious and threatening though I can't hear his exact words. Within ten seconds Calisto is following the detective back down the stairs.

Detective Sanchez-Berilla indicates a seat at the table with his hand, and Calisto, running his fingers through his disheveled stack of black hair, sits at the head to my left, where there is a breakfast setting. The two detectives arrange themselves across from me, and now we are gathered like executives at a board meeting, with Calisto our seemingly self-appointed CEO. I can see Marta's shadow hovering just beyond the open kitchen door. I pour myself a fresh, steaming cup of coffee and am glad that my hand doesn't shake.

Detective Sanchez-Berilla turns to Calisto and says in Spanish, "Señor Rivera, you told us that you were in Dolores Hidalgo visiting your mother on Wednesday night, the night of the big storm."

Calisto pulls a pack of Marlboros out of his shirt pocket, lights up, and blows a long stream of smoke into the air. "Sí," he says.

"But Detective Perez went to Dolores Hidalgo yesterday and learned from your mother that she has not seen you in many weeks—"

"A month, at least," offers Detective Perez, "even though her arthritis is very bad."

I turn to Calisto and stare at him. All this time he's been sniveling to Bibi about his sick mother in Dolores Hidalgo! Dr. Steve is right, he's a *vividor*.

"*Tengo una novia en la Colonia San Antonio.*" I have a girlfriend in Colonia San Antonio. He leans back and crosses his arms as if to say, *And what of it?*

I realize, stunned by my own talent for obfuscation, that I also have a *novio* in Colonia San Antonio. I glance across the patio. Our bedroom door is still closed, the curtains drawn. Tenney has always been a good sleeper and right now this seems like a blessing.

"Perhaps you came back on Thursday afternoon and Señora Bibienne was angry with you," suggests Detective Sanchez-Berilla. "Perhaps she was aware of your girlfriend in San Antonio?"

This, in any case, is what I think he is saying. He seems to be speaking slowly so that I can keep up with the exchange. I hear *estaba enojada*, she was angry.

I sense rather than see Detective Perez's derisive smirk. Detective Sanchez-Berilla abruptly turns his black eyes to me and says in English, "The neighbor in the house next door heard arguing on the terrace sometime after four p.m. on Thursday afternoon."

So they've been talking to the neighbors.

"I was asleep," I say, but not too quickly, holding his gaze. I realize, as I look into his eyes, that I am almost as good a liar as Calisto. I am a bad influence on my child. After this is over, if I get through in one piece, I swear, I'll never lie again. Attempting to seem helpful I add, "Calisto was not here when Tenney and I woke up and went out to the terrace to check on my mother."

"But he could have been here and left," Detective Sanchez-Berilla points out.

Calisto glares at me, his skin turning gray as the blood drains from his face. He is afraid. I don't like him but I don't want him to be the scapegoat. He's already at a disadvantage because he is Mexican and he is poor. Though . . . if Bibi changed her will he may inherit all of this. *All of this.* And then Tenney and I will be out in the street. But right now, all the arrogance in the world isn't going to save him if they decide to accuse him of malfeasance. And he was not here, that I know for sure.

I tell the detectives in an even voice, "My mother was not herself on Thursday. She was very agitated and did not change out of her negligee all day. She was drinking tequila; she never drinks tequila—"

"She was drinking straight tequila in the morning?" interrupts Detective Sanchez-Berilla.

"She was drinking Bloody Marys at eight o'clock in the morning. That is vodka and spicy tomato juice." I turn to Calisto. "You called her around then, Calisto. You said you would be late getting back."

"Sí," says Calisto, color slowly seeping back into his cheeks. "*Ella siempre estaba bebiendo en la mañana.*" I'm not sure here but I think he's saying she was already drunk in the morning, or she always drank in the morning. Then he adds in English, "I did not like to be here when she was drunk."

"So who was she arguing with at four o'clock in the afternoon?" the detective asks me. His intelligent eyes search my face for a reaction.

"She might have been on the phone," I reply evenly.

"*Ella hablaba siempre por teléfono,*" Calisto states. She was always talking on the phone. He lifts his left hand and makes a mouth-flapping motion with his fingers.

Detective Sanchez-Berilla runs his fingertips over his wrinkled forehead as if all of this is a huge puzzle to him. Finally he looks up, straight at me, and says, "Your husband dies and you run away from Dallas, Texas. Why?"

"I didn't run away, I—"

"He is accused of very bad things—"

The outside doorbell gongs, interrupting him, and we all turn our heads toward the patio where a few moments later Marta appears, leading a man who is covered from head to foot in pale dust, as if a sack of flour fell off the back of a truck while he was walking by. A rolling carry-on suitcase bumps along behind him, and he has a brown leather satchel, like a giant's purse, strapped diagonally across his chest. He's in a travel-rumpled seersucker jacket and jeans, no tie, open shirt collar. As they enter the great room I realize it's Harvey Berger. He seems much less large than I remember. He must be around seventy-three, the age my dad would have been. I stand to greet him, feeling a sense of relief, even though he may have been trying to help Bibi steal my child away from me.

"Harvey," I say, "you got here so fast."

"I flew to Dallas last night and took the first flight out this morning. I had the driver bring me straight here. The AC was broken in the car and we had to open the windows." He looks down at his dust-covered clothes. "There was some construction on the road." After a moment in which no one speaks, he adds, "I'm so terribly sorry, Merryn." He opens his arms.

Does he want to hug me? He seems positively heartbroken for me. Could he truly have been helping Bibi take my child away? She was such a good liar she probably couldn't tell the difference anymore between what was true and what she believed to be true. I feel so confused. The detectives and Calisto are watching me, their eyes like hot spotlights on my back.

Just thinking about anyone trying to take Tenney away brings a flood of tears. I collapse onto my chair and cover my face with my hands. Harvey rushes forward and fills a thick blue glass with cold water from a sweating pitcher, which he holds out to me, inches from my lips. I accept the glass and take a long, slow sip, then put it down on the place mat, noticing that the glass is thicker on one side than the other. Tenney and I went to the glass factory once and watched the workers rake and shovel broken soda, water, and wine bottles into piles, separating the fragments by color, then they melted them down in a furnace, and with a blow pipe created beautiful goblets right before our eyes, each one individual, each one flawed in its own way. The flaws are what make them special, but also fragile.

"It's important to keep up your strength at a time like this, Merryn. You mustn't get dehydrated in this heat," Harvey warns.

Calisto watches me with a look of disdain. I must remember they are my enemies. I must keep sharp.

"These are the detectives investigating Bibi's accident," I manage to say, wiping my eyes with my napkin. I tell the detectives, "Mr. Berger is our family lawyer from New York City."

The two detectives stand and shake Harvey's hand. Slowly, languidly, Calisto also rises to his feet with his hand outstretched. This is the first time I've ever seen him stand for anyone.

"And this is Bibi's protégé, Calisto Rivera," I tell Harvey. While they shake hands they eye each other like two roosters about to be pitted against each other in a ring, and I realize they may not be on the same side at all.

Harvey takes off his jacket and hangs it on one of the doorknobs, then sits to my right. He pours himself a cup of coffee, asking the detectives if they'd like some as well. Finally Detective Sanchez-Berilla says he would, so Harvey pours one for him too.

Once we've all settled down and are sipping from our cups, Detective Sanchez-Berilla turns to another page in his little notebook and says, lifting his eyes to mine, "The FBI is using this ICE agreement to meet with you in San Miguel. You are under accusation of money laundering?"

The coffee slides down my windpipe and I start coughing. My eyes burn and I can't catch my breath. Harvey Berger pats my back hard and jumps in, his tone indignant: "Mrs. Huntley's husband was killed in a tragic car accident and *he* was under investigation by the FBI. Mrs. Huntley is cooperating fully. This is actually an extremely delicate matter—a matter of national security—therefore, we cannot speak to you about the details. However, the federal agent who is already here, Special Agent K. Warnock, will share whatever information she can with you."

"Sí, she and I already conversated," says Detective Sanchez-Berilla.

Abruptly, Harvey rises and pushes back his chair. "Gentlemen, I think that is enough for today."

Detective Sanchez-Berilla hesitates only for a second before rising. Harvey is the CEO now. The detective turns to Calisto and says in Spanish, "I strongly suggest you do not leave San Miguel." Then to me, in English, "And you also must not to leave."

"I don't intend to," I reply.

"This investigation is not finished," he adds, his tone sinister as his eyes bore into me, then travel to the far wall of glass and land on the spider crack in the pane. He turns and strides out to the patio, followed by Perez and Harvey Berger, who accompanies them to the outer door, chatting amicably, one hand resting lightly on Sanchez-Berilla's shoulder as if they are old friends. I am overcome by emotion—helplessness and gratitude in a head-on collision, as if these Mexican officials have the power to decide my fate and the only thing standing between me and Mexican prison is Harvey Berger, my unlikely knight in shining armor.

In a minute Marta arrives with breakfast—stacked on one arm are three plates of fried eggs on tortillas with guacamole and pico de gallo, and in her other hand a box of tissues, which she places before me. I thank her, wipe my eyes, and blow my nose. Quick and silent as a stealth attack, she has placed a setting where Harvey was sitting and set the eggs down on top.

Calisto picks up his plate and fork and saunters out without a word, climbing back up the stairs to Bibi's quarters. I hear the door slam shut and then an echoing silence.

Harvey steps back through the French doors and glances with appreciation at the steaming huevos rancheros. He sits down and dives in as if he hasn't eaten in a week. I am unable to swallow a bite. Harvey wears silver cuff bracelets with little silver balls on the ends, one on each wrist, and some kind of shiny dark leather macramé bracelet that looks like it was made by a grandchild at camp. In a flash of acuity, I realize that all the information I have ever received about Harvey for the past twenty years has come from Bibi. She could have been lying to me the whole time.

Once he has finished his eggs, he wipes his mouth, moves the plate aside, leans forward, and says, "I loved your father. He was kind to his core. He was the best friend I ever had." He lays his weatherworn leather bag on the table, unclasps it, and pulls out some folders. "I am your godfather, after all."

My godfather? I don't believe him. "Bibi never said—"

"Oh, we never had a formal ceremony or anything, but your dad asked me to look after you. After he died . . . well, you were just a teenager . . . Vivienne wouldn't let me near you," he tells me with a rueful smile. "I could've tried harder, Merryn. But Vivienne was a mighty force to overcome."

My judgment is impaired. Nothing is what it seems. And how am I ever going to stop lying to myself if I can't tell a lie from the truth?

"Merryn, this may not be a good time, you're clearly exhausted, but there are several issues we need to discuss." He reaches over and squeezes my hand with a surprisingly strong grip. "Your father and mother . . . had their issues, as you surely remember."

What is he talking about? They were deeply in love. So deeply in love I was an afterthought. That is what Bibi always said.

"They were deeply in love . . ." I say.

Harvey pauses on an inhale, staring at me with a slightly veiled look of concern. He swallows, considers, then finally continues in the tone of a kind-hearted psychiatrist who might not want to stir up the emotions of a troubled patient: "Your father asked her for a divorce after that fiasco in Paris during the SALT II talks. That night at the Soviet embassy reception when Vivienne snuck off with Gromyko—that little folderol cost your father his career," he says bitterly. "Don't you remember when they lived apart? The State Department expected him to resign but he wouldn't, so they sent him to that dangerous and unstable political backwater, Cameroon. You stayed in Paris with Vivienne, and Henry went to Africa alone."

I feel my face closing. Nothing is making sense. I have to watch myself. "But Bibi and I did go to Cameroon," I remind him.

"Yes . . . yes, you did. Later. Your mother talked Henry into taking her back."

In Gaelic mythology, certain alleyways and mirrors lead to the land of fairies, dangerous gateways through which once you step, it is almost impossible to return. In the land of fairies nothing is as it seems. Music plays and the fairies dance

and feast all day, and time stands still. I feel as if I've stepped
through one of those gateways and will never find my way back.
Or perhaps I have been in the land of fairies all along, struck
by an enchantment that is just now beginning to break. I'm
stunned speechless.

But I have to speak, he's waiting.

"Harvey, I have no idea what you're saying. No idea at all."
My hands grip the edge of my chair so tightly my fingers have
started to ache. I slowly unclench them, attempting to appear
calm.

Harvey sighs, decides to let this go for now. He riffles
through his manila files and pulls out a document ensconced in
its own blue jacket. Bibi's will. I'm going to throw up. But everything is all right; Bibi can no longer take Tenney away from me,
that is the most important thing.

Harvey's voice drops several decibels and he says, barely
above a whisper, "Your mother's last will and testament, ex-
ecuted three years after your father died. This makes you her
sole heir, and me the executor of her estate. There are a few issues . . ." Harvey thinks for a moment, then continues, "Your
father wanted to leave you your inheritance up front, but Vivienne talked him out of it. She told him you were not responsible enough to deal with the money yourself. She convinced him
to make her his sole beneficiary. Of course, I objected, but that
woman always got her way."

All those years when I was teaching English as a second language and making so little, when I needed money, she made me
beg.

"Recently Vivienne made some grumblings about draft-
ing a new will, but I firmly discouraged her. I can't tell you
how often I've had to deal with morally dubious characters
who have managed to sweet-talk some old egoist out of a for-

tune." Swinging his arm around the great room, he adds, "If she drafted a new will and made Calisto her heir, he may get everything."

So Tenney and I very well might end up in the street with nothing. *How could she do this to us?*

Harvey takes a long sip of water and resumes, his voice still very low: "It is possible that Vivienne drew up a new will here in San Miguel."

"I . . . I have no idea."

Harvey glances toward the kitchen, then the patio, sees no one about, and murmurs, his lips barely moving though his voice remains perfectly clear, "Your mother was a difficult woman, Merryn. An extremely difficult woman. The only person who could ever get her to do anything was her father, the Dread Daddy."

"The Dread Daddy?" I repeat, unable to shake myself out of my stupor.

"Your father used to call him the Dread Daddy. It stuck. Sorry, I'm being rude. But Vivienne was the most difficult woman I've ever known. Hell, *I* couldn't get her to listen to me about anything, and God knows I tried. Sometimes she got me quite enraged. It couldn't have been easy for you, being her daughter." He waits to see how I react to this.

"Bibi was a wonderful mother, a wonderful person, I . . ."

I see something odd in Harvey's expression, I'm not sure what. I can't breathe. Tenney is approaching, her bare feet slapping against the patio stones. In a few seconds she's behind me, her thin arms around my neck.

"Tenney," I manage, "this is Mr. Berger, Bibi's lawyer from New York."

"Hello, beautiful little girl," says Harvey, reaching out to shake her hand.

"Hello," says Tenney, offering him the ends of her limp fingers.

Suddenly Harvey is tearing up, choking out words. "My God," he tells her, "you look like your grandfather."

I feel myself beginning to hyperventilate. "Excuse me," I rasp, and try not to run into the kitchen, where I open the freezer and stick my head in. I hear Tenney's solemn voice through the open doorway, muted by the sound of the compressor kicking on.

"I never got a chance to meet my granddaddy."

"I know, sweetheart. And that must be very sad for you," says Harvey. "But . . . if you like, I can be your new granddaddy, or if you'd rather, your great-uncle Harvey."

As the icy air fills my lungs I notice the shelf before my eyes is crowded with frost-covered liquor bottles—high-end tequilas, gins, vodkas—standing at attention, unmoving and yet somehow menacing, like Emperor Qin's terra-cotta army that he had made to protect himself from his enemies in the afterlife. I slam shut the freezer door and lean against it, an icy sweat prickling the back of my neck.

A movement of white across the tiles draws my eye. Sophia sits primly at Marta's feet, tail sweeping back and forth across the floor as her shiny black nose and eyes focus on the oatmeal Marta is stirring in a bowl. Marta says in a baby voice, *"Avena para mi perrita, sí, sí, sí, ahorita."* She sets the bowl on the floor and pats Sophia on the head. Sophia licks Marta's hand. I glance through the kitchen doorway across the patio. Tenney has a habit of leaving our bedroom door open and Sophia, with her finely tuned instincts, has already befriended the only person who truly counts—the one who controls the food. I must learn from this genius of survival.

Bibi told me she'd decided to make Calisto her sole heir and executor. She said that, but she was also the Queen of Liars. I need Harvey to help me figure all of this out.

I return to the great room. "Harvey, would you mind staying here with us? There are two lovely guest bedrooms downstairs by the pool. You can take your pick."

"But I wouldn't want to impose on you at such a difficult time."

"You'd be doing us a favor."

"That is very kind of you, my dear. Thank you." Then he adds in a somber tone, "We need to deal with the Dallas issue as soon as possible."

"Do you play chess, Mr. Berger?" Tenney asks hopefully. A plate of huevos rancheros sits in front of her, but she hasn't touched the food.

"You can call me Harvey, little beauty. No, I'm afraid not, my dear. Poker's my game."

"I'm a fast learner," Tenney says. "Maybe you can teach me later?"

Am I inadvertently raising a gambler? Oh, what the heck, as long as her mind is occupied, I won't interfere. "Don't be fooled," I tell Harvey with a strained smile, "you'll lose your shirt."

"Did someone say poker?"

We all turn to find Faye Peabody in the doorway, one arm raised dramatically and pressed against the doorframe. She's wearing a bright red muumuu with large white orchids in the pattern and matching red and white–striped San Miguel sandals. She has a red scarf tied around her head with a fancy bow at the top, giving her face the look of a white chocolate Easter egg.

"Pedro was just leaving so I slipped in. And who is this?" she asks, extending her bejeweled hand to Harvey, who rises and ceremoniously bows over her knuckles.

"Harvey Berger, Esquire, at your command."

"So you are the famous Harvey Berger!" She smiles delight-edly. "But you must come have comida with me!" Suddenly her lips begin to quiver. "I am so upset over Vivienne I can't stand the thought of being alone." She turns and yells toward the kitchen, "Marta! Bloody Marys, por favor!"

Tenney glances up at me from her huevos rancheros, the two yokes like filmy eyes staring out blindly from the plate. My stomach does a little flip and I'm feeling a great urge to run back to the freezer. I thought this movie was over and the audience had left the theater.

"Of course, I would be delighted," says Harvey.

Marta arrives bearing a frozen vodka bottle and the Bloody Mary mix in a tall pitcher. Two long celery stalks protrude from the pitcher like the scraggly forked branches of a red-trunked tree.

While Faye's attention is momentarily diverted by the fixing of drinks at the dry bar, Harvey turns to me and whispers, "She may know if your mother has a local lawyer and whether or not she drafted a new will. Leave it to me." This man certainly can whisper. It must be an art he cultivated in echoing courthouses and conference rooms. "I'll call the FBI lady and ask her to meet us here this evening."

"Tenney, if you eat your eggs, I'll call Dr. Steve and see if he's free this morning. Maybe he'll let you study your bug under his microscope."

She looks up at me with a sour expression. "I hate huevos rancheros."

"I thought you loved them."

"*Bibi* said I loved huevos rancheros."

"Well, what kind of eggs do you like then?" I ask.

"Scrambled."

"Then go ask Marta to make you *huevos revueltos*. She can put some manchego in there for you. And please, just tell me, Tenney. Just tell me what you want to eat."

CHAPTER
FIFTEEN

WHEN IT'S MY TURN TO OBSERVE the centipede, I lean forward and blink into the microscope's eyepieces, at first seeing nothing. After Dr. Steve makes a few adjustments, a frontal view of the insect's face comes into focus and I am confronted with a close-up of a gigantic monster from outer space. Hairy antennae protrude from its ugly head and two great pincers resembling claws surround its terrifying hole of a mouth. I scream and pull back and Dr. Steve and Tenney laugh.

Dr. Steve explains, "This is a teenager. It only has fifteen pairs of legs. It probably drowned during the storm. They breathe through tiny holes along their bodies."

But seeing it this close, it is an image from which science-fiction films are made. I step back with a shiver, and Tenney eagerly takes over, now expertly adjusting the eyepieces herself and listening to Dr. Steve while her eyes remain glued to the microscope, a very adult, calm countenance to her stooping shoulders. I don't quite recognize my little girl.

"Dr. Steve," she says without looking up, "what happens to people after they die?"

She has never asked me about this. I glance at Dr. Steve, whose dark eyes seem to be considering how to answer.

He says, "No one knows for sure. Your physical being returns to the earth, decomposes, and joins with nature once again. But as far as the spirit goes—the soul, the individual energy of that person—no one knows. I've heard of people whose hearts stopped, who died for as long as half an hour, who woke up and said they remembered everything. Sometimes they were walking along a hallway toward a bright light. Sometimes they saw all the people they loved in their lives who had died before them."

We wait for a response from Tenney, but none is forthcoming.

"No one ever said it was a bad experience . . ." Dr. Steve adds, his voice trailing off. The silence becomes oppressive. A moment later the nurse with *Dolores* on her lab coat walks in and murmurs something to him in Spanish. He responds in a quiet, forthright way and she nods then goes to the deep stainless-steel sink and begins to organize things. Dr. Steve places a yellow pad and pencil beside the microscope and says to Tenney, "Write down what you notice, what you see. You can draw if you like. Dolores has some work to do in here. We'll be right back. Tenney, I don't need to tell you—"

"Don't touch anything, I know. I'm not a baby, Dr. Steve," she admonishes, never lifting her eyes from the microscope.

The casita is empty except for the four of us. The door to the closest examining room is ajar and Dr. Steve pushes it open and indicates for me to step inside. He doesn't close the door so we can see the well-lit lab across the narrow hall. Not a sound from within.

"How are you?" he asks quietly.

"Bibi's lawyer came down from New York this morning. He really seems to know what he's doing."

"That's good."

"He thinks there may be another will. Bibi kept saying she was going to make Calisto her executor and heir." I watch his face for any minute change, like a searchlight trolling for escapees across a barren steppe, but his stolid expression doesn't shift.

Finally he says, "That's a really shitty thing for her to do."

I want to say, in defense of Bibi, *She never liked me*, but I realize, as far as justifications go, this is not very character affirming.

"She was really such a terrible bitch," he says. "I don't know how you put up with it."

I feel that unpleasant, slimy thing begin to uncoil within me. *Doctor Handsome can't keep his pants on.* "I don't know how *you* can stand it, being their doctor. Running around on your sexy motorcycle anytime one of them calls you. They say you sleep with all of them. That's how you pay your bills. Well, if you're looking for money, you're barking up the wrong tree with me. Looks like I'm going to be destitute."

His head snaps back, as if I've slapped him. Then his eyes go dim and I've never seen this look on his face before. I've gone too far. I feel terrible, I want to take it back. "I . . . I'm sorry. I can't . . . I . . . I'm jealous. I'm just so *jealous*."

"Jealous!" he laughs. "But sex is just sex. It doesn't mean anything!"

"Well, I used to feel the same way. But right now, everything I thought was true is not. Everything is upside down."

I turn to leave but in one swift movement he pushes the door shut with the sole of his boot and lifts me up by the hips and puts me down on the edge of the examining table. The sterile paper rumples and crinkles beneath me as he kisses my mouth, my neck. He lifts my tiered lavender Mexican skirt up to my waist, takes hold of one side of my panties, and slips them off. Wet soft lips, forceful tongue against my neck. He fumbles to undo the buttons of my blouse. He presses his lips against my stomach, then begins with a feathery wet tongue to kiss that usually hidden but now entirely exposed part of me, and I pull his hair. The crescendo comes swiftly and so hugely that I have to bite down on my own forearm. Then he's inside me and it's like some kind of apocalyptic earthquake, our bodies shaking and seizing, but all in total silence, a film with the volume turned off.

I'm still trying to process what just happened but he doesn't give me time to recover before he pulls away, goes to the tiny sink, and splashes water on his face. He combs his fingers through his hair, tamping it down, then dries his face with some paper towels, steps on the trash can pedal, throws the towels in—the competent doctor once again.

"I haven't fucked anyone else since I met you," he says, as if he were giving me an unpleasant diagnosis. He walks out and shuts the door softly behind him.

I stand on shaky legs, attempt to straighten my skirt and blouse, run my fingers through my hair, search for my . . . am I likely to find someone else's panties again? The thought is even more disturbing because I can't find my own anywhere. The white paper covering the examining table is torn and rumpled; I tear it off and pull a long strip from the wide roll at the head until a fresh layer covers the vinyl mattress. The silence is so complete I can hear the electricity buzzing through the overhead light fixture. I pull myself together as best I can and when all traces have been eradicated, pantyless, I take a deep breath, open the door, and cross the hall to the lab.

Tenney is still hunched over the microscope, entirely focused on her task. Dr. Steve is nowhere to be found. Dolores, hunched over the sink, is vigorously scrubbing implements of some kind. If I weren't so stunned, I'd think I made it all up.

"*Donde está el doctor Fuller?*" I ask Dolores.

She says he is seeing patients. I wait a few moments, gathering my thoughts, then tell Tenney it's time to go.

Outside, the sunlight is blinding. I dig through my purse for sunglasses. Much better now, at least I don't feel so exposed. His courtyard sounds like a barnyard. The crazy rooster crows as if it's dawn, the chickens cluck and chatter, and the baby goats bleat pitifully without a clue as to what they're wailing for.

On the way back up the steep incline through the Centro, I realize I haven't checked my phone in two hours. Two new messages from Ibrahim Ansari; one from Gordon, the Southern belle; three from Jeanne-Wallace; and one from Agent Warnock. *"I told you not to answer your cell phone, I didn't tell you not to call me back,"* says Agent Warnock.

I call her back. She tells me there are major developments. They've arrested Bucky in Houston and they're questioning him as we speak; secondly, they've set up the wiretap and we're going to do the call from San Miguel. She says she's spoken to Harvey Berger and she'll be by tonight, sometime before six p.m.

I've taken a cold shower and changed my clothes and feel almost sane, sitting at the game table in the great room playing Hearts with Tenney, when Harvey staggers in from comida with Faye. The sun is low in the sky; it must be close to five. He's still in his seersucker jacket and jeans, although he's managed to dust himself off. Sweat drenches the front of his pale blue cotton shirt and one section of shirttail is sticking out of his pants.

"My God, Merryn, that woman is a tigress. And can she drink! I'm lucky I'm not comatose. She had her hand on my knee before we'd finished our appetizers—a very nice tortilla soup with cilantro and lime, and by the time we had dessert—an excellent flan—she wanted to show me her bedroom. She said the master suite had the best view of the city. Nice view, by the way."

TMI, as Tenney would say. I am fascinated and queasy at once.

218 · THE ANGER MERIDIAN

"I knew this would be my best opportunity to find out what she knows," Harvey continues without compunction. "She was full of anticipation, so I delicately guided the conversation toward Vivienne." Now he lowers his voice to that amazing stage whisper. "Apparently Vivienne was quite vociferous about changing her will since Calisto arrived on the scene, but whether she actually did, Faye does not know. She told me Vivienne discussed the matter with a local lawyer that all the Americans use, Ignacio Suarez-Potts. It's Saturday, so perhaps he's been away from the office and hasn't heard about Vivienne's accident yet. No one is answering the phone at his office. I'm going to give him a call first thing Monday morning . . . And where is Calisto?"

"Calisto hasn't said anything to me since . . . He locked himself in upstairs and refuses to come down."

Harvey wanders into the kitchen where he asks Marta for a glass and I hear the water cooler gurgle and then he returns holding a tall, handblown green glass speckled with little air bubbles. Catching his breath, Harvey drops into the sofa, takes a long drink, wipes his forehead with a rumpled monogrammed hankie, and resumes: "After lunch she gave me the grand tour, starting with the rooftop terrace. Beautiful view. Beautiful roses and all kinds of other potted plants, even potted trees up there. Then down to the second floor, with that master bedroom and the view of the Centro. I was standing by the big bay window gazing down at the parroquia when suddenly she grabs me from behind and draws me toward the bed. She's very strong, Merryn—she has an ex-Marine trainer who makes her exercise with kettle bells.

"I had to let her kiss me, there was no way around it. She was about to throw me down on that king-size bed when I agilely sidestepped her and explained that I'm an old man with a heart condition—not true, by the way. And I've never had to use Viagra in my life but I'm sure the time is nigh. I explained to her that I'd been traveling for almost twenty-four hours straight and was not up to rigorous exercise. She backed off, probably afraid I'd have a coronary in her bed and then she'd have to deal with getting rid of my body.

"Being a widower is hard work. Ester has been gone five years now and still, everyone is constantly trying to fix me up and there are single women everywhere, jumping out of corners! I told Faye I was here on business and I'd have to take a rain check—but I was just being a gentleman. I didn't want to hurt her feelings. I'd do a great many things for your father, but going all the way with Faye Peabody is beyond the pale."

"What did Faye want Harvey to do, Mommy?" Tenney asks, curious and a little confused.

"She wanted Harvey to play Spin the Bottle with her."

"Oh," Tenney says. "Ew."

"*Ew* is exactly the right word," Harvey says.

I don't tell him that Faye will surely be back tomorrow to remind him that he promised her a rain check. I need to ask him about Beau's estate—Beau must have had savings, an IRA, life insurance. I have to stop these panic attacks. I have to breathe. I must maintain a calm demeanor. I must protect my child.

The doorbell gongs.

It's Agent Warnock.

The patio is already in shadow and I can see Tenney lying on the bed in our room across the way, the bedside lamplight spilling out through the doorway, a golden rectangle on the silvery flagstones. She knows to stay in there until this is over. Harvey sits beside me at the table, a big yellow legal pad and several pens and pencils laid out before him. Agent Warnock, catty-corner, has Agent Athas on the other end of her mobile, monitoring the wiretap from Dallas. She nods to me, her face funereal.

"The point here is," says Agent Warnock, "we've kept a lid on this so tight that no one knows anything. Beau is gone. Okay. That mousy secretary is sitting in the office answering the phone. Okay. Edward Buckingham was in Houston, and scared to crap because he had a bad feeling, now we have him. Okay. Ibrahim knows nothing, except that Beau is dead and he can't find his money. He has not been in Dallas. He has not been to the office. He has not been to your apartment. He's in the dark. He's worried about his money. Do you understand?"

I nod, silent. Finally, I build up the courage to ask, "But where is the money?"

Agent Warnock looks at me bluntly, with a masklike expression. "Apparently Beau moved it."

"Moved it? How?"

"Well," she sighs loudly, "honestly, that's none of your business. But I can tell you this: Edward Buckingham gave us everything on the YSL account in the Caymans. He cried like a little baby. But the money is not there."

"The money is not there?" I repeat, stunned.

"You're going to call Ansari back now. Just act normal," she advises. "Act as if you came down here to take care of your sick mother and you don't know a thing about anything."

I press *Return Call*. After one ring, Ibrahim picks up.

"Merryn," he says, his voice soft but pulsing with threat, "why have you not called me back? I left a thousand messages."

"My mother was very sick and I had to come down to San Miguel to take care of her. My phone was dead and I had to find a new charger. I had no idea you'd called." I glance at Agent Warnock, who nods once; everything appears okay.

"You women are not so good with the technology, yes?"

There is a slight delay as Agent Warnock listens in on her mobile. Her cheeks bloom pink.

"I was very upset," I explain to Ibrahim.

"Of course! Of course, very upset. I am very upset too. Beau was my friend. He was . . . my brother. Merryn—that girl—she meant nothing to him. Nothing. A little bit of fun. You were the apple of his eye. The jewel at the center of his heart."

I watch Agent Warnock, who rolls her eyes. Then she makes small circles with her hand, an indication to get on with it. Does she mean Ibrahim or me?

"Merryn, you have the Bootstraps checkbook, yes?"

I look at Agent Warnock, who is listening intently, the phone pressed to her ear, her knuckles white. After a short delay, she nods.

"Yes," I say to Ibrahim. "But where is Bucky? He's usually the one who signs the checks."

"As I said in my countless messages, there seems to be a little palace coup going on at the office. Bucky does not answer my calls and no one knows where he is. I fear he may have taken a little trip to Grand Cayman. They say the golf is very good there, but what a time to take a vacation, don't you agree, Merryn? That this is a strange time for Bucky to be playing golf? I have sent someone there to find him. Now, as our poor, beloved Beau is no longer with us, *you* must pick up the reigns and carry on his good works—do you understand, Merryn? You must help the children. The orphans need us. Like little sparrows who eat from the bird feeder all through the summer, you cannot stop filling the feeder in December, isn't that so?"

"Absolutely," I say. Agent Warnock's jaw muscles pulse. Harvey taps a yellow pencil eraser against the legal pad.

"You would not want your own child to be orphaned. To be

destitute. But, no worries. You help us, Merryn, and we will help you." He pauses, letting this sink in. "You must make out a little check for me. Are you listening? Make it out to *Mary's Little Lambs*, the orphanage in Kabul."

"The orphanage in Kabul? But I've never written that kind of check, Ibrahim," I say, because this is what I would normally say.

"That is of no consequence. The orphans are waiting, Merryn. Without us, they will not eat!"

"How much—"

"Just a little check. To keep us going until all is settled . . . Five hundred thousand."

"Did you say *five hundred thousand*?" I ask, aghast. Harvey looks up sharply.

"You must send it today, and send overnight to me at the following address in New York. Use DHL, Merryn. DHL, *not* FedEx. FedEx does not work well in Mexico."

"But Ibrahim, tomorrow is Sunday. It won't get there till Monday."

"Ah. Sunday. Yes. Well then, do it immediately. It is of the utmost urgency, Merryn. Do you hear me? Now take down this address."

Dutifully, I write down the address, a Saudi corporation in Midtown Manhattan. Before clicking off, Ibrahim says, his voice low and threatening, "You must not let me down, Merryn. I am not good when I am angry."

When I put the phone down, my hand is trembling. The room itself seems to breathe a sigh of relief.

Agent Warnock stands and goes out to the terrace with her phone glued to her ear, hunched over in concentration. A few minutes later she returns, her shoulders dropping in relief.

"Progress," she says as she exhales. "But where the hell is the money?"

CHAPTER SIXTEEN

Sunday

THIS MORNING WHEN I ENTER the great room I find Harvey sitting on the coral couch watching CNN on the flat-screen TV above the fireplace. The segment is about that terrible mother who murdered her toddler in New Mexico and was convicted by public opinion long before her trial. The day after she reported that her child was dragged out of her backyard by coyotes, she was seen dancing in a nightclub and partying like a person who felt free for the first time in years—in my estimation, the most telling sign of her guilt. Which is why I put away my new hat. I don't want anyone accusing me of being frivolous with Bibi not even buried yet. But why is my headache gone? Why do I feel *so much better?*

Again, I slept like a stone and would probably have slept half the day if I hadn't set my alarm. In the kitchen, I place a filter in the Krups coffeemaker and shake a pile of finely ground coffee into the cone without measuring. I pour in eight cups of water from the cooler and wait impatiently for the coffee to brew. When it's ready I carry the lacquered tray with milk and sugar out to the great room and place it on the coffee table.

"Ah!" says Harvey, delighted. "You're wonderful."

The first bar of Beethoven's Fifth Symphony blasts forth from his khaki pants and he springs up, looking a little frightened, and pulls the phone out of his pocket to read the display.

"Why did I give Faye my mobile number? I am vain, Merryn! I was flattered by her attentions. But what if she comes by unannounced? I don't think I'm physically capable of holding her off." He pushes some buttons on his phone and sets it down on the smoked-glass coffee table, watching it as if it were a scorpion.

Tenney pads in wearing her pink bikini with white polka dots. Her face, neck, and arms are browned but her torso is almost as white as the polka dots. Her ribs show through her skin. I want to say, Tenney, you really, really need to eat more. But I restrain myself. I'm afraid my face will reflect my concern.

"Mommy, let's go to Xote."

I think of the CNN piece about the mother who killed her toddler and wonder if going to a water park could be considered inappropriate behavior for a woman who has just lost her mother in a terrible accident. "I don't know, honey," I say. "I'm not sure I'm up to it yet."

"You promised we would go to Xote!" Tenney shouts.

"What is Xote?" asks Harvey.

"It's a natural hot springs water park," I explain. "The kids love it."

Harvey tells us he has not been to the hot springs in San Miguel in forty years—the last time was with Ken Kesey, and they were so stoned on "magic mushrooms" that all he remembers is being submerged in hot water up to his chest in a dark hut.

"You must've been at la Gruta," says Tenney. "Xote is way, way cooler." Her face is strained with expectation.

"I think it's a great idea," Harvey says. "A change of scenery. We'll all go."

He's right. I must keep Tenney entertained, her mind occupied. It is my job as her mother to provide this for her, regardless of the situation.

"Okay," I say with a little uncertainty.

Tenney jumps up and down, clapping wildly. "We're going to Xote!"

I wonder aloud if I should call Agent Warnock and let her know. She told us last night she is going to stay until "things are resolved, one way or the other."

Harvey says, "She's okay, that Amazon. The FBI is never very forthcoming, and Agent Warnock has been more forthcoming than most. Here's the thing: my friend, the US attorney in Dallas, told me late last night that Beau moved the money electronically out of the YSL account. They believe he transferred it to a decentralized, virtual currency on the Internet. Completely untraceable."

"What in the world is a virtual currency?" I ask, trying to shush Tenney.

"ECoins!" Tenney shouts.

Harvey and I both turn to her at the same time. "How do you know about eCoins, Tenney?" he asks in a composed tone.

"Daddy told me they were really cool. He said they were the future of currency. Let's go! Let's go to Xote!"

Harvey and I stare at each other. "What else did he tell you, honey?" Harvey asks sweetly, as if he were talking to a three-year-old. Tenney's eyes narrow in suspicion.

"Nothing. He just said eCoins were going to be the future of currency because they can't be controlled by the government."

Harvey lets out a deep sigh. "How's about I make us some world-famous Harvey Berger scrambled eggs before we go to Xote?"

While I'm changing into my swimsuit, I try to call Dr. Steve. When his voice mail asks me to leave a message, I don't know what to say. "Dr. Steve, we're going to Xote with Harvey the lawyer and we thought maybe you'd like to come." I say we'll stop by on our way out of town in about thirty minutes, and if he's not there, we'll just go on without him. I want to say much more but I don't know what, so I hang up.

When we pull up in front of Dr. Steve's house he's already outside, on the sidewalk, locking the door. He's in long flowery swim trunks, a T-shirt, flip-flops, and an unraveling Mexican sombrero, with a colorful plastic inner tube draped around his neck. Two more inner tubes and two neon-yellow foam noodles lie scattered at his feet.

Dr. Steve throws the paraphernalia into the hatch and climbs in back next to Tenney. I introduce him to Harvey and they shake hands across the open V between the front seats. He is two feet away and I feel a bright white current buzzing between us; can the others feel it too?

It is Sunday and the atmosphere at Xote is even more festive than usual. Families are barbecuing on rusty old metal grills bolted into the terraced, grassy resting areas and people sit crowded at the round wooden tables on circular benches under thatched roofs while music blares from portable radios.

I am lying back in a very hot, small pool, relieved that Dr. Steve went off to the slides with Tenney. When he's close, I fear my feelings show and it takes effort to appear nonchalant. Tenney comes running up, dripping wet, holding one of his colorful donut-shaped tubes around her waist with both arms, her elbows protruding at her sides, the bones like knobs below her skin.

"Mom, you have to come try this new slide."

"I'm happy right here, Tenney. You know I don't like those slides."

Her joyful expression collapses and suddenly I want to cry. What in the world is wrong with me? "Okay, but only if you promise to eat a *gordita* afterward. I'll do it this once." I climb out of the hot pool and follow her.

Tenney's hand slips into mine. She is smiling up at me, and I bend over and kiss her head. We climb to the very top of the white tower, where the waterslides await. We're so high up a strong wind blows, raising gooseflesh on my arms. A small, round tube with water shooting down it lies before me.

"Sit here, Mom. Put your bum in the middle. Don't forget to lift your legs or you'll rub your skin right off."

"Tenney, I don't think—"

"Come on, you're holding up the line."

Indeed, behind us a slew of Mexican children, from quite small to teenaged, are patiently waiting their turns. To my great dismay I note that not one of them is as skinny as Tenney.

What if I get hurt? Who will take care of Tenney? How can I find out about eCoins?

I'm sure the safety rules here are lax—more lax than in the States anyway. My rear is in the hole at the center of the inner tube, legs straight, feet lifted—but I don't want to go.

"Tenney, I've changed my mind—"

Tenney gives me a shove, and the inner tube plummets into the chute whose downward slant is much more pronounced than it looks from outside. I'm forced to lie back and I'm going too fast, much too fast. My heart catapults from my chest to my throat, followed by the rest of my organs. My eyes squeeze shut as the inner tube rockets down through the cylinder; I must be going a hundred miles an hour. I'm going to die. *If I live I'm going to fix my life. I'm going to become a better person.* I open my eyes to slits. The tunnel turns abruptly and I'm propelled to the left, then to the right, and I realize I'm screaming as I'm projected like a bullet from a gun into the open air, blasting into the light, the inner tube falling away as I land with a terrific crash of tumbling arms and legs into a pool of warm water. Water shoots up my nose and runs back out as I sputter and struggle to plant my feet beneath me. When I wipe the water from my eyes I see Dr. Steve standing a few feet away, up to his waist in the pool, laughing and reaching his hand out to me.

I'm still trying to recuperate when behind us we hear an echoing, deep-throated shriek, followed by several more, and soon Harvey Berger shoots out of the cylinder, his inner tube spinning away in one direction as he spins off in another, tumbling through the air and finally crashing into the water. Tenney runs down the path and stands by the side of the pool, laughing and clapping.

"How undignified," Harvey says, sputtering. "I screamed like a little girl."

"You screamed *worse* than a little girl, Uncle Harvey," Tenney tells him.

Somehow, in the last few hours, Tenney has made him family.

If they do throw me in prison, at least she will have him.

CHAPTER SEVENTEEN

Monday

A T 8:45 A.M. HARVEY AND I WALK Tenney down the mountain toward the Garza School. Four new voice mail messages from Ibrahim, asking me if I sent the check. Of course I didn't send the check. What the hell is the FBI doing anyway?

Harvey says is he's going to stop by unannounced at the Centro offices of Señor Ignacio Suarez-Potts. It is paramount to find out if she drafted a new will.

Despite the fits of anxiety that grip me throughout the day, I had another night of deep, dreamless sleep and I'm starting to worry that there is something questionable in Alberto Zaldaña's tea.

Harvey leaves us in front of the Garza School and continues on down San Francisco Street toward the jardín. Señor Garza is behind his desk, gazing at his computer screen. He glances up; I say, "Buenos dias," and he rushes out to greet us. He leads Tenney across the courtyard toward her classroom, where two new students, listless teenage girls in low-cut jeans and high-cut tank tops and too much blue eye shadow and black eyeliner sit rolling their eyes while a guitarist and a trumpeter in sombreros serenade the class with "Guantanamera." *"Yo soy un hombre sincero . . ."*

Señor Garza takes me by the arm and leads me back across the courtyard toward his office. He says, "I asked Detective

Sanchez-Berilla why he is holding your mother's . . . the body . . . so long, and he tells me to mind my own business. He is still waiting for the autopsy results and he has not ruled out the foul play from the vividor. That is right, *foul play*? Yes? But you must not to worry, everything takes a long time in Mexico. I am so sorry for your troubles. He is like an esmall dog with a very big bone, yes?" He makes his yes go large and pantomimes holding down a bone between paws, gnawing at it with single-minded intensity. I can't help but smile though my chest feels tight.

"Ah, Señora Merryn, if it were only another time . . ." He shrugs, smiles sadly. "If it were another time for each of us . . . if we were not in mourning . . ." He leaves his thought unfinished, squeezes my hand meaningfully, and I stare down at my feet, unable to come up with an appropriate response.

He smiles his kind, open smile and I feel horrible. If Ernesto Garza only knew that I am not the innocent widow he thinks I am.

He says, "In any case, I am your champion. I have told my cousin by marriage, Detective Sanchez-Berilla, to release your mother's body and go find himself something important to do. I think he is only bored." Señor Garza clears his throat, and in a more officious tone, adds, "The children after the classes today will go to Parque Juárez. Will you meet Tenney there?"

"Yes," I reply, "I will come to the park."

I step outside into the yellow sunlight and spy Agent Warnock lurking in a recessed doorway across the street. The sleeves of her safari shirt are rolled up and she wears aviator Ray-Bans, her new huaraches, and her cowboy hat. She beckons me into the shadows.

I cross the street toward her. "Agent Warnock, is something wrong?" My eyes are blinded for a moment. When my pupils adjust, I see her large pale face frowning down at me and my nose reflected twice and grotesquely large in her aviator shades.

"You signed paperwork for the charity, didn't you?"

I feel as if she just took my intestines and twisted them up like a kitchen rag. I feel physically ill. "I must have."

"You signed financial documents?"

"No, Beau never discussed the finances with me."

"We have tax returns for the charity with your signature on them."

"Oh, yes, that's right. Beau said I had to sign them. Though I never read them. But why are you bringing this up now, Agent War—?"

"Did he say why you had to sign them?" she interrupts.

"Because that's the VP's job."

"No, actually, it's not. It's highly unusual, in fact."

"Oh." I squint up at the tall agent whose expression divulges nothing. I thought we were doing so well. Why is she angry with me again?

"That *is* your signature on last year's tax return?" Agent Warnock asks. "He didn't forge it, did he?"

"I don't specifically remember because Beau would just put papers in front of me to sign. But Agent Warnock, I thought everything was good, everything was settled. Shouldn't I call Harvey?"

She just stares at me, sizing me up. "These financial documents are not a good development, Merryn." And then she sighs and adds, "Also, you should know . . . we lost Ibrahim Ansari."

"You lost him?"

"He'll probably try to contact you again. If you're not involved, as you maintain, then just call me immediately when you hear from him."

"But—are we in danger?"

"No danger at all," she states, raising her hand as if to stop traffic. Then she turns away and stalks off down the street, disappearing around the first corner.

Disquieted, I head further into the Centro, continuing down San Francisco. The sidewalk seems to be tilting upward toward my face even though I'm going downhill, and I press my fingertips against a gritty stucco wall to catch my balance. I look around, startled to see the people in the street going about their morning rituals with slow, quiet deliberation, just a regular peaceful day in San Miguel. I turn right on Hidalgo and walk down toward the north end of town. I pass an Internet café and through the barred window glimpse two rows of computer screens glowing in the dim room. Anxiety mushrooms in my chest; I fear the worst, like a person evacuated from home during a flood—all the lines are down and there is no way to find out what is really going on. But this is no natural disaster, this is all my fault. I caused all of this. Mum was right, I'm a bad person and I don't know how to manage my own life. What am I going to do?

I enter the Internet café, stepping in from the bright street, and the room is dark as a cave. In a moment my eyes adjust and I see a red macaw on a perch by the open window that leads to a barren, sun-drenched courtyard. The computer screens are too close together, but there is only one young man in the first row and he is playing a game, banging away on the keyboard. I pay the attendant thirty pesos for an hour of time and sit down at the last console in the far corner. I have to ask for help to get Google in English. The attendant walks away and I am alone in my row.

I type in the word *eCoin*. I am taken to Wikipedia. ECoins are not controlled by any centralized government and are therefore not beholden to global exchange currency rates. There has been quite a lot of noise lately about eCoins being used for illegal activities like money laundering. A link leads me to the eCoin website, which asks me to register, or sign in. An e-mail address, user name, and password are required. I close the site, erase my browsing history, and walk back out into the sun-drenched street.

Alberto's studio is closed. There is something discouraging about a padlocked door. The anxious feeling expands in my chest; I sit down on the high stone step at the foot of the door, not quite sure what to do next. On the narrow sidewalk people amble by carrying hard plastic mesh grocery bags that have the image of the Virgin de Guadalupe painted on the front, others have a well-known self-portrait of Frida Kahlo. The exhaust from the idling cars makes my nausea worse.

Alberto Zaldaña approaches hurriedly from the opposite sidewalk, his strong body carried on short, slightly bowed legs. He crosses between two cars, hefting a net shopping bag filled with mangoes.

"Good morning," he says. "I hurried. I'm sorry I made you wait."

"How did . . . I didn't tell you I was coming. Am I disturbing you?"

"*Claro que no.*"

I stand and Alberto unlocks the door and leads the way up the creaky stairs.

The large indigo room stands dark and empty, no mats on the floor. Alberto ushers me through the door at the back, which leads to a smaller room with canvas screens separating two massage tables and a waiting area—a rattan love seat and an armchair between the two windows. He indicates for me to sit. It is a spartan space, nothing extraneous, but everything bright and clean. I go to the window and look out into the narrow street, which is clogged with stop-and-go traffic.

"I will make some tea." He turns away with his mesh shopping bag and vanishes behind another door.

"I don't—"

"Everything is good," he calls from within.

He returns a few minutes later clutching a lacquered crimson tray, which he sets down on a low rattan table. Two peacocks are carved into the surface, and set out in lovely symmetry on the tray are two little Chinese teacups, a pot of tea with fragrant steam rising from the spout, and a small plate of sliced mango. The tea smells of orange blossoms and honeysuckle, perhaps a touch of bergamot.

Alberto pours the tea, offers me the plate of mangoes and a tiny fork. I take one slice, which is not too soft, and sour and sweet at once. But I can barely swallow.

"What is it, Merryn?" Alberto leans forward, gazing into my eyes. He has the long, curving nose and wide, high cheekbones of his Pipil forebears; his is a guileless face. He hands me one of the little porcelain cups. On it, a blue dragon with a red forked tongue chases its tail.

"I've made a complete mess of my life," I say.

"One of the common traits of children raised by abusive parents is that they take too much responsibility for things that are not their fault."

I jump in my seat and tea spills over the lip of the cup onto my fingers. Alberto hands me a little red and blue handspun cloth napkin.

"But I'm not . . ." My voice trails off. After a long silence I say, "I think I'd better go," and place my cup back on the tray.

"Would you like to know how I ended up here in San Miguel

running a yoga and healing center?" He looks me directly in the eye and I nod.

"The civil war in El Salvador in the eighties caused so many deaths that we children who were orphaned lived day to day, practically naked in the streets. The Catholic priests were on the side of the poor and many came to help from other countries. This young American Jesuit, Father Gerald, gathered us up and brought us to a Catholic orphanage in the capital that was a school but also had a beautiful, very old church. Father Gerald, who did so much for so many children in El Salvador, he was a good man. He saw right away I had a talent for learning, and he taught me many important lessons. We read many books. He was not close-minded in the way that some priests can be. And he became my spiritual father."

Alberto pauses, sips his tea, delicately holding the rim of the cup between two fingers. "When I finished my studies I came with him and three others to San Miguel and it was a fantastic place for me after the horror and poverty of El Salvador. Oh, there is much poverty here too, but the church does much good works for the sick and suffering. Father Gerald never treated us like *indios*, and I was quite happy. Until one day, right here in a very poor neighborhood on the outskirts of San Miguel, I almost killed a man." Alberto gazes into my eyes. I nod, trying to absorb his words while keeping my face from tensing up in surprise.

"I saw a drunken man beating his little son with closed fists. Something in my head snapped. Everything around me turned black. Then I wake up," he blinks, as if coming to, "and the drunk man is bleeding from his nose and ears and he is unconscious. You see, I had picked up a brick lying in the dirt and hit him in the back of his head." Alberto's hands lie open in his lap, facing upward, and he stares at them as if they are not a part of his body. "It was terrible. Truly, to lose control like that and not be able to remember. I suffered from what is called a rage blackout."

A rage blackout? Is this what happened to me with Mum? I shiver, as if from cold.

Alberto continues, "I believe God stopped me from killing him at the last second. The church was very upset with me. Father Gerald intervened on my behalf. I was forced to take a leave of absence from my duties as a priest."

"You're a priest?"

He nods, then says, indicating the space with a sweep of his arm, "It was Father Gerald, whose American family is rich, who gave to me the money to start this healing center."

Alberto sits back. I feel strength and calm emanating from him like a silver aura. "After that I became involved with this program called CASA, the Centro para los Adolescentes de San Miguel de Allende, for the victims of domestic abuse. But in Mexico it is very hard. There are no laws to protect women and children against family violence. And most of the time they will not come forward. Now I am working for this cause. If good cannot come of bad things, then what is the point of life?" He smiles and I don't believe I've ever seen a warmer smile in my life.

Alberto tells me that he spends one hour a day in meditation, emptying his mind to allow God in; and two hours in active prayer, asking for help for all the lost and anguished souls, but also he asks God to lift his own anger and rage. He tells me that he walks in the mountains at dawn every day, talking to Jesus and the Virgin. "They are easier for me to talk to than God because they are human and suffered as human beings." He says he has not had an episode since, but at times he still feels the presence of that dark and alien thing lurking within him.

He is waiting for me to respond. Bright sunlight pours

through the two windows, forming angled golden beams on the wooden floor.

After what seems like a long time, I ask, "Why do you tell me this, Alberto?"

"I recognize the look in your eyes; it is the same look I have in my eyes. It is the look in the eyes of all children born into violence."

"I . . . I had an extremely privileged childhood. Bibi was a wonderful person, an extraordinary woman . . ."

"You are not free," he says out of nowhere, and his voice is strangely sad. He sits impassively, his face showing no judgment. "People came from miles and miles to my village to seek my abuela's advice. She was *vidente*. In English, you call this a seer. Many in my family were seers, but it is not so good for me to advertise this, since I am a priest." He laughs easily, a light rumble rising from the depths of his chest.

He pours more pale tea into the cups. "I have been on sabbatical leave since that day. The doctors told me I am suffering from post-traumatic stress disorder. So now I am studying the healing properties of yoga and other alternative forms of therapy for anger management and PTSD. Our bishop is good, but a little old-fashioned in his views. Mine are special circumstances. Soon it will be three years and I will have to decide if I will remain a priest or become a renegade." He laughs again and slaps his muscular thighs with both hands. Then he solemnly adds, "No, I am joking. I do not want to leave the church."

Another long silence.

Tears begin to spill from my eyes and I lower my head and shield my face with my hand. "My mother hated me."

He lays his warm, soft hand on my right shoulder, where my muscle spasms always begin. I can feel the warmth like a salve.

"But that is her fault, not yours," he says gently. He takes my hand and squeezes it. His face is so deeply creased he suddenly appears much older, as old as the dry, scarred mountains around us. I look into his face and see a pinprick of light in the dark pools of his eyes. *Can he see who I really am?* I set my teacup back on the tray, my hand shaking so, the delicate china rattling against the lacquered wood.

I have to go.

Urgently I rise, telling him I have to meet my daughter in the park. My little napkin flutters to the floor. I run through the shadowy outer yoga room and down the stairs. The sunlight in the street stings my eyes as if I've just emerged from the sea.

It is not becoming easier, but harder for me to recognize what is true. I feel so confused. I think I will not return to Alberto's yoga center. The sun's brightness oppresses me and the streets are so quiet I hear only the sound of my own steps as I begin the long walk to Parque Juárez.

The two old chess players have brought a folding table and two plastic folding chairs and set up their game near the base of the cement bleachers that climb from the center of the sunken court. They've also brought their chess clock, an old-fashioned one with a wood frame built around the two white faces, and gold push-buttons on top, just like the one Tenney had in Dallas. Their audience has grown—now about fifteen people sit on the Roman-style concrete steps, watching in silence. Agent Warnock stands at the very top, on the walkway, her arms crossed, watching through her sunglasses. At least, I think, with her here, nothing bad can happen to us.

A third man is playing Tenney. He wears a pale straw Mexican cowboy hat with a snakeskin band, his face bent toward the chess pieces and hidden by the brim of the hat. I can tell by the curve of Tenney's back and the droop of her shoulders that she's losing. He has taken most of her pawns, two knights, a rook, and a bishop. She doesn't have a lot of pieces left. The man makes his move, presses the button on the clock, then looks up from under his hat with a wily smile. It's Detective Sanchez-Berilla. My knees suddenly feel like jelly. How dare he take advantage of a child? Tenney's hand hovers uncertainly over her bishop, then over the rook. Steeling myself, I walk up to the table and lay my palm on her shoulder. What skinny, frail shoulders to be carrying so much weight.

"I'm here," I say.

"Hi, Mom," Tenney says, her eyes focused on the board. I feel her shoulders relax under my hand.

The detective looks up at me from under the brim of his hat. His eyes are in shadow and reveal nothing. Has he been asking her questions? Despite the extreme heat, a shiver courses down my back. I stand to my daughter's right, my hand resting on her shoulder, and remain completely still.

Swiftly, Tenney moves one of her pieces. I know it is the bishop, but I have no idea why she is moving it. "Check," she says.

"*Carajo*," mutters Detective Sanchez-Berilla. The two old men start to guffaw, throwing their heads back and slapping their thighs, showing the black gaps in their teeth.

On the way back up to the Centro, Tenney won't talk to me. "Damn, damn, *damn*," she mutters. It took Detective Sanchez-Berilla another ten minutes to beat her. I stood beside her silently and did not interfere though I wanted to kick him in the shins. Every time I glanced back over my shoulder, Agent Warnock was there, in the distance, watching. Finally, when Tenney laid down her king in defeat, there was total silence from the crowd. I looked back toward the top of the bleachers and the path, but Agent

Warnock was gone. Tenney stood up, exhausted, and reached into the pocket of her shorts and peeled a hundred-peso note off a folded stack of bills that seems to be fattening by the day. She was making good her bet against the detective. Sanchez-Berilla held up his hands, not wanting to take her money. He offered her a rematch, but Tenney shook her head, set the bill on the ad hoc chess table, and said, "You make me have to think too hard," and pressed her fingertips to her temples. Her face was so pale the blue veins were pulsing beneath the almost translucent skin. Not a sound from the little crowd of observers.

"Tomorrow, then," Detective Sanchez-Berilla replied with a smile, sliding the bill back toward her. She did not pick it up.

"You did great, Tenney," I say now, not reprimanding her for using the word *damn* as I normally would.

"You don't know anything about chess."

"But I know you fought him hard and next time you'll win."

"He's really, really smart."

Yes, this I know is true. I'd like to tell her not to play chess with him anymore, but this would probably be the wrong approach.

We pass a blue door in the center of a stone archway in a stucco wall, *La Paz* written on a ceramic sign above the buzzer. A *For Sale* sign is posted on the door. At the back of the overgrown garden of lime trees is a recessed little coral-hued, two-story house with crimson bougainvillea cascading down the front.

"Look, a gingerbread house!" Tenney points. "That would be a perfect house for us and Sophia and the puppies."

A perfect house.

The back of my throat tightens at the sight, and for a moment I imagine us living here, with the dogs running free among the trees, all of us safe and sheltered from the world. But we have nothing.

Is there room for Dr. Steve, who can't keep his pants on?

I turn away, my heart stone-heavy in my chest, and lead Tenney up the street toward the Centro.

Just before we reach the jardín we pass a store that sells all kinds of odds and ends—school supplies, backpacks, pens, hair accessories, candy. I lead Tenney into the narrow store and ask her to pick out a small backpack for her science kit. She chooses a powder-blue My Little Pony pack that is hanging on the wall, and a pink plastic pencil holder with a lid that opens like a jewel box. I seem to forget, as everyone else does, that she is only nine years old. Emotionally she is just a little girl who likes bright little-girl things. I hail a cab outside the store and ask the driver to take us up to Montitlán.

As soon as Tenney and I enter the patio I notice that the round wrought-iron table has been moved from the north terrace to the west-facing balcony with the sprawling view of downtown San Miguel, and sitting there under the open parasol admiring the view are Faye Peabody, Harvey, and Calisto. The table is set for comida though it appears they are still on their pre-comida cocktails. Harvey spies us, gets up, and hurries over as we reach our bedroom door.

"Faye invited herself to lunch, then went upstairs and knocked on the door and invited Calisto. They wanted to eat outside but refused to sit on the terrace because they did not want to be reminded—so they made Pedro and Allegra move the table to the balcony. That thing weighs a million pounds!" All of this he says with his back to the balcony, in that whispering voice that does not carry at all.

I sense Faye and Calisto watching us, and when I turn and gaze in their direction, she wriggles her fingers at me. I wave back.

"Did Faye ask you to play Spin the Bottle again, Uncle Harvey?" Tenney asks with keen interest, and I cringe as her ringing voice ricochets back at us from every direction.

"She sure did," mutters Harvey. "You'll have comida with us, won't you?" There is a pleading look in his eyes. It's the last thing in the world I want to do, but I can't throw Harvey to the wolves.

"Of course," I say, and unlock our bedroom door. "Tenney, go wash your hands." Sophia comes skipping toward us, jumping up and down and contorting her rear end sideways like a slinky, as if she simply can't contain her joy. No one has ever been this happy to see me before in my life and my eyes sting with emotion.

"Okay," Tenney says, but goes instead to the puppy box.

I turn to Harvey and whisper, "The FBI lost Ibrahim Ansari."

"What?" Harvey whispers back. "They *lost* him? How did they lose him? Like, like, they lost their *keys*? But . . . my God, I must call that Agent Warnock immediately." He pulls his mobile phone out of his pants pocket.

While he's waiting for Agent Warnock to answer, he says, "I have no news to report on the will. Ignacio Suarez-Potts is skiing on some mountaintop in Argentina. His secretary told me he takes his vacation now because the town is empty of Americans. What a way to run a business! He'll be back in his office tomorrow afternoon. I made an appointment to meet him."

The phone rings and rings, and finally Agent Warnock's voice mail answers. Harvey asks her to call him immediately.

Tenney approaches, holding tiny Lola up in her cupped hands like an offering. "Look! Their eyes opened!" she marvels. The puppy stares out at the world with a bewildered expression. Sophia's attention is focused on Tenney's hands, but she doesn't seem overly concerned.

I tell Harvey we'll join him in a moment and lead Tenney back into our room. Once the puppy is safely in the box, we go into the bathroom and I turn on the faucet.

"You saved them," Tenney says softly, not looking up from her soapy hands. "For me. Even though you were scared of Bibi."

"I wasn't scared of—"

"You're my mom and I'll always stand up for you, just like you stood up for me."

CHAPTER
EIGHTEEN

"**Y**OU WERE SO KIND AND GENTLE with Vivienne," Faye says to Calisto, laying her pale, speckled hand over his dark one on the tabletop. "You must be in terrible shock."

Calisto seems about to burst into tears. *God, he is good.* Faye wistfully resumes stirring her posole with her soupspoon. She lifts the spoon out of the tomato-based soup and gazes down suspiciously at a kernel of hominy. "I see Marta is back to making her peasant dishes."

"I love her posole," Tenney says. Apparently so does Harvey, who has been ignoring our guests and attacking his soup like a starving man; he has already finished two bowls and is working on his third, piling the chopped fresh cilantro, avocado slices, shredded lettuce, and fresh-squeezed lime on top. Tenney watches him, smiling delightedly at his unusual behavior. In an imitation of Harvey, she piles an excess of avocado and cilantro into her bowl.

Calisto pushes his bowl away, sits back, and lights a cigarette. A blue glass ice bucket stands on the table and sticking out is a bottle of Dom Perignon. Calisto lifts it out of the ice and fills Faye's and his own flutes.

"Don't you love this champagne?" Faye asks Harvey, her tone suddenly flirtatious and light, though it carries a sour edge. "I was saving it for a special occasion."

Harvey hasn't touched his glass. "Lovely," he says.

"Can I have more posole, Mom?" Tenney asks. I glance doubtfully at her bowl but it is empty, just a few flakes of cilantro floating on a thin layer of red broth. Tenney has never asked for seconds in her life.

I feel like throwing my arms in the air and shouting, *Hallelujah!* Calmly, with perfect self-control, I reply, "Sure, Tenney," and reach for the serving bowl and ladle.

Faye says coyly, "So, my dear Merryn, I hear you were seen frolicking at Xote with Doctor Handsome. According to my sources, you were having an *awfully* good time."

She turns to Calisto as if they're conspirators in this matter, and he wears that nasty smirk which makes me want to throw my iced hibiscus juice in his face. My mind flashes once again on the young mother partying in the nightclub when she should have been home mourning.

"I insisted on Xote," Harvey says. "Tenney needed a change of scenery. In fact, we had a wonderful time. I haven't been on a waterslide in, oh . . . I don't know if I've ever been on a waterslide, come to think of it."

"Uncle Harvey screamed like a little girl!" Tenney adds, laughing.

"No wonder no one answered the door when I stopped by yesterday. And here *I* was thinking you were avoiding me." Faye pats Harvey's free hand; he keeps his eyes lowered and focused on his soup. "And how is everything going with the FBI?" she asks cheerily.

"We can't talk about that," Harvey replies shortly.

"Oh-oh!" cries Faye. "Well, I hear Doctor Handsome has a new *patient*. The Brain Drain Lady from Berkeley, California. A widow. Rich, rich, rich! But booooooooring."

A hot point of pressure nags at the right side of my jaw just below the ear, as if someone is turning the tip of a nail there, marking the spot before letting loose with a hammer. *Oh, please, not the TMJ.*

"He doesn't like to be called Doctor Handsome," Tenney pipes up. "He's Dr. Steve."

"Dr. Steve . . . hmmm," says Faye in a singsong voice. She taps a hard crimson nail against her flute, which Calisto promptly refills. The ethereal bubbles rise and pop in the air.

"I think I could eat this posole every day for the rest of my life," says Harvey.

"Me too!" chirps Tenney.

"Ha-ha-ha!" says Faye to Harvey. "That shows where *you* come from! Your ancestors probably fled a village pogrom on some frozen Russian steppe. This is 100 percent peasant soup! But I thought your people didn't eat pork."

"I *love* this soup," I chime in, though I've never given this soup much thought. "So that must make me a peasant too." I smile brightly. Faye and Calisto stare at me with their mouths agape and in that moment I realize I really do love the way the large white hominy—kernels for a giant—crunch so satisfyingly between my teeth. I also realize the discomfort in my jaw has miraculously vanished.

"I don't recognize you, Merryn," says Faye shortly. "You were always such a . . . nice, *quiet* girl. You're clearly not yourself."

A hot wind rises from the valley, jiggling the parasol and filling the air with powdery dust. Harvey covers his bowl with his hand. The dust coats my tongue and teeth.

No, I'm definitely not myself.

Faye asks with bright enthusiasm, "So, *did* Vivienne draft a new will?"

Calisto suddenly looks up, alert as a meerkat standing guard atop his burrow. Harvey looks across the table at Calisto and asks point-blank, in an equable tone, "Have you found a copy of a new will, Calisto? Anything in her papers up there?"

With a flourish, Calisto reaches into the back pocket of his skintight jeans and pulls out some folded papers that have curved to the shape of his rear. He leans across the table and offers the square of papers to Harvey, holding them between two fingers like a cigarette. "She made a new will," Caliso says with a condescending air. "And Bibienne told me I am essecutor of her estate."

I don't move an inch as the world goes black around the edges. Harvey slowly unfolds the sheets, plucks his slim reading glasses out of his breast pocket, puts them on, and begins to read. After two seconds he says, "This document is not signed."

"It is only a copy that Bibienne has gave to me," Calisto says.

I glance at Faye, whose vanilla-icing face seems to be glowing with fascination.

Harvey tosses the sheets in Calisto's direction. "Until a new will is produced that is signed by Vivienne and witnessed, I will remain the executor of her estate. In the United States of America we have what is known as a Dead Man's Clause, which means that the spoken words of a deceased person have no standing in a legal dispute. This document means nothing."

Calisto doesn't say anything but his brow furrows in concentration, his gaze unfocused. Then, turning to Faye, he delicately pinches between two fingers an errant strand of her pale hair that was dislodged by the recent gust of wind, and tucks it delicately behind her ear.

Harvey pushes his chair back, the metal screeching against the flagstones, and looks at his watch. "It's getting late." As he stands he adds, "We have to get to work, Merryn. It's been a lovely lunch. Calisto, until all of this is settled, I will have to ask you to vacate the premises."

Ever since Faye had her eye lift her shiny eyes have a slightly startled look, so it is difficult to tell, but she seems for a moment positively stunned into immobility.

Harvey goes to pull back Faye's chair. She resists, shaking him off, and remains firmly planted in her seat.

"No point wasting good champagne." Faye lifts Harvey's untouched flute by its delicate stem and upends it into her red mouth. "If you are no longer welcome here, my dear Calisto, you are entirely welcome to stay with me. I have a number of gorgeous guest rooms . . . In fact, you could practically have a whole floor to yourself."

"I will take the Mercedes," announces Calisto, rising elegantly to his feet. I see no reason to say no, if it will get him out of the house.

Finally Faye stands, a little unsteadily. Tenney runs ahead of them, across the patio toward the garage door. She opens it wide, steps aside to let them pass. They never look back, walking with their glassy eyes forward. Tenney closes the door behind them and starts to laugh into her hand.

"What a terrible woman," Harvey says, gazing at me somberly. He seems exhausted all at once, moves slowly as if his joints ache. "She's almost as mean as your mother. No wonder they were such good friends."

"Bibi only wanted the best for me. She wanted me to be happy." I don't even think about what I'm saying, the words fly out on their own.

"Look how well that turned out!" he counters bitterly. "Your mother turned you into a doormat." He shakes his head and sighs. "Based on the conversations I had with Vivienne, I'm quite certain she spoke to you the same way she spoke to me, so really, you don't need to defend her to me."

Feeling dizzy, I lean against one of the stone pillars, trying to relax my wooden face.

The sky is turning pink and lavender in the west . . . Yes, she isolated me. We lived an isolated life. I was afraid to look past the version of the world she presented to me. I see now that I lived as if under a totalitarian regime, a cowering slave in a cult of personality. But what do you do? What do you do when everything you once believed to be true is taken away?

"Let me try Agent Warnock again." Harvey hits some buttons on his phone and holds it to his ear, waiting, when the doorbell sounds.

We stare at each other. Tenney runs through the archway toward the front door and I yell for her to stop, but she disappears. A moment later she returns, her expression questioning. Standing just behind her with his hand grasping her shoulder is Ibrahim Ansari. He wears a gray sports jacket and an ascot tie. With him is another man, a muscular, scary-looking Arab in a dark suit. This must be his bodyguard. I have seen them before, lurking in the dark corners of banquet halls, listening to their earpieces and whispering into microphones.

Ibrahim squeezes Tenney's shoulder and she flinches. Harvey's face completely drains of color. He slips his phone into his pocket and places his left hand flat against his chest as if he is having heart pain.

"Harvey—" I say.

"I'm fine. Don't worry about me." His mouth is a tight, thin line.

"Merryn, darling!" calls Ibrahim Ansari, smiling brightly, arms wide, as he steps toward me and pulls me into a suffocating hug. "We thought we'd stop by and see how you are faring."

I forget how easy it is to travel when you're so rich you have your own plane.

Sophia is barking harshly behind our closed door. Out of the corner of my eyes I see that Tenney has slipped away, pressing herself into the wall, moving stealthily toward our bedroom between the pillars of the protected walkway. I force myself to keep my attention focused on Ibrahim, so he will ignore her. The bodyguard pushes his way past me. He trots on a boxer's light feet across the patio and through the French doors and into the great room. He steps out onto the terrace, gazing dispassionately at the view, then approaches the outside kitchen door, and my heart leaps into my throat. I know Marta is in there washing the lunch dishes. He leans in, apparently sees nothing out of the ordinary, and reenters the great room, nodding in silence.

Ibrahim takes me by the arm and guides me into the great room. "Where is everyone?" he asks, looking around as if he's arrived late for a party. The bodyguard closes the swinging kitchen door and stands in front of it with his arms behind his back, legs slightly spread. There's a weird bulge in his suit jacket. He has a gun.

"It's siesta time," I say, though really I have no idea what time it is. The sky in the east is already beginning to darken.

Harvey walks to the piano and leans on one elbow against the lid like a man listening to a player in a cabaret.

"This is my uncle Harvey," I say.

Harvey calmly watches the bodyguard, who looks around, eyes pausing here and there.

"This is Beau's friend Ibrahim Ansari," I say to Harvey.

"How do you do," says Harvey, not offering his hand. I realize, and am amazed, that Harvey is not afraid. He is old, but he is not afraid, and Ibrahim seems to sense this.

"Merryn," says Ibrahim, going toward the bar. He looks at

the bottles, picks a Chivas with a silver label, and pours a generous shot into a glass. "What is going on? The office tells me that all day no package is arriving from Mexico. Did you use DHL like I told you?"

"I didn't write the check," I respond. "I've never signed checks for Beau's organization before, and Beau—"

"Beau was foolish," says Ibrahim, his voice going suddenly quite cold. I glance at the bodyguard, whose eyes seem impassive and disinterested as he watches us. "But you see, a great deal of my money was entrusted to Beau and I must get it back. The money in the Bootsraps account is nothing—a mere pittance."

"I counseled Merryn not to write the check," Harvey replies with bold calm. "I'm her uncle but I am also her lawyer."

"Then you are a foolish man as well. Where is this checkbook?"

"I don't have it," I say quickly.

"Beau said you were not a threat. That you were quiet as a lamb. Are you quiet as a lamb, Merryn?"

"The checkbook is in Dallas," I state. "I don't have it."

He comes toward me, but Harvey steps in front of him. In my peripheral vision I see Tenney standing in the doorway, a white blur at her feet. The bodyguard grasps Harvey by the shoulders and literally lifts him aside.

"Then you and the child will be coming with us back to Dallas," says Ibrahim, reaching for my left wrist and squeezing it in a viselike grip. "Where is the rest of the money, Merryn?"

In a flash Sophia is upon him, growling like a pit bull as her jaws clamp down on his ankle. Ibrahim shouts and the bodyguard kicks Sophia like a ball so that she flies through the air and lands hard against a plush armchair, rolls once, and gets back on her feet, charges Ibrahim again, growling furiously as she tries to take hold of him.

Marta pushes the kitchen door open and freezes there, her

mouth in an O. The bodyguard pulls out his gun and aims it at Sophia.

"Stop! Sophia!" I shout.

"Stop!" Tenney throws herself over the dog.

"I *hate* dogs," mutters Ansari.

At once I hear that wild drumbeat in my head as my vision grows dark around the edges, as if I'm in a tunnel of some kind.

"I am not going anywhere with you!" I yell, my whole body prickling with adrenaline as I try to break free of Ibrahim's grasp. "I won't be pushed around by you. You have no right. You have no right!" Suddenly I remember a move I learned in a self-defense class fifteen years ago at the West Side YMCA, and as if on autopilot, my right hand clenches into a fist and the ridge of my hand makes hard contact with Ansari's nose. He shouts something in Arabic and lets go of me to grab hold of his nose. The bodyguard steps in and, with one little hooking movement, knocks my legs out from under me. In a moment, Harvey is kneeling beside me on the tile floor, trying to help me up.

Harvey seems so small beside this bodyguard with his muscle-bound arms and thick neck. "You people have no class at all. No class at all."

Ansari presses a silk handkerchief to his bleeding nose.

"All right," I say, out of breath as if I've run ten miles, "I'll go with you. But leave my child out of this. Leave her here with Harvey and I'll go with you."

"Do not consider calling the police," warns Ansari, gazing at Harvey as he lifts the rocks glass of Chivas and pours the scotch into his mouth.

With Ibrahim on one side and the bodyguard on the other, I feel my knees buckling as they press me forward. The bodyguard opens the front door of the house. A shiny black SUV with tinted windows idles in the street just beyond the door.

The street is suddenly ablaze with sirens, red lights flash-ing. *Federales* standing in the flatbed of a truck wearing helmets, their faces covered by black cloth, point their assault rifles at us. Agent Warnock in her dark blue pantsuit runs across the street. Agent Athas, in a black T-shirt and jeans, appears out of no-where and points a sidearm at the bodyguard's temple.

"Don't even think about moving," he says through gritted teeth. "Because I really feel like shooting you right now."

"You, sir, are under arrest," Agent Warnock says to Ibrahim Ansari in a perfectly conversational tone.

In less than five minutes Ansari and his bodyguard and chauffeur are taken away in plastic handcuffs, the black SUV has been driven off, and Agent Warnock guides me back through the darkening house to the great room, where my family waits for me in a strangely peaceful silence. Sophia lies on her side, panting, on Tenney's lap. Harvey goes to the bar and takes a long swig from the mouth of the Chivas bottle.

"My God, Merryn," he says hoarsely, "I haven't had so much excitement since I hung out in San Miguel with Ken Kesey."

"I could use a drink myself," Agent Warnock says. "But I'm still on the job."

"Madam," says Harvey, "if I may—you people really do have a lot of nerve, using my client as bait."

I slide down to the floor with my back pressed to the wall of glass.

"We knew they were landing at Guanajuato-León Airport. We've been tailing them. We got the whole thing on tape. Every-one hates the feds, but *someone* has to catch the bad guys. And trust me, the richer they are, the harder they are to catch. It's a very satisfying occupation. Now let me check on that dog. I was an army medic in my former life." Agent Warnock crouches be-

fore the child and the dog and with sure and gentle hands, begins to palpate Sophia's abdomen and rib cage.

"Ah, she has some pain here, maybe a bruised rib, but nothing too serious." She checks Sophia's back legs, bending them
in and out. "Good news: nothing broken on this doggie here."
Then she says to Tenney in a low voice, "You remind me of myself when I was your age. I was always alone, or with my dad. He
was a criminal investigations agent with the IRS. You can beat
that wily detective at chess. You have the right kind of approach,
but you're very young and you lose your focus more easily than
adults. Use that to your advantage. Trick him."

"Hmmm," says Tenney.

Then, all at once, Special Agent Warnock stands, wipes her
palms on her suit pants, and walks toward me. I stand on shaky
legs. "Well then," she says in a formal, businesslike tone, "the
US attorney will be in touch."

"W-what?"

"I'm heading to the airport. Gotta get Ansari back to Dallas.
Lots to do. Lots of paperwork to take care of. We'll be in touch."

"But . . . but . . . you're just . . . going to leave us here?"

"Leave you here?" she echoes, as if confused.

"But . . . things aren't . . . resolved yet with the . . . police."

"My job here is done," she says, and puts out her hand for a
formal, no-nonsense shake.

CHAPTER NINETEEN

CALISTO APPARENTLY SLEPT AT FAYE'S HOUSE. He did not return last night, and his clothes are still upstairs in the guest room closet.

This morning I let Tenney go back to the Garza School. Things have to seem normal for her, whether they are normal or not. Allegra took her down by cab and Harvey and I went up to Bibi's master suite to look for documents. Of course, Calisto has already conducted his own thorough search and if he didn't find anything, neither would we. The walk-in closet was flung wide open and from it wafted a ghost of Bibi's sharp Mademoiselle perfume, stopping me in my tracks. Her elegant porcelain face gazed down at us from the walls, black-and-white close-ups of Bibi in her youth. I realized with a strange shudder that I hadn't breathed a whiff of Beau's Clive Christian cologne in five days.

Bibi's bedroom and little study alcove looked like a disaster area, as if a tornado had passed through—sheets and blankets in a tumble on the king-size bed, empty beer and tequila bottles and glasses, ashtrays overflowing, the file cabinet open and papers and letters scattered everywhere. Harvey and I looked through them but did not find anything pertaining to a new will.

We returned to the kitchen and he asked Marta to call a locksmith to change the locks on the front door. The locksmith told Marta on the phone that he would be here *ahorita*—right now—which, Marta explained, could mean anything from today to next week.

Back at the dining table in the great room, I'm overtaken by a spell of dizziness, so Harvey escorts me across the patio to my room. Maybe I drank too much coffee.

"This has been an incredibly stressful few days," he says, "why don't you lie down for a bit?" In a while he will be going downtown to talk to the lawyer, Ignacio Suarez-Potts, and we will know whether or not I'm destitute.

I enter the bathroom and run the sink's tap, cupping handfuls of cold water to my face. In the mirror above the sink, I stare at my reflection. Dark crescents surround my eyes. *Who the fuck are you?* I ask her, or she asks me.

And what happened that day when Mum fell, and why can't I remember?

I turn away and enter the dark bedroom, where I collapse facedown on the bed and sink into a kind of deep darkness.

I find myself in our Dallas living room, where a gigantic aquarium stands on some kind of dais, illuminated by a fluorescent bulb inside the lid. The water in the aquarium is opaque and green. Why is there an aquarium here? I've never had an aquarium, or wanted an aquarium. I approach and peer into the murky tank. A shadow, a black finlike shape, passes close to the glass, something large and dark slithering in the water. The disturbed water splashes over the top, causing the protective lid to jump, and I recoil. What if the lid isn't heavy enough and the thing leaps out? Who feeds it? Should I try to feed it? What does it eat? Should I try to flush it down the toilet? The tank is much too big to empty by myself. And anyway, I don't want to see what's inside. Maybe if I just leave it, it will eventually starve to death. But this too feels wrong, cruel. I'll know it's in there even if I try not to think about it. Unable to decide, I wait for someone to come and tell me what to do. But no one comes. I feel guilty. It's not this thing's fault that it has to live in a green, murky tank, utterly neglected. It is not tame. I continue to wait. I look at the kitchen wall clock: 3:07 a.m. *Oh*, I think, *I'm in the anger meridian.*

I come to suddenly, to find Sophia licking my face. Emerging from the depths, I turn toward the digital clock. It's 12:55 p.m. I'm going to be late to pick up Tenney at Parque Juárez. Did Sophia somehow know this? Or did she sense I was having a nightmare?

"Good girl," I mumble, throwing my feet over the side of the bed and slipping into my fisherman's sandals. I grab my purse and run out the door. On the corner of Cuesta de San Jose I wave down a cab. We make it to the corner of Aldama and Diezmo Viejo, the northwest entrance of Parque Juárez, by a quarter after one.

I run to the basketball courts, approaching from the upper path. The two viejos are kicking back in the second row of cement bleachers, drinking Dos Equis beers. Señor Garza is behind them, on the third step, looking a little scandalized at their casual demeanor. A number of spectators pepper the cement benches, immersed in the match. Tenney's skinny legs are tucked beneath her, her feet in pink sneakers hanging off the back of the folding chair. She looks so small. I climb down the steps and sit beside Señor Garza, who squeezes my hand.

Tenney stares at the chess clock; I gather she's running out of time to make her move. Sanchez-Berilla is stone-faced under the brim of his hat.

The viejos acknowledge me with quick nods as they light filterless, strong-smelling cigarettes. Tenney makes her move and slaps the button on the top of the clock. Sanchez-Berilla only takes two minutes to counter, sliding his queen all the way across the board. There is a slight shift, a murmur passing like a draft through the audience. Tenney seems unperturbed. She calmly looks over her options.

My little girl scratches at a mosquito bite on her arm, such a childlike gesture, yet she's playing chess against this silver-haired adult who terrifies me. She promised, win or lose, this would be the last match.

Sanchez-Berilla looks up from beneath his hat, his black eyes focused on me as I sit wearing what I hope is a passive, neutral air. In my mind I'm thinking, *I hope she trounces you, you son of a bitch.* This must be anger I'm feeling—this hot, uncomfortable thing slithering up from my core. Should I get up and stand by my daughter's side? I start to rise, but Ernesto Garza gently presses down on my hand.

After what seems an interminable time, Tenney slides her own queen forward and hits the button. Sanchez-Berilla frowns, surprised. He takes many minutes to decide his next move. When he hits the clock button, Tenney rapidly once again moves her queen and says, "Check."

"Ay, dios mio," mutters Sanchez-Berilla, and in front of us the two viejos start cackling and stomping their feet. One of them says, "That nephew of mine, thirty years and *nunca—nunca he ganado*—I have never won."

The detective's next move seems indecisive, but he finally lifts his hand off his bishop.

Tenney moves quickly. "Check mate," she says.

The audience breaks into applause. Detective Sanchez-Berilla accepts his loss with alacrity, laying down his king. Out of his pocket he pulls a billfold and riffles through it until he finds a 200-peso note, which he slides across the board to Tenney. She takes the bill, then extends her small, white mosquito-bitten hand and he offers his strong, large, muscular, hairy dark one.

Detective Sanchez-Berilla turns toward me and for a long,

silent moment, seems to size me up. I return his look impassively, realizing I haven't washed my face or brushed my hair and am still dressed in the gray linen shift I wore this morning. I approach the chess table, trying to still my frantic heart.

He takes me by the elbow and walks me a few paces away. Tenney follows us with her eyes.

"Your daughter is very intelligent," says the detective.

"Yes," I say.

"And you, you got along with your mother?" he asks suddenly.

"We had a perfect life. I had a wonderful childhood. Bibi was a wonderful woman. Everybody loved her."

"I ask because of the loud voices arguing on the terrace at four p.m. in the afternoon on the day your mother falls to her death."

"I think the neighbor was mistaken. Bibi was probably on the phone."

"Well, perhaps," he allows. I don't respond. Then he says, "Your niña, she says at first that she was with you the whole time, asleeping. Then, she says she went upstairs to her abuela's room to find a toy and came back down and finds you on the terrace. What do you think of this?"

"I think your tactics are unjust. Like your chess game. She's only a little girl." A drop of sweat trickles slowly down my spine. We're coming up on the hottest part of the day and the sun is beating down fiercely on the unshaded areas of the park. My mouth is dry, my tongue stiff. My heart feels suddenly heavy, as if it is having a hard time pumping blood through my system. "In America it is illegal to question a minor without a parent present."

"Ah, but this is not America. In any case, we were just talking. Chattering, as you say."

"I am going to speak to my lawyer about this. I don't think

this is right." I feel as if I'm regaining my footing now.

"We will conversate another time, yes?" He puts his hand out, as if to guide me back toward the group gathered around the chess table, but I don't want him to touch me, to feel me sweating, trembling, so I step ahead of him. Tenney is still at the table, her worried eyes focused on me.

A moment of blankness, a feeling of displacement, overcomes me. I am not sure how we've ended up here but Tenney and I are walking along a wide path in some unknown corner of the park. On both sides loom enormous Mexican elms with deeply fluted gray trunks and vast root systems, the greenery dark and impenetrable. Egrets roost in the tall trees, their croaking cries wild and tropical, like the jungle in Cameroon. At the first shady bench, I drop down and breathe into my cupped hands.

"Mom," Tenney whispers close to my ear, "there's something I need to tell you. Dad said not to tell you unless we were in serious trouble. I think we're in serious trouble now."

"What is it, Tenney?"

"I have the e-mail address and user name for the eCoin account."

I turn my face toward her, inches away from her tawny eyes. In the sunlight the specks of gold in her irises seem even brighter. "What are you saying, Tenney?" I whisper.

"Dad told me." Her voice is barely a murmur. "He made me repeat them back, like, ten times. He said you'd have the password."

"Oh my God, Tenney. Have you told anyone this?"

"Of course not," she snorts, as if I'm silly.

Above us, in a wild crescendo of croaks and cries and flapping wings, the roosting egrets take flight, a white tornado rising in the pale blue sky.

"Come, quickly." I take her hand and pull her to her feet.

We hurry along the path amidst the huge elms, and practically run through a pair of painted, earth-red pillars at the corner of the park. We cross an ancient square where aged cement public laundry basins are lined at a right angle against two walls. I lead Tenney on a circuitous route through the old and elegant neighborhood, Spanish colonial houses painted that deep, earthy red, flowering purple vines cascading down their outer walls, through the narrow twisting streets, back toward the north end of town and the dark little Internet café on Hidalgo.

This time there is no one inside; we have the place to ourselves. I pay the thirty pesos to the bored attendant and sit down with Tenney at a different computer in the back row.

I type in the website name: *eCoins.com*

Whispering, I ask, "What's the e-mail address, Tenney?"

Standing beside me she leans in, her breath hot and warm against my ear: "sumpter1861@gmail.com."

"And the user name?"

"100meteryacht."

Now the password. The password requires at least one number and one uppercase letter, no spaces.

That day on the beach in Grand Cayman he said, "I'm going to buy us a yacht as big as a cruise ship. That's when you know you've made it. When you have your own hundred-meter yacht." And then he added in a strange voice that made me think he was perhaps a little insane, "Always remember this: ten steps ahead. That's the secret."

He might have put the uppercase letter in the middle, but that would not be Beau's style. He would choose the most obvious and the easiest, because he did not think very highly of my reasoning capabilities. That would be his way. With trembling fingers, I type: *10Stepsahead.*

I have to answer three security questions, which I realize

immediately he designed especially for me. *Wedding date, birth of first child, name of first pet.* We never had a pet. Beau was allergic to animal hair.

I remember suddenly that I once told Beau about Arsène. We had grown so distant in the past few years, the man I had come to know was not someone with whom I would have normally shared this painful story. But we had tried to be close, once. Lying in bed after making love, perhaps this was even the night Tenney was conceived, in the dark, he told me about his failed first marriage. He told me his wife left him for a much richer man—a cattle baron. Beau said he would never get divorced again. Feeling closer to him than I ever had before, I told him about running into the French couple on the Pont Neuf, and how I'd become so depressed I'd wanted to kill myself. This exchange echoes in my mind now like the pleasant ringing of a distant bell.

Staring at the computer screen in the dark Internet café, I type: *Arsene Lupin.*

The account opens. It contains 210,000 eCoins. Tenney, standing beside me, gripping my shoulder, gasps.

"All this carrying-on for only 210,000 dollars?" I mumble, astounded.

"Mom," she replies impatiently, "look here," pointing. *"One eCoin is worth $199.67.* That's . . ." she takes a moment to figure it out in her head. "$41,930,700."

I stare at the screen, unable to assimilate this information. And I have absolutely no idea what to do.

Just as we reach Bibi's house the front door opens and the locksmith in blue overalls steps out into the street, carrying a heavy and ancient-looking leather tool kit. Behind him is Marta; she hands me a new key.

We walk through the archway into the patio, bright light to darkness, to light again. Harvey is on the balcony, leaning against the balustrade, a black silhouette against the white dome of the sky. He gazes down on the city baking in the dust and the heavy midday heat. Tenney goes into our room and I hear her talking to Sophia and the puppies in her high-pitched, little-girl voice.

"I talked to Suarez-Potts," Harvey says as I approach. My eyes ache. "Vivienne apparently did go to him and he drafted a new will for her, in which she made Calisto her executor, and in which she left him the house and what's left of the money, which is not much. But she never signed it. She kept putting it off, then Suarez-Potts went on vacation. She must have realized her mistake." He pats my arm, as if to reassure me. "It's all yours, Merryn. As it should be."

It's yours by accident, I tell myself. This could have gone either way. This morning I had nothing but the cash in Blueberry's battery compartment. Now I'm suddenly rich.

$41,930,700 worth of eCoins in a hidden account. Opium money. Beau must have known about the opium, or he turned a blind eye to it. I doubt he ever even considered that Ibrahim might be funding extremists. But then, Beau came from a family who'd once owned slaves. Denial on this scale takes a lot of work. I should know.

Or maybe Beau did know and that is why he pulled the money out of the Caymans. Maybe he found out. Or maybe this is only a fraction of the total sum.

On the way back up the mountain from the Internet café, Tenney was thinking, counting, her lips moving as she mumbled to herself. Then she said, looking up at me with feverish eyes, "We could buy enough polio vaccines for an entire country. Millions of polio vaccines . . . We could build a children's hospital!"

"But it's not our money, Tenney," I said.

"Do you know how much a hundred-meter yacht costs, Mom? Do you? I did an Internet search. Two hundred million dollars! There's even one owned by some sheik that has a jewel-encrusted steering wheel! You think that's *their* money? You think they *earned* it?" She was furious now, her eyes ablaze.

I laid my hand on her shoulder. She shook me off and marched on up ahead. *She's right*, I thought. *No one needs a diamond-encrusted steering wheel on their $200 million yacht.*

". . . And I also talked to the US attorney in Dallas," Harvey is saying. "There's still some negotiating to be done, but they're going to offer you immunity in exchange for your testimony. Isn't that good news?"

I drop into one of the canvas armchairs in the shade of the balcony's overhanging archway. Beyond the balcony the sun crashes down on the city and burns behind my closed eyelids.

"Merryn, are you all right? You've gone suddenly pale," says Harvey. "I'll get some limonada." He hurries off toward the kitchen. In a minute, he's back carrying a glass. I drink it down and the limonada is so cold it feels solid going down my throat.

It looks like I'm going to have to keep on lying for a long time to come.

After comida, Harvey heads downstairs for a nap and Tenney and I stretch out on our king-size bed. Sophia jumps up and settles between us. She presses her spine up against my stomach and I scratch her chest. She flips over onto her back, lifting her front paws, her eyes dreamy with delight.

A furious ringing of the outside bell disturbs the hot afternoon. Tenney doesn't move; she must be asleep. I go to answer it, realizing as I run barefoot through the patio that I'm a disheveled mess, still wearing my linen dress from this morning.

I open the door to find Calisto standing there, the Mercedes idling behind him in the middle of the street.

"I come for my things," he says. Calisto doesn't appear to be any angrier than usual, so I go back inside and press the garage door buzzer and let him drive the car in. I follow him upstairs. Allegra has been up to clean and Bibi's white room seems alien and strange. Calisto walks down the hall and into the guest bed-room. He flings open the closet and begins throwing his clothes onto the bed. Then he stops, stands still, as if at a loss. All these expensive clothes must be new, I think, accrued while he lived here with Bibi. He glances around, seems to realize he doesn't have a bag or suitcase to put them in.

His face, for the first time since I've known him, loses its superior smirk and he looks like a lost child. If Bibi had signed the new will, I'm sure Calisto would have thrown us out in the street without a moment's hesitation. But right now I don't feel victorious.

"Bibi must have suitcases somewhere you can borrow."

He nods once, mutters, "Suitcases," and returns to Bibi's room. He throws open her enormous walk-in closet and that ghostly whiff of Mademoiselle perfume knocks me backward into the edge of the bed. Stacked on narrow shelves on one side of the closet from floor to ceiling are hundreds of pairs of San Miguel shoes in different color combinations. Calisto snorts and shakes his head. "My mother lives in a shack of bricks with a tin roof, two rooms. No toilets. The walls do not even have paint."

Up above on a top shelf are her Vuitton suitcases, her "trou-seau" gift from her daddy. Calisto picks a couple at random and throws them on the floor. He drops, almost collapsing, onto the one with a hard frame. He pulls out a pack of Marlboros and lights a cigarette. Hunched over, legs wide apart, he smokes like a campesino sitting on a stoop on market day, watching the world go by. Now I understand his self-centered greed. It was not born of arrogance and entitlement, but of fear and want and, yes, of resentment.

"Would you like to keep the car, Calisto?"

His head snaps back in surprise. "You are saying I can keep the Mercedes?"

"You seem to be attached to it. We need to find the deed so I can sign it over to you. You'll have to deal with the insurance. I don't know how that works in Mexico. But I will pay Bibi's insurance for the next few months, until you get that straightened out."

A long silence.

"Do you have anyplace to go besides Faye's house?" I ask him.

"You . . . you Americans. There are ten people living in my mother's shack. You think it is easy for me to learn English? Learning to dress good? My family, they live like animals. They have nothing."

Alberto said, *If good cannot come of bad things, then what is the point of life?*

"How much money would you need to get your own place, to start your own life? A business, maybe?"

He stares at me, his eyes full of suspicion and defiance. "Why you would help me? You have no reason to help me."

"My mother would have wanted me to help you."

Calisto's mouth twists downward at my words. "Your mother was . . ." His eyes glaze over and for a moment I fear he's going to start crying. He grabs fistfuls of the hay-like hair on each side of his temples, the cigarette smoldering between his fingers, and gazes up at a luminous photograph of young Vivienne, her white, flawless neck extended, her dark eyes and hair shining. "Your mother, every day she was changing her mind, *I give you this money, I don't give you this money*. She had me swinging from a stick like a toy for a cat." In a low voice he adds, "Your mother was . . . a cunt."

I gasp; he gasps. Wide-eyed, we glance nervously around like children who accidentally lit a box of matches on fire. Vivienne stares down at us from the walls. The harder I try to protest, to object, the stronger the nervous urge to laugh grows, rising from my chest until I'm snorting out my nose and Calisto is practically bent over double, holding his stomach while smoke roils out of his nose.

Finally we regain our composure. I swipe at my eyes with the back of my hand. He tamps out his cigarette in a bedside ashtray.

"You will have all the money you need," I tell him. "No se preocupa."

He pulls himself up off the suitcase and squares his shoulders, smoothes his designer jeans. "I will start a car service," he says. "I am very good with cars and old American ladies. I will find out exactly how much I need and you will be my business partner. Now, I am going to see my novia. I am going to ask her to marry me. I am bringing her good news today, no?"

Calisto bows low, like a Spanish *caballero*, and backs out the door, leaving his clothes behind.

Harvey, Tenney, and I are watching CNN in the great room. The profligate murdering mother from New Mexico has been acquitted by a jury of her peers and a major New York publisher has offered her an undisclosed seven-figure sum for her story. The entire world seems to be in a red fury and on the screen people are apoplectic and screaming at each other.

Tenney has fallen asleep with her head on my lap and Harvey's eyes are at half-mast though he's sitting upright with his feet on an ottoman. I wake him and walk him to the stairs, then carry sleeping Tenney into our bedroom and pull down the silver bedspread and tuck her in, leaving on the bathroom light. Sophia and I head out through the dark patio for her last walk. As I unlatch the front door, I hear a motorcycle roaring up Cuesta de San Jose. Damn my heart. I used to have such self-control. I could do anything and feel no emotion.

In a moment, a single headlight appears around the corner and grows larger as it jiggles its way up the street. Dr. Steve pulls to a stop in front of the door and sets one boot on the sidewalk. He removes his helmet and runs a hand through his dark hair. "I know it's late. I've been thinking about you all day. I haven't heard from you and I . . ." His voice trails off.

"I'm taking Sophia for her walk." The dog paws at his knee. He reaches down and scratches her ears.

He turns off the engine and sets his helmet on the seat. Together we amble up the middle of the deserted street toward the Charco, our footing unsteady on the rounded cobblestones. He takes my hand and the warmth of him travels up my arm and into my chest. "A lot of talk in town today about the take-down. How are you doing?"

"I'm glad it's over. I had nothing to do with any of it."

This much, at least, is true.

When we reach the end of the row of houses, I turn and gaze at the city spread out below us. The stars glow palely across the great dome of the sky, and bits of mica in the road glint brightly, giving the impression of a mirror to the sky. The flat-roofed houses lining the street are like dark steps descending the mountainside. A few yellow lights twinkle peacefully in the valley, the mountains guarding us like sleeping giants curled up on their sides.

Dr. Steve steps behind me and presses me to his chest, crossing his arms over my shoulders. I can feel his lungs expanding and contracting. Sophia's tail thumps gently against my calf, and I think, *Don't trust this. You can't even tell a lie from the truth.* I can feel my heart pumping hard and wonder if he can feel it through my skin.

"Faye called me. Apparently Calisto told her to go to hell." At this, he laughs in amazement, with childish delight. "Faye was furious. She said Vivienne never got around to signing the new will and Calisto gets nothing, but Calisto told her you offered to give him money to start a business, which turned him 'all uppity'—in her words. That's an amazing thing to do. Not many people would do that." He runs his smooth, warm palm from the crook of my neck to the end of my shoulder, a balm to my aching muscles. A cool wind flows past us on its way down the mountainside, raising a cloud of fine dust that I can feel on my tongue and teeth, and I hear Bibi's voice in my ear, carried on its current, *She surely isn't the first rich American lady to be seduced by your Doctor Handsome.*

Dr. Steve's face is a black silhouette in the darkness.

"Why should *they* have the right to treat people like slaves?" I say. "What did they ever do in their lives to have the right to treat people like that? And the worst part is, we convince ourselves that we're free when we're not free at all."

He takes a step back, as if I've physically pushed him away.

"I'm sorry," I say, "I was talking about myself. Not you."

He takes my hand, and we head down the deserted street, Sophia trotting ahead, watchful and alert. When we reach Bibi's front door, Steve leans in and kisses me gently on the lips.

"You're right," he says simply, with no fanfare, no open question at the end, no demand for a response. "I keep pretending that it isn't so, but it is. Fucking for money is fucking for money, no matter what you call it."

"But we've all done that, one way or another," I say. "And I for one am just not going to do it anymore."

CHAPTER
TWENTY

I STEP OUT OF THE MARKET on Homobono after dropping
Tenney at the Garza School and find Detective Sanchez-Berilla
waiting for me, wearing white athletic shoes and a dark suit.
It is just past nine a.m. and the streets are abuzz with activity, as
if people are hurrying to get everything done before the heat of
the day sets in. Behind the detective a dusty black car idles in the
middle of the narrow street, coughing out dark, noxious fumes.
About five vehicles wait patiently behind it, no one honking,
which is a little scary here in San Miguel; they must all know, or
at least sense, that he is someone important who can do things
like this with impunity.

"Please, come with me," he says evenly.

I am certain I am going to be arrested. I look around for other
policemen, but we are alone. He holds his arm out, indicating
the passenger seat. For about three seconds I consider calling
Harvey Berger, who is feeling bruised and exhausted and resting
at home. But that would probably seem to Sanchez-Berilla like a
guilty act, a hostile response. The detective trots over, opens the
door, and holds it for me; I settle in with my mesh bag of apples
and manchego cheese wrapped in wax paper. He drives north
into the valley, past what I think of as the edge of town because
from here on out the houses are not crowded together, side by
side, but spread apart, and there is more dust and potholes and
vegetation. We cross a narrow bridge over a creek that is barely

a rivulet this time of year. Once again he parks at the edge of the sidewalk where no one else would dream of parking and gets out, not even bothering to lock the door.

"Come, I wish to show you something," he says in a friendly manner, and with that he disappears into a space in the shrubbery and starts climbing up the steep mountainside. I follow him up the narrow, pebble- and rock-strewn path. The sun is still fairly low, just having peeked its head above the mountains. It's a hard climb and I'm sweating, though the landscape on this side of the mountain remains in shadow, dark and cool.

We climb for fifteen or twenty minutes, and when the path cuts into the steep rock face, Detective Sanchez-Berilla reaches out and grasps my elbow. He holds me steady as I step on uneven ground, rocks sliding out under my fisherman's sandals. The land is wild here, dry and weedy, with mesquite and cacti all around. In the east the mountains glow brightly in the fresh morning sun. We keep on climbing, giving a wide berth to an enormous cactus with needles as long as my little finger, our breaths heavy in the thin air.

Finally we reach an outcropping, a flat plane the size of a baseball diamond. Detective Sanchez-Berilla is not as out of breath as I am, probably because his body is long-adapted to this altitude. He stops and gazes down into the canyon, where the river and the reservoir lie in the deep blue shadow of the mountains across the divide. I realize with a start that we are standing across the ravine from Balcones, and I can see Bibi's red house perched on the edge of the mountainside among its neighbors, its retaining wall of blond stone gleaming in the golden light. The flat land shelf two hundred feet below the house cuts through the greenery like a pale, horizontal scar. That is where she fell and where she lay broken. And still, even here, I feel nothing.

"I like to walk here," he says. "I like to clear my head after thinking too much during the days."

I don't say anything.

"Many people walk here in the afternoons," he adds.

If he had something, we would not be standing here. We would be down at the police station.

"That is a beautiful house," he muses. "How much is a house like that worth, do you think?"

"I have no idea. But I will know soon since we intend to sell it. Why? Are you interested in buying it?"

He laughs, a little snort of air. "Ah, no." He shakes his head, then gazes off across the canyon like Gatsby looking over the bay toward Daisy's green dock light. "I remember when there was no houses here. Now there are so many I am worrying about the water. Where will the water come from?"

"Yes," I reply hollowly, "I worry about the water too."

"Calisto Rivera was with his novia," he says, as if this is a perfectly reasonable progression in our exchange. "There are three other witnesses. And anyway, I am told he is not the one who will inherit your mother's estate."

"Well, that was not known until yesterday, when Señor Suarez-Potts returned from his vacation."

He turns his dark eyes to me and, with that penetrating gaze, asks quietly, "You do not like the vividor and yet you are giving him money for a business. Why is this?"

"Because he deserves it, after all the shit he put up with."

"What . . . *shit*? You did not love your mother?"

"That is the wrong question. Did I like the way she behaved? No. She cared only for herself. People like her will destroy this place."

"Interesting perspective." He nods with a certain solemnity.

"My mother held people hostage. I don't know what you

want me to tell you. If you are asking me if I miss her, no. I do not miss her."

He doesn't respond, just stares out across the deep gorge with a contemplative expression.

"I don't know what you want from me," I say. "You need to close this investigation so we can all move on."

"Ernesto Garza, the husband of my deceased cousin, God rest her soul, is—how do you say in English?—a little *enamorado* of you. I fear he is going to ask for your hand in marriage. I do not want you to break his heart."

"Señor Garza is one of the kindest people I've ever met. He is my friend. But I will never marry again."

"Perhaps I should warn him before he . . . makes an embarrassment of himself. So. What will you do, now?"

"My daughter and I intend to stay in San Miguel. I'm going to help Dr. Fuller build his children's hospital, and I'm going to work with Alberto Zaldaña in his center for abused women and children. If good cannot come of bad things, Señor Sanchez-Berilla, then what is the point of life?"

"Ah," he says, nodding. "Then let us go."

EPILOGUE

WE HAVE BEEN WALKING for three days on a rocky, unpaved path along the side of the two-lane highway. The air is crisp and cool but the winter sun is bright and there has been no rain. The sky is a ringing blue, with a few puffy clouds sailing by on the wind. Today is the last day for Tenney and me; we will be picked up by a bus and driven back to San Miguel, but most of the pilgrims will continue on for six more days, to the church of Our Lady of San Juan de los Lagos in Jalisco. Alberto Zaldaña will walk the whole way, as he has every year since he came to San Miguel.

The San Juan de los Lagos pilgrimage takes nine days on foot from San Miguel, across the campo's rocky terrain. Three days ago, seven thousand people of all ages gathered in front of the parroquia and headed out together. The streets were lined with clapping and cheering well-wishers, handing out oranges, water, and juice. Tenney and I are walking to help raise money for Alberto's program against domestic violence. We are raising money for every kilometer we walk, with Alberto and the Mexican teenagers and their mothers who have sought help at the center, and several other American women volunteers. Tenney loves the center; she spends her afternoons there doing her homework while I volunteer, teaching the children English. Just a few months ago Alberto's organization received a very big donation from an anonymous source, but he still insists on leading his group on the pilgrimage.

All day long the pilgrims sing and pray. *Santa María, Madre de Dios, ruega por nosotros, pecadores* . . . There are entire families of believers, even young children, who intend to walk the whole nine days, to stand in the church before a little sugar-cane paste statue of *La Virgen* which is more than four hundred years old. It is said that after this long and grueling journey, whatever you ask of La Virgen will be granted.

The sun sinks behind the mountains, casting an orange glow over the rugged terrain. Tenney loves the campsites at night, the fires burning in oil drums, the singing and the music, strangers bonded by the single desire to reach their destination. It is like an endless holiday.

In front of me, Alberto pauses and breathes deeply into his abdomen, advising others to do the same. He offers a child water from a large plastic bottle that he carries in a side pocket of his weighty backpack. The path is littered with rocks and there seems to be no end to the journey, only the rhythmic sound of thousands of feet walking and the rough wind blowing through the mesquite and cacti. I stumble over a stone and Tenney grabs my arm.

"Mom," she says, "can we keep going all the way to Jalisco?"

Alberto turns his head and smiles at us. "There is plenty of food. I hope you did not think it would be easy to be my friend."

I am out of breath, but not from nerves. My lungs have not seized up in eight months. What does Tenney want to ask La Virgen?

I've walked away scot-free. Bucky took a plea, though he had little to offer besides the empty Grand Cayman account. He insisted he knew nothing about Ansari funding extremists. He got fifteen years in federal prison, but it's not a bad one, as far as prisons go. He even gets to play tennis, I hear. Ibrahim Ansari was swallowed up by the NSA machine. In the end I didn't even need to testify.

"Please, Mom. Can we?" Tenney glares at me. She wants an answer. She looks so healthy, has grown two inches and gained seven pounds in eight months.

"We'll have to send a message back to Steve," I say. "He'll worry otherwise." *Doctor Handsome, who can't keep his pants on,* is rich, though he says he has no idea where the money came from. One morning, there it was in his bank account. He's building a brand-new children's clinic and I tell him jokingly that all that sex with the old ladies must have paid off. At least now, this makes him laugh.

I crouch before my child. "It's a long way to Jalisco. It's six more days."

"I know. But I want to keep going."

"Is something wrong? What do you want to ask the statue, Tenney?"

In the last six months we have electronically funneled millions upon millions to help organizations in war-torn areas of the world, yet she is still restless, dissatisfied. It is never enough.

She whispers urgently in my ear, "I want to know what happened to Bibi."

For a few seconds I gaze steadily into my daughter's gold-flecked eyes. "Bibi was drunk. Her foot caught in the hem of her dressing gown and she lost her balance. I couldn't get to her in time."

Tenney's face glows in the waning light. "You'll never lie to me, Mommy? Never?"

"Never."

She throws her arms around my neck and says, "La Virgen already gave me my wish. But can we still keep walking?"

"Yes. Of course."

* * *

Sometimes I dream of that day. The red-tailed hawk passed so close he seemed to be looking at us, his keen golden eyes appraising. For a moment I floated off on his black-tipped wings, and down below I saw the terrace bathed in yellow light. On the wrought-iron table's glass top, the sweating ice bucket, the tequila bottle, the tonic, her purse, her phone. Her cigarettes, her lighter. Her ashtray lying on the coping of the low retaining wall as she sat, rocking slightly, over the abyss.

I talked to Harvey Berger and I'm suing you for custody of Tenney.

A punch to the solar plexus, catapulting me back into my body. I couldn't breathe. She looked at me with a petulant smirk, as if she felt entirely justified in her actions. Hot blood flooded my head. I could hear it pulsing like some wild tribal drum behind my eyes. She stood, as if the matter were now closed, but the pointy heel of her slipper caught in the hem of her gown. As she tried to untangle her foot I noticed, almost clinically, that she was annoyed because I was taking too long to come to her aid. Even as I rushed toward her I thought, *She won't be happy until she has it all, eats us alive, and it's killing her, and all I have to do is nothing.* And so, three feet away from her, I stopped.

She saw my expression and said, *Oh,* as if she suddenly didn't recognize me. Her hands shot out, her cigarette toppled over the edge, her silver rings flashed. Her red nails clawed at the air but I remained still as a statue and watched her tip backward over the coping. Her satin slipper with the ostrich feathers shot out and crashed into the windowpane.

In that moment, it was easy to step over that invisible line, but now, looking into Tenney's unflinching eyes, I realize that it was not a thin line at all but a deep canyon and Tenney will always be on the other side, and I will never be able to cross back to her. But that is a small price to pay. Every day I wait for the old feelings of shame, of guilt, of horror, to overtake me like a rain flood from the mountains, but they don't come.

The Mexican woman who is only forty but seems more like sixty and had her jaw wired shut after her husband punched her pauses to rest beside Alberto, bent over with her palms on her thighs. Alberto offers her a straw from which to sip from his water bottle, then pats her on the shoulder.

"Just a little farther, my friends," he calls out. "Let us now offer a silent prayer as we walk the last kilometer to the camp."

I feel the vibration of thousands of silent voices rising into the darkening sky like a flock of carrier pigeons beating their white wings.

I am here, God. I am waiting.

Acknowledgments

Johnny Temple is a true visionary and our twenty-year friendship has been a beacon to me through some very dark literary days. Trena Keating, my agent and longtime friend, offered invaluable guidance in the shaping of my characters and in the unfolding of this "unreliable narrator." Laurie Loewenstein and Taylor Polites, my tireless friends, read every draft and offered crucial suggestions. Nina Solomon, Barbara Taylor, Justin Kassab, and Tyler Grimm helped me through various "logjams" along the way.

Beverly Donofrio generously shared her San Miguel home; and Laura Fraser and Eva Hunter shared their knowledge of the architecture, flora, and fauna of that magical city.

Lauren Ciavarella Stahl advised me on federal prosecutorial practices; Matthew Crowe and Taylor Polites helped me understand my characters' money-laundering and tax-evasion schemes.

Louie Lizza gave me clear and simple directions on all matters pertaining to chess.

Terri Taylor, who was displeased by my original take on Dallas, Texas, straightened me out, and has the honor of being one of two liberals I've ever met from that great city (though she insists there are others).

Dr. Richard E. Cytowic explained the rudiments of Gram staining; Dr. Richard Goldberg allowed me access to his American Optical microscope and shared its fascinating history.

Sandra Castro and Carlos Wolstein kindly helped with Mexican culture and correct grammar.

Father Gerald Gurka, who prays for me even though I am not of the faith, candidly answered all my questions concerning the Catholic priesthood.

Eyrna Jones-Heisler loved me unconditionally and supported me through these many drafts.

I could not have written this book without each and every one of you.